PULL THE TRIGGER

BLACKTOP BRETHREN MC BOOK 1

SAMANTHA CONLEY

Editing by Full Bloom Editing

Cover Design by Amanda Walker PA & Design Services

CHAPTER 1
SHERIDAN

"WE HAVE TO CELEBRATE!" Kenna declared as she pulled the tape off the cardboard box.

"I have to unpack," I countered, emptying the box on the bed. The clothes fell out in a heap. God, I hated unpacking.

"Come on, Sheridan. This is a big deal. New city, new house, new job. You need to live a little."

"Please," I scoffed. "I need to get this house in order."

"When was the last time you went out and had fun?" She threw herself onto the mattress and looked at me.

I paused, picking up the clothes. I couldn't remember. Wasn't that pathetic?

"Exactly. You haven't since Ellie was born."

"Being a single mom doesn't afford me a lot of time or money to be going out," I retorted, placing the clothes in the dresser.

"You're not being a bad mom if you do something for yourself every once in a while."

"I couldn't agree more, Kenna," my mom sounded off from the doorway into my bedroom.

"Great. Why don't you gang up on me?"

"Here's what you're going to do, honey." Mom walked over to me and pushed my dark hair behind my ear like she did when I was little.

"You and Kenna are going to go to that nail place she likes and get your nails done. Chill out and relax. Then you'll go pick out a new outfit and a couple of sets of scrubs that you need for work."

She placed a finger on my lips when I argued.

"No, you are going to listen. Go get one of those iced coffee things that you like. Have dinner and go to a club or whatever you girls do. I'll take Ellie with me for the night. Ray and I will stay here and finish getting everything unpacked."

"Mom," I groaned. "I can't afford all that right now."

"It's my treat."

"No, I'm no—."

"Do not make me play the guilt card, Sheridan Diane."

"You better listen to her, kid," Ray, my stepdad, called out from the kitchen.

"Fine, but I will pay you back."

She made a sound in the back of her throat.

"You're so strong, Sheridan. Stronger than I ever was at your age. I'm sorry you had to find that out. Us McCleary women are made of tough stock, but you'll burn yourself out if you don't make time for yourself."

"Amen," Kenna chimed in, and I cut my eyes to her.

"Traitor."

She stuck her tongue out and grabbed the bath towels out of the box. "Your bath or the one in the hall?"

"Mine."

"I'll get Ellie's room set up before we leave for the night."

On cue, my three-year-old daughter came barreling into the room with our dog Ripper hot on her heels. She squealed as she climbed on the bed and knocked over the pile of clothes there.

"Eleanor Rose," I warned.

She turned to me with her big hazel eyes wide. It was like looking in a mirror at my younger self. Mom was right, those McCleary genes were strong. The three of us bore a striking resemblance. Mahogany colored hair, hazel eyes ringed with dark green, and petite frames. Mom looked more like an older sister than someone who gave birth to me. It would have been nice if our genes had included a little more padding in the chest area. I kept waiting for my boobs to come in, but they never did.

"Sorry, Mommy. I'll pick them up." She slid off the bed and reached for the clothes closest to the edge. Even at her age, she was tiny compared to other kids her age.

"It's okay. Why don't you go put your toys up in the toy box, okay? Gigi can help."

"Ellie, do you want to stay the night with me and Ray?" Mom asked as she bent down to help.

Her eyes lit up, and I glared at my mom. Oh, that manipulator.

"Yesssss!" Ellie squealed. Mom smiled at me in triumph.

"I hoped you would."

"Can Ripper come, too?" Ripper's ears perked up, and he cocked his head as if asking too.

"Of course, he can. You make sure you bring his food and blanket with us."

"Yes, ma'am."

Ellie tore out of the room as fast as her legs could carry her.

"Damn it, Mom."

"Now you have no excuse." She tossed her hair and walked out.

"I forgot how great your mom was."

"She's a busybody. She—"

"Loves you," Kenna finished for me.

"I know, but I hate people doing things for me."

"Look, we've been best friends for years. I'm going to be straight with you. We missed you. She's glad to have you and Ellie close by. Let her spoil you a little. It's been over three years since you've been in the same state. She has a lot to catch up on."

"I hate it when you make sense."

"Lucky for you, it's not that often," Kenna laughed.

"If we're going to do this, we better get going," I agreed with reluctance.

As Kenna and I walked out the backdoor, Mom slipped Kenna her credit card in some weird secret handshake. Like I wouldn't notice?

We piled into Kenna's Kia Soul, turned up some Kelly Clarkson, and headed to the mall. We belted out the lyrics at the top of our lungs. I felt lighter than I had in ages. Maybe it was time for a little R&R. I was just going to sit back and soak it all in.

Later that night, Kenna pulled up to a popular country bar that she went to on her nights off. She tended bar at another place, but she didn't want to spend her nights off there, too.

"You ready for this?"

"I guess," I breathed out.

"Forget for a little while that you're a mom. You're just Sheridan. Here to have some fun and let loose. We'll have a few drinks, make a sorry attempt at line dancing, and forget all our troubles for a few hours."

I followed her inside after we bypassed the line, waiting to get in. The bouncer gave Kenna a wink when a couple of people bitched about us cutting the line, but they shut up quick when he glared.

"Thanks, Brian," Kenna patted him on the arm when we passed by.

"No prob, K. Don't cause any trouble," Brian laughed.

"No promises," she called over her shoulder as we walked in.

The music was loud, but it drowned out the myriad of conversations of the patrons inside. People lined up around the dance floor or were seated at the tables that overlooked the dancers. We weaved around people and found an empty two-person bar top.

"Isn't this place great?" Kenna asked as she sat down.

"It's loud."

"Lord, you're not that old, Sheridan."

"I feel like I am."

"What can I get you to drink?" a waitress asked as she approached our table.

"We'll take two margaritas on the rocks and an order of nachos."

"Got it. Be back in a jiffy."

It was only a couple of minutes before she placed our drinks on the table. Kenna picked hers up and gestured towards mine. Glasses in hand, we toasted.

"Here's the deal. Tonight, there is no talk of kids, jobs, bills, or responsibilities. Okay?"

"Deal," I agree. Kenna downed her margarita in one long gulp.

Lord, what did I get myself into?

Three margaritas later, we were out on the floor dancing in time with the others. I hadn't felt this free in a long time and I liked it. I didn't care that I was messing up the steps or turning in the wrong direction. Kenna put me back in line. The tequila helped.

On a step, I turned and caught the stare of a man leaning on the rail. He flashed a smile at me, and it wasn't the dancing that made me have a hot flash. Lord, that smile was melt your panties off hot.

It was nice to know that I wasn't dead in that department.

The song finished and Kenna and I returned to our table. It wasn't a minute before a fresh round of drinks landed on the table.

"We didn't order these," Kenna told her.

"From the gentleman over there," she answered and pointed toward the Panty Melter. He tipped his beer in our direction.

"Well shit," Kenna laughed. "Never would have expected to see him here."

"You know him?"

"That's Levi. He hangs out at Shooter's a lot."

"He's cute," I drawled. She sputtered out the drink, the concoction dripping down her chin as she stared at me with wide eyes.

"We may need to cut you off," she laughed, wiping the liquid off her face.

"You don't think he's cute?"

"He's downright smoking hot and he knows it."

"He's one of those?"

"He's not an asshole about it. He's a nice guy, for the most part."

I tipped up my drink and downed half of it.

"Yummy," I stated, licking the salt from my lip, listing to the side before I caught myself.

"You stay here. I'm going to go get us some water." Kenna stood up and disappeared into the crowd. I swayed in my seat to the beat, closing my eyes to soak it in.

"Would you like to dance?" The voice came from over my shoulder.

I looked up and saw Panty Melter behind me.

"I don't know how," I confessed, staring into his brown eyes. The corner of his mouth kicked up in a half grin.

"I'll show you."

He reached for my hand and tugged me out of the chair. Keeping me close, he maneuvered us onto the dance floor. He gathered me close to his body and moved. My feet had a mind of their own and followed his lead.

I leaned my head on his chest and breathed deeply. He smelled so good.

"Thank you."

"For what?"

"You said I smelled good."

"I said that out loud?"

"Yes, you did," he chuckled.

I lifted my chin and looked up at him. Our eyes caught and held. Heat flared in his eyes, and I let out a little whimper. He leaned down and brushed his lips across mine.

I don't know what the hell happened after that, but my body took over and told my mind to hell with it. I clutched his black shirt in my hands and pulled him closer. He deepened the kiss and palmed my ass with his big hand. I lost all sense of where I was and what I was doing. All my focus was on the way his mouth felt on mine.

It had been so long, too long. My long dormant libido flared to a fever pitch when my back pressed against a wall. Panty Melter pressed into me, and he was all I could feel. His hand slid up my thigh and wrapped it around his ass. My other leg followed suit without his prompting. His body pressed between my open thighs, hot and heavy, and I thought I'd explode from the contact. He rocked his hips and the hard bulge behind his fly hit me in the perfect spot. I gasped against his lips. His mouth quirked up, and he kept up the rhythm.

"You going to come for me?" he whispered in my ear.

And damn if that didn't do it for me. The friction, his scent, and that voice were all I needed. Sparks flared from my core up into my body. He caught my moan with his mouth and continued to work his hips, extending my release. I broke away, breathing in gulps of air as he slowed. My face heated when related slapped me. I dry-humped a guy I didn't know from Adam in the hallway of a bar. I laid my head on his shoulder in embarrassment.

"You okay?" His breath ghosted across the tip of my ear.

I nodded, unable to find my voice.

"Want to get out of here? My place isn't too far."

What the hell did I do now?

"I can't. I need to get home to my daughter." I placed my hands on his chest and pressed.

"Daughter?" That had him backing off. My body cooled as he put distance between us.

I ducked under his arm and made my way back to the table. Kenna was looking around as a man spoke to her. Relief flashed in her eyes when she saw me.

"Where the hell did you go?" She barked out, giving me a once-over. Could she tell what I'd been doing? Shame had me ducking my head.

"Restroom," I mumbled. "I'm ready to go home."

She looked over my shoulder and back at me.

"Yeah, I think it's time for us to get out of here."

I led the way out front, and we got into her car.

"Sheridan, are you okay?" Worry tinged her voice.

"I'm a slut," I moaned, leaning my head back against the headrest.

"Girl, you are the farthest thing from a slut. They don't go three years without getting laid."

"Oh, God. Take me home before I make an even bigger fool of myself."

"Nothing bad happened, right? He didn't force you to do anything?"

"He didn't have to. My body was on board. At least we didn't go all the way."

"Then what the hell are you upset about?" Kenna asked, confused.

"I dry-humped him until I got off."

She busted out laughing.

"What?"

She looked through the windshield and shook her head. "Nothing, but I think we need to cut you off at two margaritas from now on."

She put the car into reverse and backed out. I kept my eyes closed. Two margaritas hell. I wasn't drinking again. At least the tequila didn't make my clothes fall off.

CHAPTER 2
SHERIDAN
TWO MONTHS LATER

"NO, no, no! Damn it. Don't do this to me!" I screamed, tears burning my eyes. I eased over onto the shoulder before the semi-bearing down on me flattened me like a pancake. The temperature gauge redlined as smoke billowed from under the hood of my beater car. Barely making it over the white line, a truck blew past, horn blaring, and rocking my car as I crawled to a stop.

"Why does this shit keep happening to me?" I hit the steering wheel with each word, the cracked plastic stinging my hands. Sickness rolled through my stomach, bile burning in the back of my throat.

Digging my cell phone out of my purse, I called Dr. Collins, my boss, since the vet clinic didn't open for another half hour.

"Sheridan, good morning," his deep, jovial voice rang in my ear. I could picture him grinning, a smile stretching his white-bearded cheeks. He reminded me of a skinny Santa Claus.

"Hello, Dr. Collins. I wanted to let you know I'm going to be late this morning. I'm having car trouble." I winced, waiting for the disappointment. I was still on my probationary period. Being late was an excuse to get fired, right?

"I'm sorry to hear that. Anything I can do?"

"No. I'm going to call a tow truck—" At that moment a semi roared by inches from my car. A shriek ripped free from my lips.

"Sheridan, where are you?" Concern laced his words.

"On Highway 46."

"That's a dangerous place. Please stay in your car."

"I am, don't worry. Look, Dr. Collins, I really need this job."

"Don't worry about that, Sheridan. You get to the office when you can. I'll let Tracy know."

"Yes, sir."

My next call was to my mom.

"Hey, Sheridan. How's the new job?" she asked as she answered the phone.

"It's good, but I need a favor."

"Sure, love. What do you need?"

"Can you look up a number for a towing company for me?"

"Did that damn car break down again? I told you that you need to get something more reliable for you and Ellie." Great, just what I needed on top of this crappy morning, a lecture from my mother.

"I know, but I don't have the money right now."

"I told you I'd loan you the money. Is Ellie with you?"

"No, I already dropped her off at daycare."

"Where are you?"

"Sitting on the shoulder of Highway 46, near exit 20."

"Let me call Ray."

"No, I—" The phone beeped as she disconnected the call. "Need the number. Damn it, Mom."

I banged my head back against the headrest. Just what I needed, for my stepdad to get involved. Don't get me wrong, I loved the man. He'd been in my life for over a decade now, but, as a deputy sheriff, he could be a smidge intimidating. Okay, he could scare the crap out of you if he had a mind to.

Ten minutes later, a red tow truck passed by before pulling sharply over onto the shoulder. Turning on the lights atop the cab, it backed up until it was close to my front bumper. The driver's door opened, and a large black boot appeared, followed by a jean-clad leg. The rest was just as impressive. A broad chest covered by a tight black t-shirt. Swirls of ink peeked out from beneath the edge of the sleeve.

Sullivan Towing and Recovery was written across the back in bold, bright red print. A black ball cap covered his head, shading his face from the blistering sun blazing down. He slammed the door shut before striding around the back of the truck, coming to the passenger side of my car. Bright blue eyes rimmed in navy peered down into the car as he motioned to roll down the window. With a huff, I took off my seatbelt, peeling myself off the hot vinyl of the seat. Crawling over the center console, I rolled down the window. Manually. Nothing electric in this bitch. The corner of his mouth quirked up, revealing a dimple on his left cheek.

"I couldn't help but notice you're broken down. Can I give you a lift somewhere?" He leaned on top of the car. His voice raised to be heard over the rushing traffic.

"How much it is gonna cost me?"

"Usual fee is one twenty-five."

My stomach dropped. That'll cost me more than I have in my checking account. And I hadn't bought groceries this week.

"I'm sorry, but I can't afford that. I appreciate you stopping."

He rubbed a hand across his clean-shaven chin, gaze narrowed.

"Look, I can't leave you stranded on the side of the road. I'm headed to the yard, anyway. There's a garage next door. I can drop your car off there."

"I still can't afford it. I'm sorry."

"Nothing to be sorry for." He stood, walked to his truck, and climbed inside. The yoke attached to the back of the truck lowered and his reverse lights came on. Within seconds, he secured my car.

My mouth hung open in shock. What the hell did he think he was doing?! Checking the mirror, I swung open the door and jumped out to meet him in front of my car.

"I told you I can't pay you!" I fumed.

"And I told you I'm not leaving you stranded on the side of the road. I'll drop you off at the garage, but I can't in good conscience leave you sitting here with a car seat in the back."

"And what is your boss gonna say if you're out here giving free rides?"

"Not a damn thing. Names Sullivan. James Sullivan." He stuck out his hand.

"You're the owner?" I scoffed, placing my hand in his.

"One of them. Call me Sully." He smiled at my disbelief. "My dad opened the shop, but my brother and I are partners with him."

"I guess you don't have to worry, then. I'm Sheridan," I replied, sheepish. Just then, another semi rushed past, the force nearly blowing me off my feet.

"Time for you to get in the truck," he said, taking my arm and guiding me to the passenger side.

"Wait. My purse," I argued.

"It's not going to get lost between here and the garage," he replied, opening the door and putting me inside.

Old rock music played inside the cab. At least he had good taste, but if AC/DC's *Highway to Hell* started playing, I was bailing the hell out. A few minutes later, we pulled into a parking lot of Jameson's Automotive Repair. Sully pushed a few buttons, and I watched as my car lowered to the ground next to an open bay door.

"This is your stop." He smiled. "Come on."

I followed Sully inside the dimmed interior. Music blared from atop a tall red toolbox. The smell of oil and sweat permeated the hot air. A large fan offered the tiniest bit of relief from the relentless heat as it hummed. A red truck was parked inside with its hood propped up, and another bay held a blue car. The music from the radio briefly interrupted the conversation coming from beneath the hood between two men, one noticeably older than the other.

"Yo, Trigger, you got a customer," Sully bellowed from the doorway, making me flinch with surprise. Trigger? What the heck kind of name is that?

"Rooster's in the office," a deep voice rumbled. Shivers ran down my spine when I heard it. Wait-Rooster?

Sully glanced over to the left through a window.

"Looks like he's on the phone. This young lady broke down on the highway and could use some help," Sully quipped back.

Metal clanked against the concrete. From underneath the front of the truck, a pair of legs appeared. Wheels squeaked as he rolled out on a creeper, the thing mechanics used to slide under a vehicle. Navy pants became a white top streaked with what looked like grease or oil.

It stretched taut across his abdomen, and I looked away before he caught me gawking like he was a damn thirst trap.

But like a magnet, I couldn't help myself. Muscular arms covered with ink. A short dark stubble obscured his sharp jaw as if he forgot to shave before he left the house this morning. His head turned to the right, revealing eyes the color of honey. They widened slightly when he saw me. His lips kicked up in a grin before he climbed up off the ground.

"What have you brought me, Sully?" He winked in Sully's direction as he wiped his hands on a red rag. His gaze roamed from the top of the ponytail on top of my head to the pink sneakers on my feet.

Oh geez. Another guy who thought he was God's gift? No thanks.

"This is Sheridan." Sully thumbed in my direction. "Sheridan, this loser is Levi Jameson."

"We've met."

"We have?" I tried to recall.

His eyes narrowed.

"My mistake. Nice to meet you, Sheridan. Name's Levi." Trigger stuck out his hand.

"Levi? I thought your name was Trigger." He engulfed my hand in his. Had I imagined the sparks when he touched me? By the look in his eyes, I thought he felt them, too.

"Trigger's a nickname. My mom named me Levi."

"Nice to meet you."

"Can you tell me what happened?"

"I was driving to work, heard a pop, it redlined, and here I am."

"Found her sitting on the shoulder. Decided to help her out," Sully added.

"Helping the damsel in distress." Levi narrowed his eyes at Sully.

"Fuck off, Trigger. It's called being a nice guy. Try it sometime."

"I'm a nice guy."

"When you're trying to get into their pants," Sully muttered under his breath.

But I heard him and so did Levi. He subtly scratched his nose with his middle finger, glaring at Sully. My eyes narrowed on Levi. Why did he seem familiar?

"Where'd you break down?" Levi asked when he focused back on me.

"On forty-six."

"Damn, that's a rough stretch. Lots of accidents."

"Semi nearly blew me off the road," I laughed.

"Doesn't surprise me. You're a little bit of a thing." He smiled at his teasing.

"I may be small, but I'm mighty. Never underestimate a short girl."

"Unless you need something off the top shelf," Sully laughed.

"You hush. I've had to make do my whole life. I've learned to scale a counter with the best of them."

"Now you see why I couldn't leave her stranded," Sully added.

"Yeah, you're a genuine hero." Levi rolled his eyes.

"Would you be able to take a look at it?" I asked to break up the tension between the two. It seemed as if Levi was put out with Sully saying anything.

"I can get to it this afternoon. Just leave me your number and I'll call you."

"Oh, crap, my phone!" I hustled out to my car, leaving the two men staring after me. It was lying on the seat where I had dropped it earlier. Seven missed calls.

"Oh shit," I muttered.

I hit the missed call alert. The phone rang once before Ray picked up.

"Where the hell are you?" he barked.

"Sorry. I got a tow."

"Your mother is freaking out right now. She thinks you've been kidnapped or some shit."

"Damn, I'll call her." No wonder Ray was riled up. Nothing affected him the way my mother did.

"Where. Are. You?" Ray bit out each word.

"Jameson's Automotive Repair."

"Be there in five."

The line went dead. Why did that sound like a threat? I called Mom back to let her know I was safe, and Ray was on his way.

"Sorry about that," I blurted, walking back into the work bay.

"Boyfriend?" Levi quirked a brow.

"No. My mom. I told her I broke down, and she was worried."

"Never piss off your mom," Sully laughed.

"I'll be able to look at it this afternoon. Need to call your boyfriend or someone for a ride?"

"Ray's on his way," I muttered distractedly as I looked for his SUV.

"I'm going to need your number so I can call you with the estimate. Come with me and I'll have you fill out some paperwork." Levi turned and walked toward the door to the office.

"Yeah, sure." With a last glance over my shoulder, I followed.

Levi slid a clipboard across the chipped laminate counter.

"Fill this out for me," he ordered, handing me a pen.

I filled out the standard things—name, address, phone number, make and model of my piece of crap car and what brought me in.

"Is 'the car went boom' an appropriate answer here?" I laughed, pointing at the line.

"That'll work," he chuckled.

"Yo, 5-0 in the house," Sully stated from where he had set up sentry into the office.

"Oh, that's Ray."

"You belong to a cop?" Levi asked, brows drawn.

"What?" I asked, not understanding what he meant.

"Your boyfriend's a cop?" He drew out as if to make sure I understood each word.

"No, Ray's my stepdad."

"Just as bad," Sully muttered.

"You guys have a problem with cops?"

"No, not really. They seem to have a problem with us."

Oh shit, what kind of place had Sully brought me to? Was my car going to be safe here?

"Sheridan?" Ray's voice echoed throughout the building.

"I'm in here, Ray. Just filling out paperwork."

As Sully exited the door, Ray entered. It wasn't usual for me to see his authoritative side, but it was out in full force today. He raised his aviator shades and took in the room. His gray eyes, hard and assessing, landed on Levi and then me.

"Everything good?"

"He said he'll be able to take a look at it this afternoon."

"Good. I'm Ray Jensen." He held his hand out to Levi.

"Levi Jameson."

"I've heard good things about your shop." His tone suggested they better be true.

"We've got good guys working here," Levi agreed, looking around at the other workers who were staring at us.

Ray nodded his head, and they eyed each other. Something passed between them, but for the world, I didn't know what.

"If you're ready, Sheridan, let's get you to work."

"Is there anything else you need from me?" I asked Levi, breaking his and Ray's staring contest. He glanced at the paper.

"Everything looks good. I'll call you when I know what's wrong with your car."

"Thanks."

"Go grab Bug's car seat before you forget," Ray barked out.

"Yes, sir," I mumbled, walking out the door.

"Car seat?" Levi called out.

"Yes, for my daughter."

"Good thing she wasn't with you when you broke down, huh?"

"It was."

As I pulled out Ellie's car seat from the back, Ray walked out. He plucked the seat from my hands and put it in the back of his cruiser.

"Let's get you to work," he said, slamming the rear hatch.

"Wait, Sheridan," Levi called out, jogging over to Ray's cruiser. "I need your keys."

"I guess you do," I laughed to cover my embarrassment. How the hell was he going to move my car or start the darn thing without the keys!?

I pulled the keys out of my pocket and placed them in his palm. My fingers grazed his skin and sparks kissed my fingertips. His eyes held mine, and the intensity was enough to make me flush. Pulling my hand back, I climbed into Ray's cruiser. Why did he seem so familiar? A memory teased my mind, but it fleeted away before it fully formed.

As we pulled out of the parking lot, Levi had propped himself up against one side of the bay, watching us drive off with massive arms folded across his chest. The slight breeze ruffled his dark hair. My eyes caught his and my heart sped up in my chest. The intensity ensnared me. His eyes promised me things. Things I wasn't sure I wanted to know. I sunk back in my seat as we turned onto the road.

Why did I think today was going to change something monumental in my life?

CHAPTER 3
TRIGGER

AS SOON AS the cruiser pulled out onto the street, Sully burst out laughing.

"Man, I thought you had game!"

"Fuck off," I muttered, fighting the urge to chase after the SUV. What the fuck was wrong with me?

"She is gorgeous, though. A little on the small side." Sully elbowed me as he planted himself next to me on the wall. He pulled a pack of gum out of his back pocket. He offered it to me before pulling out a stick. The scent of cinnamon wafted on the breeze when he removed the wrapper.

"Fuck yeah, she is."

"Not your usual type, though."

And I couldn't argue with that fact. I liked them blonde, busty, and easy. That's why I usually stuck to the club girls. They knew the score. We fucked, and we were done. No feelings, no attachments. They didn't even say anything if I took a couple of different ones to my bed on the same night. Or at the same time.

But this girl was different. I hadn't been able to get her out of my mind in weeks. And she didn't remember a damn thing! Or she was a fantastic actress. Either way, it was a big hit to my ego that she didn't remember me, and I'd been living out the memory of her dry-humping me each night in the shower. I looked over at his grinning ass.

"Why don't you stop being a pain in my ass, Sully, and help me move that pile of shit into the bay."

"I've got to get to the shop before my old man raises hell."

"Tell him you were bringing in her car. Business is business, man."

"Except I did it for free. Old man is going to tear me a new one."

"You fucking pansy," I chuckled and pulled out my wallet. I pulled out enough bills to cover the cost of Sheridan's tow. "That'll keep you straight with him."

"What the hell? She got some voodoo going on that I don't know about?"

"Fuck off."

But what was it about this girl? She was small, barely coming up to my chest. Her boobs looked nonexistent underneath those scrubs, and I couldn't even get a glimpse of her ass. Her eyes, though? I'd never seen anything prettier. Gold spiked with emerald shards, and a dark green ring encapsulating it. Thick dark lashes framed them. And then her plump pink lips? Fuck what I would give to see them wrapped around my cock. My dick throbbed at the visual.

"Voodoo may be a possibility," I muttered. But I don't have a clue what that girl did to me.

"Boys, you need some help?" Rooster, my dad and owner of the shop, came up behind us.

"We've got it. Sully just brought us in a junker."

Rooster eyed the car with disdain. "How much can we get for it?"

"We're not taking it for scrap, Dad. It belongs to someone else. She broke down on the road and Sully towed her in."

"Be cheaper to buy something else, I'd wager. We've got several jobs lined up. Add it to the list and get to it when you can." Rooster shook his head and went back to the office.

"Prez didn't seem too impressed."

"Lots of shit going on with the fight coming up and the party."

"Let me know if I can help, Brother."

"Always. Get the hell out of here. I've got work to do." I patted him on the back and went back inside.

After getting the other mechanics on their assigned jobs, I started my day. Three brake jobs and a serpentine belt later, it was time for lunch. Dad rolled up in the company truck with bags of barbeque from a spot up the street. Sweat trickled down, well, everything, as he waved me into the office.

"Give me a second to clean up and I'll be right in." A chin lift acknowledged my words.

When I came out of the restroom, all the guys sat around the picnic table outside with a Styrofoam container. Nestled under some trees, the guys found shade from the scorching sun.

"In here," Rooster barked out when I opened the office door.

I walked through the waiting room into his private office. In one hand, he held a sandwich, and the other was typing on the keyboard.

"Sit." The decades-old chair creaked under my weight.

"How are things coming along?"

I pulled the Styrofoam contained toward me and lifted the lid. The scent hit me hard. My stomach grumbled in response.

"I've got the catering set up for the family party. I'm waiting to hear from the DJ. Kegs are ordered. Brenda agreed to tend bar."

"What about for the kids?"

"There's a place on Lexington that does those blow-up things. I was going to rent one or two of those. How would you feel about getting a lifeguard for the pool?"

"Not a bad idea. Everyone will be drinking, and I'd feel better knowing someone is watching," Rooster agreed.

"We'll just have to remind the guys to keep their hands to themselves."

"Good luck with that," I laughed.

"What about the fight? How's Hammer looking?"

"How does he always look?"

"Watch it, boy," Rooster warns.

"He looks great. We've been working on takedowns and floor work."

"Not like many people get that big bastard down on the mat."

Hammer was another member of our club, the Blacktop Brethren. My dad and his best friend founded the club back in the eighties after they got out of the army. Dad became the president and Brass the VP. A few others from their unit moved close after they were discharged and joined too.

I'd grown up with the club and several of the younger members I'd known since birth.

"Hammer will make us a killing if anyone bets against him."

"No one's that stupid," I scoffed.

"I'm not so sure, son. I've heard that the one entry is a ringer. Used to fight professionally before he was kicked off the circuit for fighting dirty."

"At least we know. It's not like we have a ton of rules. Hammer knows the risks."

"Shit can always happen." He eyed me hard, and my stomach cramped. I placed the sandwich down.

"I know."

I used to be the prizefighter for our club. When I was younger, I had a hair-trigger temper and would get into fights all the time with the smallest amount of provocation. In high school, I got jumped by a bunch of older guys and got the shit kicked out of me. An older guy found me and helped me out. After taking me to the emergency room and meeting my parents, Gus took me under his wing. He owned a martial arts studio, and my parents were happy to sign me up. He taught me to control my anger and focus. I learned a lot from that old man. Later, the only fights I got into were the ones in the cage. And I was damn good. Until one night, it all came crashing down.

I could still hear the chanting of the crowd. The sweat dripping down my face mingled with the blood from my busted eye. I could tell the ref was about to call it and got in one last punch. The blow caught the kid straight on the jaw and it was lights out. I remembered him falling, his head bouncing off the floor with a crack. As soon as he hit, I knew something was wrong. Rooster and Raze, my best friend, took me to the far side of the ring while the others rushed in. I stared as they tried to get him to wake up. The paramedics rushed in and placed him on a backboard with a brace around his neck.

That was the last time I saw him alive. His father, president of the

Devil's Reign MC, promised that I would pay for killing his son. A son that he put in that cage. It was my last time in a cage, too.

"Trigger," my dad called my name, snapping me out of the past.

"Sorry, sir."

"I didn't mean to dredge up old memories."

"It's fine."

"I just want both of you to be prepared for anything."

"We will be."

"We've had eight more fighters sign up since the last time. We'll have a record-breaking crowd coming in. We need to bump up security."

"I'll talk with Sully. He has a few friends that have done security work since getting out of the service."

"We'll need more of everything."

"I'll get on it. I was thinking about hitting up some of the food trucks in town and having them set up for a share. Shooter may let us use a couple of his bartenders and wait staff if we need to."

Shooter was another member of the club that owned a bar and grill in town. After he retired from the Marines, he moved here to Noble and opened a restaurant. It didn't seem like a logical choice for a former sniper, but what the hell did I know?

"This weekend we need to work on the bracket and make sure everything is lined up. We don't need any fuck ups."

"The metal detectors for the Barn should be here in two weeks. It'll give us time to get them installed."

The Barn was a large warehouse on the outskirts of the city where we held our events for large gatherings. Four times a year we held a tournament for underground fighting, which was our big money maker. Other people also rented out the Barn for other uses to keep the cash flowing into the club.

"Keep me apprised of everything. With this many more fighters, it makes me a little antsy."

"No problem, Dad."

"Eat your damn lunch and get back to work."

"Yes sir," I laughed.

Around three o'clock, I got to look at Sheridan's car. Dad was right.

It would be cheaper for her to get another car than fix everything that was wrong with this one.

"Fuck, this is not good," I muttered as I loosened another bolt.

"That bad huh," Sully stuck his head under the hood.

"She needs a new radiator, water pump, belts. Hell, the whole engine needs to be worked on."

"Damn, she will not like that. She couldn't even afford the tow."

"That's not good. I thought she was a nurse or something. They make decent bank."

"Don't know man. Maybe her baby daddy ain't helping like he should."

"Fucker," I grated out. "Can't stand a fucking deadbeat."

"Who knows what the situation is?" Sully shrugged.

"Guess I'll call and give her the news."

I walked into the office and pulled up her sheet. Dialing the number, I propped myself up on the edge of the desk.

"Hello?" Her husky voice sends a shock straight to my dick. With her diminutive size, you'd think she'd have an airy voice, not something that should be on a phone sex line.

"Sheridan? This is Levi at Jameson Automotive."

A heartbeat passes before she answers me. "What's the damage?"

"You need some extensive work. Your water pump blew, and the fan belt went into your radiator. You're going to need to replace them."

"Shit, that doesn't sound cheap."

I winced.

"Your serpentine belt also needs to be replaced or you'll be stranded on the side of the road again. It'll come apart at any time."

"Damn it."

"I'm sorry—"

"How much?" She cut me off.

"You're looking at around seventeen hundred dollars for parts and labor."

Silence.

"Sheridan, are you there?"

"Can you have it brought back to my house, or should I call Sully?"

"What?"

"I can't afford seventeen hundred dollars right now. I just had the transmission rebuilt in the thing two weeks ago. It wiped me out."

"Look, maybe we can work something out. I can try to find some used parts that'll cost less."

"It'll still be too much."

"We can work out a payment plan or something," I rushed out.

Why was I so desperate to help this chick out?

"You can do that?" Her voice was hopeful.

I looked at the sign above the counter. *Payment required at time of service.*

"Sure," I lied through my teeth. "I even have a loaner car that you can use in the meantime." In for a penny, in for a pound, right? My dad was going to flip.

"I don't know about this. It may take me a while to come up with the money. My job is barely covering my bills as it is."

"It'll all work out."

"From your lips to God's ears."

"Do you need me to come pick you up after work?"

"No, my best friend is going to be giving me a ride."

"I can drop off the loaner at your house," I offered.

"We can come by and pick it up. There are probably some papers I need to fill out for it."

Eyeing the door to my dad's office, I moved further away. The last thing I needed was her showing up here asking about her loaner.

"It'll be easier for me to drop it off. Is the address you put on the form where you'll be?"

"Yes, I should be home by five thirty. Six at the latest."

"I'll plan on six just in case."

"Thanks, Levi. I really appreciate all of this."

She disconnected the call, and I placed the receiver down. What the hell was I getting myself into?

"I know you did not just tell a customer that they could pay out their repairs and have a loaner car." Dad's voice boomed from behind.

Fuck.

"I'll take care of it."

"You better. I don't run a damn charity."

CHAPTER 4
SHERIDAN

"IS YOUR DAD PICKING YOU UP?" Tracy asked as she walked up to the counter.

"No, Kenna is."

"That's a damn shame. That is one fine-looking man." She tapped her long red nails on the counter.

"He's married to my mom," I reminded her.

She smirked at me before sauntering off.

"Girl, she will try to get her claws into him. Mark my words," Gladys warned as she handed me the next chart.

"Ray won't give her the time of day. He thinks my mom hung the moon."

"That's how my Henry was. I miss that man."

"If I can find a man who loves me the way Ray does my mom and Henry did you, I'll be lucky."

"Your time is coming, honey. Better get in there before Dr. Lansky throws a tantrum."

"Wilbur," I called out, and an elderly man stood. Next to him was a giant Saint Bernard attached to a red leash. "Good morning, Mr. Adams. We're going to room two as soon I get Wilbur's weight."

The dog behaved and stood still on the scale. I pulled a treat from my pocket and, with Mr. Adam's permission, snuck it to Wilbur.

"Wilbur is just here for his yearly exam, Mr. Adams?"

"Yes, he needs his shots and his preventatives."

"All right. Let me get Dr. Lansky for you and we'll get Wilbur all fixed up."

With a huff, Wilbur lay down on the floor. Thank goodness I didn't have to get the dog onto the table. He was bigger than me.

Exiting the room, I flipped the flag that said the room was ready for the doctor. I grabbed the supplies to draw Wilbur's blood and placed them on the counter.

"Sheridan, my dear, I'm glad you made it to work safely," Dr. Collins called out, pulling off his dirty coveralls. It was his day to make farm calls, and it was always a dirty process.

"Thank you for being understanding, Dr. Collins."

"Things happen that are beyond our control. Did everything get worked out?"

"Sort of. They're going to let me pay it out."

"My dear, I don't want to speak out of turn, but if you need, I can loan you the money."

"I wouldn't feel right, Dr. Collins."

"The offer stands. You're an excellent employee, Sheridan. If I can help you out, I will."

"Sheridan, get in here and get Wilbur's blood drawn," Dr. Lansky snapped from the door to room two. I picked up the supplies.

"I'm coming right now."

"Gerald, it's my fault. I delayed Sheridan," Dr. Collins smoothed it over.

"Sorry, Craig, I didn't see you there. Wilbur needs a full panel and his routine shots."

"Yes, sir." I scooted by Dr. Lansky and went into the room.

Wilbur took everything like a champ and got another treat before heading to the checkout counter.

"That's the last one," Gladys groaned when the spoiled poodle and her owner walked out the door hours later.

"I need to clean up the last room and I'll be finished."

"Kenna's picking you up?"

"Yes. She has the night off."

"You two don't get into too much trouble, then. Goodnight."

"Goodnight, Gladys. See you in the morning."

"Let me know if you need a ride or anything, honey. Give that little girl a kiss from me."

The door shut behind her as I turned the key in the lock and flipped over the open sign. This place gave me the creeps when I was the last to leave. I hurried through the place, sweeping, mopping, and wiping down the table. With everything cleaned and stocked for tomorrow, I was ready to go home. My phone dinged in my scrubs pocket.

Kenna: I'm here.

Me: Give me just a second. I just finished up.

Kenna: No worries. I hit the taco stand up the road for dinner. Margs to go, baby!

Me: You're a lifesaver.

In the last room, I double-checked, making sure everything was in place before leaving. A hand caught the door before I closed it.

"Shit!" I screamed, thinking someone had gotten inside.

"Sorry, Sheridan. I didn't mean to scare you," Dr. Lansky said with a smirk. "I couldn't help but overhear earlier that you were having trouble paying for your car repairs. I'd be more than happy to help you out."

"Thanks, but I've got it taken care of."

"I bet we could come to a better arrangement." He trailed a finger down my arm.

Revulsion pulsed through me.

"Spend some time with me and I'll make sure everything is taken care of."

Outside, Kenna honked her horn.

"I've got to go," I rushed out, leaving him standing there. Outside the staff entrance, Kenna sat with her car idling.

"What's wrong?" She asked as soon as I sat in the seat.

"Dr. Lansky hit on me. I feel like I'm going to throw up."

"That's gross and sexual harassment."

"Oh, it's not like that."

"Bullshit. That's how it starts."

"I need this job, Ken."

"I know, but you don't have to put up with that shit. I told you to come work with me."

"I may have to take you up on that. I've got to make some extra money to pay for my damn car."

"You need a new car," Kenna stated.

"When money grows on trees, I'll get one, but right now it's not in the cards. This job barely covers everything." My chest tightened. "I feel like I'm a horrible mother."

"You are taking care of yourself and your daughter. You pay your bills, food is on the table. You are doing great as a mom. Ellie knows you love her and are always there for her. That's what matters."

Kenna's voice was tinged with jealousy. Her mother had abandoned her when she was young, leaving her with her elderly grandmother. Her grandmother had been great but in poor health and was unable to deal with a young child. She passed away when Kenna was sixteen and Kenna had to fight to stay out of foster care.

"If I get another job, that's more time away from Ellie. I feel like I'm missing so much already."

"Ellie has tons of people who love her. It's not like you're going to be leaving her with strangers. You know your mom and Ray will watch her whenever and I will too if I'm not working."

"I don't know what I would do without you guys."

"That's what friends are for. Speaking of, do we need to go get Ellie?"

"No, Mom was going to grab her early. Ellie mentioned wanting a new toy, so I'm sure Mom took her shopping."

We pulled into the drive of my house. Grabbing the food bags and jug of margaritas out of the back seat, we walked into the house. Blessed cool air rushed over my skin.

"God, it feels good in here," Kenna moaned.

"Amen. If the air goes out, I will curl into a ball and die."

"Don't mention that with the way your luck has been running," Kenna chided. "Are we swimming?"

"Hell yes. Let me get changed."

"Where's Ripper?"

Normally my German Shepard meets us at the door, but today he's noticeably absent.

"That's weird. Ripper!"

Nails scrabbled across the hardwood as he barreled down the hall. Like a bullet, he rushed at us.

"There he is." Sinking my hands into his thick fur, I give him a good rub down. He melted into me with each scratch and rub. "Such a good boy."

Then a stench hit the air, and I remembered where Ripper got his name.

"Oh, God, that stinks," Kenna waved a hand in front of her face.

"Ripper, outside," I coughed, eyes watering from the smell.

With his head ducked, he went out the doggie door.

"I couldn't imagine having to be trapped in a car with him all day smelling like that," Kenna laughed.

Ripper was a retired police dog. There had been an accident that affected his ability to smell causing him to possibly be wronged when called out. Ray had gotten him to come live with us after he retired from the force. Ripper's old handler was a friend of Ray's and with him getting a new canine partner, it was a peaceful transition to our home. Ripper adored Ellie and appointed himself her protector. I felt better knowing he was in the home with us.

"Ellie must have snuck him a treat or something. That new food we put him on has made a world of difference."

"Go get changed. I'm ready to get into the pool."

I thought my luck had finally changed when I found this house to rent. Ellie and I had been living in a rat-infested hell hole for a couple of years before we moved to Noble. I was looking for a new place to rent when I received an email with the link to this place from a realty firm.

Touring the place, I knew I could never afford the rent, much less furnish the place, but the agent said that I qualified for a program that assisted with the rent, and the place was furnished. I signed on the dotted line as soon as I could. It had truly been a blessing for Ellie and me.

"Be right back."

I hurried down the hall into my room and pulled out the red bikini from the top drawer of the dresser. Within minutes, I changed and headed out the back door.

Kenna sat poolside, her long tanned legs slowly moving through the water. Her blonde hair was tied in a knot on top of her head. From here, I could see the tattoo of the birdcage with its open door on her left shoulder.

"Hurry and get over here," she commanded, holding a glass of margarita above her head.

"You don't know how much I need this," I moaned, taking the glass from her and taking a big gulp.

"No, girl, I know how bad you need this," she laughed.

A few minutes later we lounged on floats in the pool, sipping margaritas and splashing water on ourselves to keep cool.

"Tell me about this mechanic. You sounded kind of excited on the phone."

I sputtered, spraying the last sip of margarita.

"Excited? To find out it's going to cost a mint to fix that crap car I've got?"

"Yes, excited. Was he hot?" Kenna peered at me over the top of her shades, green eyes bright.

"Maybe," I replied with a smile.

"Hot damn. It's about time you noticed a hot guy. Did he get your number?"

"Um, yeah, how else was he supposed to call me back?"

"Good point. Did he call you from the shop's phone or his phone?"

"The shop phone, I guess. It just showed the number."

"Damn. If it was his phone, you could save it and call him up for a little booty call."

"Kenna!"

"What?" she asked with a shrug. "You need to get laid."

"I can't believe we're having this conversation. I haven't had enough alcohol for this." I drained the rest of my glass.

"Remember what happened last time you got drunk," Kenna warned.

"Don't remind me," I groaned. "I swore off alcohol after that night. You're a bad influence, Ken."

"Hush it. You needed to let loose that night. And boy did you," she laughed.

Most of that night was a blur and Kenna refused to tell me what embarrassing thing I did. Every time she brought that night up, she'd look at me and laugh like a loon.

I heard a car pull into the driveway followed by the door opening and shutting. Assuming it was my mom bringing Ellie home, I called out.

"We're in the back."

But instead of my mom, the object of our conversation walked through the gate.

CHAPTER 5
TRIGGER

"HEY, Hammer, you mind if we make a brief side trip before we head to the gym?"

"It shouldn't be a problem. What's up?"

"Need to drop off a car at a customer's house." I rattled off the address.

"That's Mom and Dad's Street," Hammer remarked.

"Really?" That was surprising, as Hammer's parents lived in a very nice neighborhood. How the hell did she live there and not be able to afford car repairs? Maybe her mortgage took all her money? Who the hell knew?

"Is this Sheridan's place?"

"Yeah. You know her?"

"She lives next door to my parents. Mom has watched her kid twice."

"What do you know about her?"

"Why?" My non-answer was enough for him. "Ah, hell, you're interested in her? She's not your usual type, Brother."

"Sully already pointed that out," I bit out.

"Sheridan's single, has a little girl, and works at a vet clinic. I think that's what Mom said."

"Any man in the picture?"

"Not that I know of. Mom tried to set us up when Sheridan first moved in," Hammer chuckled.

That was laughable. If Sheridan wasn't my type, she sure as hell wasn't Hammer's. At a little over six and a half feet tall and three hundred pounds, Hammer liked his woman on the tall, curvy side. The more tits, hips, and ass they had, the more he wanted them.

"You know we're going to stop by my parent's place? I'd never hear the end."

"And your mom's going to feed us?"

"Of course. That's what Italian mothers do."

"Come on."

I hopped in the Nissan Sentra that I had picked up for a steal to make a few extra bucks and drove to Sheridan's house. Hammer followed behind in his jacked-up Chevy truck. It took us about twenty minutes to reach the subdivision. The houses that lined the streets were all new and cost a pretty penny, according to the billboard on the side of the road for the next phase that was opening.

Either Sheridan was lying out her pretty little ass about not being able to afford the repairs, or she had a sweet ass deal going on.

I pulled into the driveway of a one-story brick home. The flower beds were a bevy of colors, and the lawn was freshly mowed. Mom would be impressed. Hammer parked his truck in front of his parents' place and gave me a quick wave before he headed inside.

Once I shut the car door, I heard Sheridan's voice call out that they were in the back. The Kia Soul I'd parked behind seemed familiar, but I couldn't place it. The gate wasn't locked when I lifted the latch. Feminine laughter floated on the breeze when I walked through. And nearly stumbled when I saw the two women wearing skimpy bikinis floating in the pool. Sheridan's head whipped toward me; jaw dropped.

"Hey, Trigger," Kenna called from her perch. "Fancy meeting you here."

She gave me a little finger wave before staring over at Sheridan, who was trying to get off her float. The plastic squeaked as she fumbled, flipping it over. Her arm stayed above the water, cup right side up.

"Didn't spill a drop," Kenna crowed.

Sheridan came up sputtering and wiped the water off her face.

"It's empty."

"Kenna," I acknowledged, attempting not to laugh. "I thought your car looked familiar."

"My girl had a shit day. Thought I'd make it up to her."

Her girl? My head went crazy at the thought.

"Sorry, Levi. I thought you were my mom. Give me a second to get dried off."

"Don't rush on my account," I commented, watching her lithe body move through the water.

The red bikini highlighted her small pert breasts, nipples hardened from the cold. The red ties rested on her slim hips, but her ass was glorious, high and round. And those thighs? God damn, I wanted them wrapped around my head as I devoured her.

My dick hardened in my pants, and I tried to adjust myself. Kenna caught me and broke into a husky laugh.

"At least I know that the feeling is mutual," she smirked.

Sheridan hurried, picking up a purple towel and wrapping it around herself. I held back a groan at the loss.

"I didn't realize it had gotten so late. I'm sorry. What do you need from me?"

You laid out bare in front of me?

The words almost slipped out.

"Nothing. I parked the car behind Kenna's. Insurance and registration papers are in the glove compartment if you need them. I filled up the tank and checked all the fluids. Everything's good to go. She may not be pretty, but she'll get you where you need to go."

"You don't know how much I appreciate this. Kenna said her boss is hiring. I'm going to pick up a few shifts there to help me pay you back quicker."

Her words made me smile since Kenna bartended at Shooter's, which was a popular hangout for the club members.

"No rush. Like I said. I'm going to look tomorrow for the used parts. I'll get it done as fast as I can."

"Yo, Trigger, where you at?"

"In the back," I called back to Hammer.

He peered over the fence as he let himself in.

"Where's he at?"

"Who?" I bit out. As soon as the words left my mouth, a giant black and tan bullet shot out of the house with a deep growl.

"Holy shit," I breathed out as he ran my way.

"Ripper, heel."

The dog skidded to a stop and froze.

"Sit," Sheridan commanded. "Good boy."

"Damn, that's a big dog."

"He's the best." She beamed, petting his head.

"That dog will take you down in seconds," Hammer remarked, coming up beside me.

The dog released a low growl as we moved closer.

"Good to know."

"Hi, Michael. It's good to see you again. How's your mom?"

"Being stubborn as usual, but otherwise good."

"Sheridan?" another voice called out.

"In the back, Mom."

The gate opened once again, and a dark-haired sprite raced inside. Dodging adults, she landed on the dog with a giggle.

"Ellie, what have I told you about doing that to Ripper?"

"Not to," she replied, voice muffled as she was face-planted in the dog's dense fur.

"I swear that girl will be the death of me," an older version of Sheridan trudged in laden with shopping bags.

"Let me get those for you, ma'am." Hammer hurried over and divested her of the bags.

"Thank you, Michael. Sheridan, I didn't realize you were having a get-together."

"We're not." Sheridan looks around the yard. "I'm not. Levi was dropping off the loaner car."

"Levi, is it?" The woman eyed me up and down with eyes the same shade as Sheridan's. If it weren't for the faint lines around her mouth and eyes, I would swear she was Sheridan's older sister.

"Levi Jameson, ma'am."

"Good lord, don't ma'am me. Makes me feel old. Call me Sheila. I appreciate you helping my daughter out. I've been telling her she needs a new car, but she doesn't listen."

"Mom—"

"Sheila, there are margaritas in the pitcher. Help yourself," Kenna called out from the water, saving Sheridan from getting into an argument with her mom.

"Thanks for the offer, but I need to get going. Ellie wiped me out."

The child, who was running around the yard chasing the dog, laughed.

"Thanks for picking her up, Mom."

"Anytime, sweetie. If you need anything, let me know. Bye, guys."

"I think you may have had a glimpse of your future," Hammer whispered. "And it doesn't look too bad."

"Mommy, can I swim, too?"

"Go get your swimsuit and you can."

"Yay," she squealed, running for the door, Ripper hot on her heels.

"She sure is cute. How old is she?"

"She's three going on fifteen."

"This is a nice place you got here," I remarked, taking in the pool and outdoor kitchen area.

"Thanks. We like it. It's an improvement on the last place."

"Where did you move from?"

"Colorado. I was going to school up there until I just couldn't manage it anymore."

"What were you going to school for?"

"I was pre-veterinarian. I couldn't pull off a full load of classes, work, and take care of Ellie. So, I moved down here to where my mom and stepdad are."

"Are they helping you pay for this place?"

She narrowed her eyes at my question.

"What's that supposed to mean?"

"This is a nice house. I couldn't help but notice the billboard on my way in. These go for a mint."

"Uh-huh," she said, and the hair on the back of my neck stood up.

That was never a word you wanted to hear a woman utter. Along with fine.

"You know what? It's none of my damn business." I threw my hands up in surrender.

"You're right. It's not your business but seeing as you're helping me out and I assume you think I'm trying to pull one over on you since I told you I don't have the money to pay for my repairs I'll tell you the truth." With each word, she poked her finger into my chest.

Was it sad that it was getting me hot? She got sexier being pissed off.

"I rent this place and I qualified for help to afford it."

The last words caught in her throat. Her eyes welled with tears. She blinked them back as she turned away from me.

Pride is a damn hard thing to live with. Especially when you needed help.

"Honey, it is none of my business. I'm glad that I can help you out."

"Mommy look! I did it myself!" A small voice exclaimed.

Both of us looked at her. I swallowed a laugh as her mother groaned.

She'd gotten dressed by herself all right, but it was all wrong. The straps of her swimsuit crossed in the wrong direction.

"Ellie, my goodness." This time it was her mother who laughed. "Let's go get you fixed up, okay?"

Sheridan ushered her daughter back into the house without a backward glance at me.

"Trigger, I don't know what you're thinking or if I like it," Kenna said from beside me.

"Stay out of it, Kenna."

"She's my best friend. She's been hurt before. If this is just going to be a dump and go for you, leave her the hell alone."

"A what? A dump and go? What the fuck does that even mean?"

"You're usual bullshit. Your fuck'em and leave'em life. She's too good for that shit."

"Tell me how you feel, Kenna."

"I know what went down at the club that night. That wasn't her.

The real her. She doesn't remember a damn thing from that night, and I haven't enlightened her."

"She doesn't recognize me?" I pouted and Kenna laughed.

"No, she only remembers being hungover as hell the next morning and swearing that she was never going drinking with me again."

"I thought she was pretending when she saw me earlier."

Kenna shook her head before narrowing her eyes at me.

"I like you, Trigger. You're upfront with the woman and I respect that. They know what they're getting into. Sheridan's different.

"I figured that one out already."

"Then you're already ahead of the game. I don't want to see her hurt."

"What if she hurts me?" I frowned down at Kenna.

"The only way that'll happen is if you fuck up."

She turned and walked back to the pool, leaving wet footprints on the concrete. "She may be the best thing that will ever happen to you. You'll have to wait and see."

"Guess I'll get that chance if she's going to be working at Shooter's."

Kenna grimaced.

"What?"

"That may not be such a good idea."

"Why? I can be a good boy." I winked, and she barked out a laugh.

"I'll believe it when I see it. I didn't know it was you she was talking about. Shooters may not be the best place for her to make some extra cash."

"Why not? All the waitresses seem to make enough cash each night."

"Nessa," she said as she held my gaze.

"Nessa? What about her?"

Nessa was one of our club girls and another waitress at Shooters.

Kenna snorted in disbelief. "Really? You don't see where there may be a problem?"

Even Hammer chortled.

No, I didn't see what the problem was.

But it wouldn't be long before I figured it out.

CHAPTER 6
SHERIDAN

I FOLLOWED KENNA INTO SHOOTERS. The place was well-lit and busy for a weekday lunch. It wasn't the dive I thought it would be. The plate-glass windows allowed light to pour in. Three separate dining areas had heavy wooden tables and chairs spread out, plenty of room in between. Plush, burgundy booths lined the outer walls, while old metal signs boasting motor oil and gasoline companies dotted the walls. In the center was a dance floor was an elevated stage to host the live music on weekends.

"Three butt funnels," I laughed out.

"What?" Kenna looked at me strangely.

"Butt funnels."

"What the hell is a butt funnel?"

"We've been friends for years and you don't watch Bar Rescue?"

"Uh no. Unlike someone I know, I have a life and don't watch crap TV."

"You take that back." I smacked her arm. "Jon Taffer is a legend. And those butt funnels drive drink sales."

"Still don't get it."

"It's the openings around the dance floor. They're narrow on purpose, so if two people pass through, they turn and face each other.

They make eye contact and, bada bing bada boom, the man is buying the lady a drink."

"You're crazy," Kenna blurted out.

"It's the lack of adult conversation and spending a lot of late nights up with Ellie," I muttered.

"Hey, Dave," Kenna shouted down to the end of the bar where a short, thin man was wiping down the bar top. "Shooter in his office?"

"Yeah, he was a few minutes ago."

"Thanks," Dave replied with a nod, turning back to the customer who had walked up.

Kenna weaved her way around customers toward a darkened hallway beside the bar.

"His name is Shooter?" I asked in confusion.

"It's his road name. His real name is Alex, but he won't answer to it."

"I do when I have to," a voice rumbled out of the doorway Kenna turned into.

Kenna stopped short, and I walked into her back. I peered around her side and saw what made her hit the brakes.

The man was older but in great shape. His muscular chest was sprinkled with dark hair. Sweat dripped down his taut abdomen as he finished buttoning his pants. He had to be around Ray's age, but he was damn fine. With his eyes locked on Kenna's, he reached down and picked up a black t-shirt off his desk.

Kenna opened her mouth to speak but clamped her jaw shut when the door to the left opened and a blonde woman came out, adjusting her top. Kenna's back straightened and her fists clenched.

"Should have shut the damn door," Kenna barked out.

"Nessa, why don't you head on out," Shooter instructed the woman as he pulled the shirt over his head. It was a damn shame, but I wouldn't say it.

Nessa strolled up to us on what looked to be five-inch stiletto heels, with a smirk on her face. "Might want to fix your makeup. You look a little used," Kenna bit out.

"Bitch," Nessa seethed as she pushed past us.

"Kenna, there's no need to be rude. Introduce me to your friend."

"Sheridan, this is Shooter. He owns the place."

"Are you going to hide behind her all day?"

"Sorry," I muttered, coming to stand beside Kenna. The tension between the two was so thick I could have cut it with a knife. "It's nice to meet you."

"Kenna told me you're looking for a part-time job. Have you waitressed before or tended bar?"

"I've done both."

"Are you easily offended? Some of this crowd can be a little rough around the edges."

"Not really. I worked at a college bar. If you've had to put up with drunken frat boys, you can put up with a lot. I don't know if anything could be worse."

Shooter smirked, and I wanted to swoon. What happened that I kept running into all these popular men?

Kenna wasn't unaffected by it, either. Her face stayed impassive, but I could tell.

"Kenna, grab her an application," Shooter ordered. "Can you start this weekend?

"Yes, I can."

"Come in at two on Saturday. Get a feel for the place. We'll see how it goes. If you don't run out crying, I'll see about adding you to the schedule for a full weekend."

Elation swamped me. I started bouncing up and down.

"Thank you. I won't let you down." He smiled at my excitement.

"Don't forget to bring your ID and social security card for the paperwork. Kenna can get you some shirts to wear."

"Let's go." Kenna turned toward the door.

"It was nice meeting you!" I called out, following behind her.

"You too, Sheridan," Shooter's voice rumbled out behind me.

With one last stop at the bar, Kenna grabbed a manila folder and headed for the door like her ass was on fire. The crowd parted as she rolled through.

"What's the hurry?" I rushed to catch up with her much longer stride. Being short sucked sometimes. Especially when your best friend is seven inches taller than you and all legs.

She slammed her hands against the door open and it flew open, slamming into the brick façade. I cringed, waiting for the sound of shattering glass, but it never came.

"Nothing. Just want to make sure you get back to work on time," she muttered, digging in her purse for her keys.

I'd taken an extended lunch today with Dr. Collin's approval since I told him I was interviewing for a second job. After I reassured him I wasn't leaving the clinic, and it would not be permanent, he was fine with it.

"I still have half an hour left. I thought this would take us a lot longer," I assured her as we hurried to her Kia Soul.

"That gives us time to grab some lunch, then." She smiled, but it didn't reach her eyes.

"Is there something going on between the two of you?"

"Who?" When I looked back at the building, she huffed out a breath. "No, there's nothing going on between me and Shooter."

"Do you wish there was?"

"No. He just knows how to push my buttons." She opened the car door and climbed in.

I didn't mention that he hadn't done that today. He'd only had sex in his office, and we'd almost caught him in the act. I knew when to keep my mouth shut.

"How about Whataburger? My treat."

"That sounds good. I haven't had it in forever." I clicked my seat-belt closed as she started the engine.

"Who was that girl, anyway?"

"That's Nessa, bitch extraordinaire," Kenna hissed out.

"Don't like her, huh?"

"Whatever gave you that idea?"

CHAPTER 7
SHERIDAN

THE NEXT DAY at work was busy. A popular doggie daycare had passed around a virus and I had seen and smelled more diarrhea and vomit than I ever had in my life. The smell lingered in my scrubs and hair. Not even my loaner car was spared. As soon I got home from work, I stripped down by the back door, threw the clothes in the washer, and raced for the shower.

When I got out, my mom and Ellie were cooking dinner.

"Hey, guys." I walked over, giving Mom a peck on the cheek and picking up my girl. She wrapped her arms around my neck and squeezed for all she was worth.

"Did you let Ripper out?"

"Yes, ma'am. He's outside pooping."

"Ellie, for goodness sake," my mother huffed out.

"What?" Ellie's eyes widened. "Can we swim tonight, Mommy?"

"Not tonight. I'm tired. How about a movie?"

"Elsa?"

I resisted the urge to roll my eyes. It would be freaking Elsa. If it kept her quiet, I didn't care at this point.

"Sure. You can watch Elsa. We'll eat, take a bath, and get into our jammies."

"Okay. Gigi is making mac and cheese."

"Oh, is she?" My mouth watered. Mom's macaroni and cheese was amazing. I could never make mine taste like hers, even though she had given me the recipe. Sneaky woman wasn't giving up her secret.

"Regular for Ellie and buffalo chicken for you."

"That sounds amazing. I appreciate it."

"Rough day at work?"

"It was a killer. Stomach bug times about twenty."

"Please say no more," Mom rushed out, turning a little green around the gills. She didn't do well with sickness. I don't know how she made it through my childhood after my dad died.

"I won't," I promised. "Are you eating with us?"

"No, Ray and I are going out for dinner."

"He's off on a Friday night?"

"Yes, and I'm taking advantage," she winked, and I shuddered at the implication. "What time are you dropping Ellie off tomorrow?"

"Around one?"

"That's fine. We'll take her to daycare on Monday and you can pick her up after."

"I thought I was going to pick her up Sunday morning?"

"She might as well spend the weekend at Gigi's house."

At my disheartened look, Mom laughed. "You can come over for lunch on Sunday. Will you work that day, too?"

"Saturday is my trial by fire, so to speak. If I do ok Shooter said he'll give me more days on the weekend."

"You'll do fine. You come from tough stock."

"Too bad more height didn't come with it," I chuckled. Mom narrowed her eyes at me. "I'm kidding, Mom."

"Dinner is ready. Just add the chicken and sauce to yours. I've got to get ready for tonight." She gave me and Ellie a kiss. "Y'all have a good night and I'll see you tomorrow."

"Love you, too, Mom. Don't have too much fun tonight," I teased.

"Love you, Gigi!"

Later, after we ate dinner and Ellie had her bath, I passed out about halfway through the movie with Ellie singing *Let It Go*.

The next morning, I made Ellie some pancakes when Kenna

showed up. With dark bags under her eyes and hair in a messy bun on top of her head, she looked like she had a rough night.

"Please tell me you have coffee," she groaned, dropping her head on the counter when she sat down.

"Lucky for you, there's some left."

I poured her a cup and slid the bottle of creamer closer to her. She ignored the creamer and downed the cup.

"It must have been a terrible night."

"Super busy. Everyone wanted to ignore the last call. It took over an hour to clear out the place after we closed."

"Good tips?"

"Hell yes." She grinned. "I'm just worn out."

"You didn't have to come over so early. Do you want some pancakes?"

"Ken Ken, have pancakes with me!" Ellie screamed, slamming herself into Kenna's legs.

"Sure thing, kiddo." Kenna picked her up and placed Ellie in her lap. "What are we putting on them? Cheese?"

"Ewww, no." Ellie scrunched up her nose. "Butter and syrup."

After stuffing ourselves, Kenna grabbed the shirts she had left in her car. She tossed me the red one.

"Try it on."

"It's my size. It'll fit."

"Go try it on and let's see," Kenna ordered.

"Fine." I turned my back and whipped off the shirt I was wearing. Sliding on the red one, I turned to face her.

"See, I told you it would fit."

"Is this child-sized?"

"Do you have a push-up bra?"

"Really?" I huffed out.

"Do you?"

"Maybe? I'll have to check. I haven't worn one in years."

"Throw on a pair of shorts too," she called out as I walked down the hall. "The shorter the better."

"You've got to be kidding me," I muttered, entering my room.

My bed was a rumpled mess of blankets. I pulled up the covers and straightened the pillows, knowing that Kenna and Ellie would end up in here sooner rather than later.

The top drawer of my dresser housed my everyday undies. It wasn't going to be in there. I kneeled to the bottom drawer that rarely ever saw the light of day and started digging.

At the very back, laid a black bra I hadn't seen in a very long time. "Am I going to do this?"

I pulled the shirt over my head, unsnapped my old bra, and put on the black one. My barely B cups filled out to a C with the extra padding. Then I grabbed a pair of denim shorts that I wouldn't think to wear outside of my house.

"I look like a damn hoochie," I remarked when I walked back into the living room.

"No, you don't," Kenna laughed. "Trust me. You'll see hoochie tonight."

Kenna picked up the bottom of the shirt and tied it into a knot, leaving a good portion of my stomach bare.

"The fewer clothes you wear, the more money you'll make."

"I don't know if I can do this. It's not me."

"Smile and flirt. That's all you need to do. Trust me."

Tugging down the top she gave me, I walked into the back door that Kenna told me was the staff entrance. Knowing she would be here later tonight gave me the boost of confidence that I needed. I still felt uncomfortable as hell in this outfit. At least she relented and let me wear my Converse. There was no way I could have worn heels, as she suggested.

The kitchen was bustling after the lunch rush and preparing for the evening crowd. One guy nodded at me as he loaded up the dishwasher. I waved back and walked further in.

"Sheridan, right?" Dave asked as he rounded the bar.

"Yes, that's me."

"You can put your bag down here. Did you bring your ID and stuff?"

"Sure did." I pulled them out of my wallet and handed them to him.

"I'll make a copy of them right quick and then we'll get you started."

"All right."

He walked off down the hall where Shooter's office was.

I leaned up against the bar and looked out over the room. There were still plenty of full tables, even though it was an odd time of day. Several pool tables were situated over to the side and another room just beyond that was roped off.

"That's Nessa's area back there," Dave stated, coming up behind me. "There's a motorcycle gang who hangs out back there, and she deals with them."

"Motorcycle gang?"

"They call themselves a club but whatever. I'd avoid them if you can. Nessa's possessive, and can be a pain in your ass if you get on her bad side."

"Roger that. Avoid Nessa and that room. Got it."

"It'll make for an easier night."

Three hours later, I had served several tables and mixed some drinks. I nodded at Kenna when she came in.

"How's it going?"

"Not too bad. The system is the same as the last place I worked."

"Good. Give it a couple of hours and this place will be hopping. Make sure you take a break before then."

"I think I'm taking my dinner break in an hour."

"Okay. Nessa will be coming in soon. Make sure you spend as little time with her as possible."

"What the hell is the deal with this Nessa? Dave warned me off her, too."

"She's a vindictive bitch, plain and simple. She sees any female as competition for attention and she'll do anything to make your life hell if she can."

"Who pissed in her Cheerios?"

"Who knows? She's been that way as long as I've been here. She wants to put her stamp on all the men of the Blacktop Brethren."

"Who are they?"

"The local motorcycle club. You've already met a couple of them."

"I have?""

"Trigger and Hammer."

"Levi and Michael?"

"That the mountain of a man?"

"Yes, that's him," I confirmed. I knew he rode a motorcycle from the times he came to his mom's house. It was hard not to hear it coming up the road.

"Dave said they're a gang," I whispered.

"Dave's just jealous. One guy screwed his girlfriend, and it's pissed him off ever since. Can't believe Shooter still lets him work here."

"Why would he care?"

"He's one of them."

"Oh, shit. That was Nessa with him in the office, right?"

"Yes, being her usual whore self," Kenna uttered.

"Ladies, let's get back to work," Dave stated as he walked by. "Quit the chit-chat."

"Sir, yes, sir," Kenna barked out and saluted.

"Smartass," Dave laughed and kept going.

Kenna wasn't lying. By ten o'clock my feet felt like they weighed a thousand pounds apiece and my arms could barely hold up the tray. But the tips were rolling in. Nessa had come in earlier in all her glory. She ignored me and walked straight back to her section and stayed there unless she needed to get them another round of drinks. I hadn't seen Levi or Michael come in, but the back room was packed with men wearing black vests declaring them members of the Blacktop Brethren.

Several ladies had ventured close enough to catch the guy's attention, but a harsh word from Nessa scared a few off. I wanted to laugh at the way they retreated, like a dog with its tail tucked between its legs.

I picked up the tray from the bar that held several mugs of beer and weaved between the patrons. It was a definite disadvantage to only be five foot one. I couldn't see over anybody!

Someone knocked into my side, causing the mugs to shift on the tray. I tried to keep them balanced, but it was too late.

One by one, the mugs fell over, splashing beer all over me, the floor, and the customer on my other side. He turned, knocking the tray out of my hands.

"You fucking bitch," he shouted, bloodshot eyes narrowed, balling up his fist.

I froze, waiting for the hit.

A hit that never made contact.

Inches from my face, a hand reached out and caught the fist. A wall of black filled my vision as my savior stepped in front of me.

"What the fuck do you think you're doing?"

"That bitch spilled beer all over me. I'm going to take it out of her hide."

"It was an accident, dumbass. And if this is how you treat women, I suggest you leave."

"You gonna make me?"

My hero nodded.

Then I was surrounded by more men. All wearing the same vest. The words Blacktop Brethren MC surrounded a wicked-looking skull and pistons.

I held my breath waiting for the fallout. As small as I was, I would get trampled in the melee. A large hand landed on my shoulder, causing me to glance up and over my shoulder. Michael smiled down at me from his towering height. His brown eyes twinkled with mirth.

"Don't worry, Sheridan. You're fine."

I believed him.

When I looked back, the man in front of me had turned and now faced me. Levi smiled down at me.

"Already getting into trouble, huh?" Levi laughed.

"Mom always said I was a magnet for trouble," I laughed nervously, relieved that it was him. My heart picked up speed at the look of concern that he gave me. He eyed me up and down, looking for any injury. I gave him points for not lingering on my nonexistent cleavage. He cupped my cheek, rubbing his thumb across my skin. It tingled in its wake.

"You okay?"

"I'm fine. Thanks for saving me."

"Anytime, doll." When he dropped his hand, my skin became cold, aching to have his touch back.

"Trigger, come on," Nessa whined, coming up behind Levi and wrapping herself around his arm. "I got your drink."

"I'll be there in a minute." He never took his eyes off me while he patted her arm.

She pouted up at him before glaring at me. Even though I knew I had done nothing, she had declared me an enemy.

"I'm good," I muttered, backing away from the pair. "You go have a good time and I need to get cleaned up and grab some more beers."

"Make sure you get Dave to come clean this up before someone injures themselves."

I gave him a thumbs-up before I lost myself in the crowd.

"Kenna, I need another round of beers. My last ones bit the dust."

"Is that what was going on out there?"

"Some guy backed into me and knocked them over."

"Hey, Dave. Got a spill on the main floor," Kenna yelled across the bar.

Dave gave her a nod of acknowledgment.

"I think I made an enemy of Nessa," I blurted out as she pulled the beers.

She winced. "Damn, I was hoping it would at least be a week. What happened?"

"Some guy took offense to getting soaked in beer and decided to introduce his fist to my face."

"And?"

"Levi stepped in and told him the errors of his ways."

Kenna hissed in a breath.

"Then the other guys showed up."

"That'll do it. You got the attention that she craves from the guys she considers hers."

"Are they?"

"Are they what?"

"Hers?" I asked, annoyed.

"I don't think any of them are in a relationship. She likes to think she's queen of the castle, but unless her pussy is a drug and they're addicted, it's all in her head."

"Whose pussy is a drug?" Shooter growled out, coming up behind Kenna. She stiffened, almost dropping the last mug of beer she placed on the bar.

"Wouldn't you like to know?" Kenna breathed out. "There you go, Sheridan. It's time for my break." She wiggled from where Shooter had her trapped against the bar. Shooter's gaze followed as she hightailed it away from us.

"How's your night going, Sheridan?" He leaned against the bar; arms crossed over his chest.

"Not bad. One incident, but nothing I couldn't handle."

He snorted.

"What?"

"Nothing, babe," he laughed. "Nothing at all. I think you may fit in here after all."

Smiling, I picked up the tray and walked into the crowd.

CHAPTER 8
TRIGGER

"TRIGGER'S IN LURVE," Sully crooned when we got back to the room.

"Fuck off, asshole." I shoved him to the side as my brothers laughed.

"I don't want to hear you say shit about me saving the damsel in distress ever again."

"What was I supposed to do? Let the fucker hit her?"

"Here's your beer, Trigger," Nessa rubbed up against me, her titties grazing my arm.

Any other night that would've gotten my attention, but my gaze was on the petite brunette who seemed to take up most of my thoughts.

"It's almost my break time if you want to take a trip out back," Nessa whispered to me.

"Appreciate the offer, but I'll have to decline. Why don't you hit up Savage?" I suggested. "He's been having a rough week."

She pouted her cherry-red lips at me but moved over to Savage, where he was sitting on a stool in the corner. She threw herself into his lap and glared at me.

"Man, you are asking for trouble," Wrench laughed.

Wrench was another brother I had grown up with. He owned the garage that was on the same block as my dad's. Wrench and his brother, Demon, were magic with tools and paint. Where Dad and I worked on the usual repairs on vehicles, Wrench did modifications. He could do anything to make a vehicle go faster or pimp it out with an amazing paint job.

"Where's Demon at?"

"Who knows? I haven't seen him today." Wrench upended the bottle of beer he was holding.

"I thought you had that Mustang to finish up this weekend?"

"We do. I've been working on it most of the day, but Demon flaked on me," he bitched.

"He seems to do that a lot. Need me to come over and help tomorrow?"

"I'd appreciate it. The customer is coming at ten Monday morning, and I promised to have it ready."

"No problem. How early you want to start?"

"Depends on how late the party ends tonight." Wrench grinned.

"Seen something you like?"

"New girl. Wouldn't mind taking her for a spin."

At the mention of Sheridan, my hand tightened on my beer.

"Leave that one alone," I ground out. Wrench's brows shot up in surprise.

"It's like that, huh?" Wrench smiled.

"No, it's not like that, but she's not one to play around with."

"I hear you, brother."

"Good." I tilted the beer bottle to my lips, downing the cold brew.

"Need another one?" Nessa appeared at my side.

"Sure, babe," Wrench told her, handing her his empty.

"I'm good. Thanks, though."

Nessa shrugged her shoulder and walked out.

Conversations carried on around me, but I couldn't focus on them. From where I was standing, I could see the main floor and Sheridan making her way across with another heavy ass tray. How the hell she held it up, I didn't know.

When I looked back, I noticed that Raze and Sully had gathered around the table with Wrench and me. The only ones missing from our crew were Demon and Hammer. Hammer had headed home after the incident on the floor to rest up. Since he was the club's fighter, we needed him in tip-top condition for the fight coming up in a couple of months. As for Demon, if his brother didn't know where he was, no one else did either. Those two were thick as thieves. Or they had been until Demon started on a downward spiral. I guessed fucking up and losing the best thing that had ever happened to you would do that.

The five of us had been inseparable since we were little kids. We'd raised hell throughout school. Demon was a year older than me, Hammer, and Raze. Sully and Wrench were both the youngsters of the group. By the time they had graduated high school, the teachers breathed a sigh of relief.

"Hey, Trigger, are you even listening?" Raze elbowed me in the side.

"Sorry, man. What did I miss?"

"After the fight, I'm headed to Vegas for a tattoo convention. You want to tag along?"

Raze owned a tattoo parlor in town and was always in demand. He booked out for months at a time and people traveled from all over to get inked by him. His body was a testament to his love of body art. His entire torso, back, and arms were covered and his legs were well on their way. The only places free of ink were his neck and face. He was sporting two lip rings and a hoop in his nose.

"I think our boy might be occupied," Sully taunted.

"If he hasn't tired himself by then," Wrench added.

"Fuck you guys."

"What did I miss?" Raze asked, looking at each of us.

"Nothing," I bit out.

"Our boy has a crush," Sully laughed.

I threw a French fry at him.

"Who's the girl?"

"New waitress," Wrench answered.

"That was fast."

"Nah. He met her for the first time the other day. Her car broke down and I hauled it to the shop."

"She going to work off some of that payment?" Raze wagged his brows at his innuendo.

"Don't talk that way about her," I growled.

Raze spewed the drink of beer he had just taken across the table. Wrench wiped his face, sending him a dirty look.

"Holy shit." Raze eyed me with surprise.

"What?"

"Nothing, Brother. She's working tonight?"

"First night. Lover boy here saved her ass earlier."

"What happened?" Raze's eyes darkened with anger.

"Some douchebag wanted to get physical."

"Bouncers didn't step in?"

"I don't think they saw it. She's a little bit of a thing."

"Where is she?" Raze craned his neck to see out into the main room.

Wrench turned his head to look. "She's walking towards the bar." He nodded in her direction.

My eyes were drawn to her ass. The shorts she was wearing were bordering on indecent and if she bent over, I'd be able to see what she was wearing underneath.

"Damn, she is small. Nice ass, though," Raze remarked.

"Watch it," I warned.

"No offense. Just calling it like I see it."

"What are you looking at?" Nessa asked, coming up beside the table.

"New girl," Raze answered.

Nessa's eyes narrowed on Raze.

Now I understood what Kenna meant about Nessa. She didn't appreciate having our attention diverted from her when we were here.

"I doubt she'll be here long," Nessa huffed. "She doesn't have what it takes."

Nessa flounced off without asking if we needed anything. She was our damn waitress, after all.

"No, we didn't need anything," I muttered.

Sully laughed. "I'll make a trip to the bar. The usual?"

We nodded as he scooted back his chair.

"Be back in a few."

"What was wrong with her car?" Raze asked.

"What's not wrong with it? It's a piece of shit. Dad wanted to scrap it."

"Ouch."

"I take it she didn't agree?"

"I didn't mention it to her. She didn't have enough money for Sully to tow her in."

"Shit. How's she going to pay for repairs?"

"Lover boy is letting her pay it out," Sully imparted, coming up to the table.

"How the hell did you get your dad to agree to that?" Wrench asked in surprise.

"He doesn't know," I uttered.

"Fuck. He's going to kick your ass when he finds out."

"He also loaned her a car, so she wouldn't be on foot," Sully added.

Raze looked at me with disbelief.

"She has a little girl. I couldn't leave her stranded." I shrugged my shoulders. Why did I feel the need to defend myself? I was a nice guy.

"You have it bad," Wrench quipped.

"She's just some chick. I had a moment of weakness."

The table erupted in laughter. They didn't believe that anymore that I did.

I stayed a lot longer than I planned. Last call was about twenty minutes ago, and the place was clearing out. Most of my brothers had left and went to our clubhouse which was about seven miles outside the city limits. Normally, I was with them ready to lose myself in club pussy. But not tonight.

Tonight, I watched as Sheridan made her way around the rooms cleaning up empty bottles and trash. There were only a few patrons left. She smiled up at one as he handed her a wad of bills. I saw red but shut that shit down. She wasn't mine.

Not yet anyway.

Where the hell had that thought come from?

The guys were right. I had a crush. I refused to call it anything else.

"You ready to go, Trigger?" Nessa asked, rubbing up against me.

"Huh?" I dragged my attention away from Sheridan. "I'm going home in a few minutes. I need to get some sleep since I'm helping Wrench out in the morning."

"We could go in the back real quick," she offered. She reached down and cupped my dick. It didn't even perk up.

"Not tonight."

Her brown eyes narrowed on me, then her head turned in Sheridan's direction where she was talking to Kenna at the bar.

"She won't give you what I do. Remember that," Nessa hissed, as she squeezed my dick a little too hard.

I headed out and stood by the back door, waiting for Sheridan to appear. Shooter kept the place well-lit, but it was still the middle of the night. It wasn't safe for a woman to walk to her car alone.

Had it bothered me before?

Hell no.

Now the thought of Sheridan being out here where someone could attack her made me sick to my stomach.

The heavy metal door opened, revealing Sheridan and Kenna. One bouncer, Zeke, brought up the rear. He nodded in my direction before letting the door shut behind the girls.

"Busy night, ladies," I remarked, and both let out a startled scream. Sheridan clutched a hand to her chest.

"Damn it, Trigger. You scared the crap out of us!" Kenna griped. "What are you doing back here?"

"I wanted to see how Sheridan did on her first night."

"It was good. Thank you for saving me in there. I wasn't looking forward to getting decked by some guy."

"I'm sorry you were put in that position. If a man can't treat a woman with respect, he doesn't deserve to be called a man."

Kenna covered her laugh with a cough. Sheridan glanced at her over her shoulder.

"Let me walk you to your cars." I gestured toward the back where the employees were parked. "Does someone walk with you out here every night?"

"The bouncer or Shooter if he's here," Kenna remarked.

"Good."

Kenna's car parked the closest to us and she got in first.

"Night, guys. Sheridan, I'll call you in the morning."

"Not too early. I plan on sleeping in for a change," Sheridan quipped.

Damn, I wanted to give her a reason to sleep in.

"Be careful driving home." Kenna shut her door with a thud.

Sheridan's loaner car was parked three spaces down. Kenna honked as she passed us by. We arrived at the driver's side and Sheridan dug in her bag for the keys.

"Why do they always fall to the bottom?" she muttered as she moved things around. "Found them," she crowed and yawned.

"You're worn out."

"I haven't worked like that since I left Colorado."

"Did you waitress there?"

"Yeah. It was decent money for a part-time job."

I took the keys from her hand and unlocked the car door. She slid in and reached for the keys.

"Have you had any trouble with the car?"

"No, it's been fine. It's nice to have one where the air conditioning works all the time."

"Yours doesn't?"

"It doesn't get very cold. In this heat, it barely makes a dent."

Something else for me to check on Monday.

"What was that look?"

"What look?" I asked.

"I don't have the extra money to fix the air. Get that out of your head."

"I don't know what you're talking about."

"Somehow, I don't believe that."

"When are you working again?"

"Shooter's giving me Friday and Saturday nights for now. More if I want them, but I need to spend some time with my daughter."

"Who's keeping her tonight?"

"She's staying the weekend with my mom and Ray."

"You're lucky they live close."

"I am. It was hard when she was smaller, and it was the two of us. My mom's always ready to step in and help." She yawned again.

"Get yourself home and get some rest."

"A hot shower and my bed sound heavenly."

Damn right, they did. I needed to get out of here before I offered to wash her back.

"Be careful driving home."

"Good night, Levi," she said with a smile and shut the door.

I went to sleep that night dreaming of that smile. All alone in my bed and I couldn't have been happier.

CHAPTER 9
TRIGGER

"WRENCH, YOU IN HERE?" I knocked on the metal door that was ajar.

Wrench's bike wasn't out front, but it wasn't unusual for him to park it inside when the garage was closed.

"Fuck, don't yell," came a voice from my right. Wrench emerged from the shadows, rubbing a hand across his head.

"Hungover?" I laughed. I flipped on the overhead lights. The bulbs flickered before flaring to life. Wrench shielded his eyes from the onslaught.

"Fuck yes. Why did you let me drink so fucking much?" He groaned.

"Would you have listened?"

"Probably not," he conceded.

"Here." I tossed him the bottle of ibuprofen I picked up on the ride over.

"Thanks," he replied, catching the small white bottle.

"Got you this, too." I hand him the bottle of red Gatorade. "Figured you might need some fluids in you."

"I'm getting too old for this shit," he complained, opening the bottle.

"Man, don't say that."

"It's true. I turned thirty last month and you're knocking on that door. These late nights aren't as easy to bounce back from as they used to be."

"But they sure are fun," I countered.

"Are they?" He shook his head. "I don't know, man. There has to be more out there."

"Like what?"

"If you call me a pussy, I'll beat your ass," Wrench warned.

"Noted."

"I want what Deke has with Lydia."

Deke was an older member of the club and Wrench's uncle. Wrench and Demon lived with him after their mother died from cancer. Lydia was the epitome of a great wife. She supported her old man and the club but didn't take any shit. She'd kicked a few of the club girls' asses for trying to touch her man. Not that Deke wanted any of that. He only had eyes for Lydia.

They reminded me a lot of my mom and dad. They'd had their issues throughout the years but always came out stronger on the other side.

A lot of the older members weren't as lucky. They'd either gotten divorced or fucked up and lost the best things that could have happened to them, leaving them bitter and jaded against women.

"That's not being a pussy. That's being a man and seeing what a good woman can do for you. You just need to make sure you're ready for that when she comes along."

"Amen. I don't think I'm going to find her hanging out at bars, getting drunk on the weekend."

"How did Deke meet Lydia? I don't think I ever heard the story."

"It was a turtle in the middle of the road," Wrench laughed.

"A turtle?"

"Yes. There was a big alligator snapping turtle in the middle of the road. Lydia had stopped to move it because she was afraid it would get run over. When she went to pick it up, the damn thing spun around and nearly got her fingers. When Deke rolled up on his bike, she had taken the floor mat out of her Jeep and was trying to push it across the road. The damn thing was massive, at least eighty pounds."

I could picture tiny Lydia attempting to scoot a huge turtle with the floor mat.

"He said it was the stupidest thing he had ever seen and he had to help her, though. He parked behind her, then went over, picked the damn thing up, and carried it across the road. When he crossed back, she looked up at him and he was lost."

"That explains the turtle tattoo he has."

"He got it the next day. He knew she was special."

"How did he know?"

"The moment their eyes met, he knew. It was a punch in the gut."

That hit a little too close to home. Was that the reason I couldn't get Sheridan out of my head?

"Just luck of the draw that he stopped to help her."

"Or that she's soft-hearted about animals. What if she had given up after the damn thing nearly took her finger off? They would have passed right by each other."

Both of us stopped to think of the consequences if that had happened. Deke was on a treacherous path before he met Lydia. If they hadn't met, he would have ended up in prison or dead. Wrench and Demon would have had to go into foster care or go to some obscure family member on their dad's side.

"Lydia said it was fate." He drained the rest of his drink. "Let's get to work. We have a ton to fix if he's picking this up in the morning."

"Still no word from Demon?"

"No," he bit out.

"No one knows where he is? Not even Mads?"

Wrench shook his head.

"Mads said he called her, but it was a shitty connection. I've called all the club members and the girls. No one's seen or heard from him in a couple of days. It's not the first time he's hit the road to clear his head when shit's going down." Wrench hesitated. "He worries me."

"It's bullshit that he's left you here to do all this by yourself. It's both of your business."

"We will have words when he shows his face."

The next morning came a hell of a lot quicker than I would have liked. Wrench and I had worked late into the night to get the Mustang finished, but we did it. If it wasn't already spoken for, I was tempted to buy the thing myself.

My shower felt so good pounding down on my sore muscles I stayed in too long. Dad was going to kick my ass for being late. I pulled into the donut store and picked up a dozen kolaches as a peace offering.

I parked my bike next to a rental car parked off to the side of the building. All the bay doors were open and heavy metal music blared from the radio. I walked into the lobby and bypassed the counter, going straight to Dad's office.

"You're late," he uttered, not looking up from his newspaper.

"I brought breakfast."

"Did you get the jalapeno ones?" He looked over the rim of his glasses at me. He knew me too well.

"That and regular."

"Heard you helped Wrench yesterday."

"I did. That Mustang is a fucking beast. I wish I could be there when the owner shows up and sees it."

"I heard the guy's a real hard ass. Some hot shot from Arizona."

"Wrench did a wicked paint job on it," I added.

"The boy has skills. I'm thinking about having him do some work on my shovelhead."

Dad had been working on rebuilding the old Harley Davidson that he had found in a scrap yard. He'd put a lot of time and effort into making it run like new. I think it may have been one thing that made my parent's marriage work. Each had their own hobbies. Dad would spend time out in the garage tinkering with something and mom would paint or do craft projects. They didn't spend every waking moment with each other. They were their own person, but they fit together.

"Dad, can I ask you something?"

"Sounds serious."

"It is."

"Hit me."

"How did you know Mom was the one for you?"

"Damn," he chuckled. "You know the story of how we met?"

"It was at a bar, wasn't it?"

"It was. Your Mom was something else. A couple of us guys went to the bar that wasn't far from base. Figured we'd blow off a little steam and find some women. We walked into this bar. No idea who the hell was playing, but the place was packed. You couldn't move without bumping into someone."

"We found a table and made the guys who were sitting get up," he chuckled at the memory. "We ordered some beers and had started drinking them when your mom came up to the table. She looked at each of us and demanded to know where the other guys were."

"She wasn't happy to learn that we'd made them leave; tore into us. All of us were twice her size and she didn't give a shit. One guy made a comment that she didn't like, and she dumped a pitcher of beer over his head."

"Mom?" I asked in disbelief. "My mother did that?"

"Damn right, she did. I knew right then and there that I wanted her. The next day, I knew I wanted her forever."

"Please do not expand on that," I pleaded, even though I knew what he meant. The thought of my parents having sex was not something I wanted to think about. Who the hell did? "Nothing else. You just knew?"

"Yes, but that didn't mean I didn't have to work to convince her. She thought I was an arrogant hothead and didn't want a damn thing to do with me. It took a hell of a lot of time and effort for me to get her to be with me."

"Do you ever regret it?"

"Not a damn minute. Your mother is my world. Why all the questions?"

"Just wondering. Wrench and I were talking last night."

"You're getting about that age."

"What do you mean?"

"I wasn't much younger than you when I met your mother. There's a certain point in your life that you want more."

"My life is pretty damn good as it is," I argued.

"I'm not saying it's not. I was like you before your mother. Looking for the next good time. Eventually, you grow out of that and want more. Some people do it earlier than others. Some never do. If you're asking these questions, I think you're getting there."

"Fuck, Dad."

"At least I didn't say what your mom would. *My little boy is growing up*," he mimicked.

"Shit. I'm going to work."

"Get on that brake job on the Ford."

"No problem." I shut the door behind me.

Standing at the counter when I came out was one technician, Jeremy, and a man I didn't recognize. He stared at me with scrutiny before focusing on Jeremy once more.

"Trigger, you're working on that Cavalier, right?"

At the mention of Sheridan's car, I froze.

"I did," I answered, coming up beside him. I stopped in from of the other man. "Why?"

"I can't find it in the system. This gentleman wanted to pay for some repairs."

"Why don't you head back in, and I'll take care of it." Jeremy gave me a grateful look and went back out into the bays.

"What can I help you with?"

I noticed that the man was wearing a long-sleeved shirt. Not something you see every day in this heat.

"I think he told you what I wanted," he grated out.

"We don't give out information about our clients. Only the owners or their designated agents."

"Jeremy was ready to give it to me."

"He's still new, and I'll make sure he knows that he can't do that. Now why don't you tell me who the hell you are and why you're asking about that car?"

He rubbed a hand across the back of his neck.

"Look, I don't want any information about her. I want to help pay for the repairs."

"Who the fuck are you to her?"

"Duke. Sheridan is, was mine."

"Not anymore." It wasn't a question.

"No, I fucked that up."

"And?"

"I'm trying to make things right the only way I can." He pushed up the sleeve of his shirt and revealed a tattoo I knew.

"Fuck," I hissed. "You're part of the Devil's Reign?"

His dark eyes narrowed, but he nodded.

"How the hell did she get messed up with the likes of you?"

"She lived in the apartment across the hall from my mother."

"In Colorado? That's a little out of your territory."

"Yes, it is. Mom had a stroke, and I had gone there to help her. Sheridan would cook for her and bring it over. One thing led to another."

"Did she know who the hell you were?"

"No. I didn't wear my colors around her. Mom didn't like it. Sheridan thought I was a regular guy."

"Jesus, man," I breathed out.

"I know. It was fucked up. I fell for her when I had no business bringing anyone into my life."

"Why the hell are you here now? How did you know her car was in the shop? Does she know you're here?"

"No, she doesn't, and I want to keep it that way. No one can know I'm here."

"Not even your club?"

"Especially them."

"I don't know how I feel about this."

"Look, I get it. You feel something for her." I stiffened as he threw those words out. How the hell could he tell that?

"She's easy to love. Why don't you meet me somewhere tonight and we'll get this straightened out?" He pulled out his wallet and extracted several hundred-dollar bills.

"Use this for her repairs. I know I can't pay for it all or she'd be suspicious."

"That car needs a ton of repairs. It would be cheaper to scrap it than fix it all."

"If I thought I could get away with buying her something new, I would. I'm doing what I can."

"There's a place over on Bellevue Street. A little hole in the wall called Crawford's. Meet me there at eight."

The diner was empty when I arrived, with only a couple of old-timers sitting at the counter drinking coffee. The rental car from earlier was parked in the corner. I killed the engine on my bike and placed my helmet on the handle. At the last second, I pulled off my cut and tucked it into my saddle bag.

The bell jingled when I pulled the door open. Verna looked up from behind the counter and smiled.

"It's been a while, Levi."

"Yes, ma'am, it has."

"Grab a seat wherever." She waved a hand over the place.

"I'm meeting someone."

She looked me over and noticed what I wasn't wearing. She nodded.

"In the back booth."

I nodded my thanks. Sliding into the booth, Duke looked up from the white ceramic mug in front of him.

"Did you order anything to eat?"

"No, wasn't sure how long this would take."

"Verna, can I get two specials, please? And a Coke?"

"Sure thing, Levi."

"Foods great here. I'd hate for you to miss out," I told Duke when he looked at me with narrowed eyes.

"What do you want to know?" Duke asked, wrapping a hand around the mug.

"Is Sheridan safe?"

"From me?" He looked up in surprise.

"You, your club, does it matter?"

"She's safe from me. That's why I did what I did. About the time she told me she was pregnant, one of my brothers told me that our President was getting suspicious of me spending so much time in Colorado."

"Why did that worry you?"

"Cobra is a mean bastard. He's not above using family members to keep us in line. Before Sheridan, he didn't have any hold over me and it ate at him. I couldn't take the chance of him finding out about her or the baby."

"Why not tell her the truth?"

"She wouldn't have understood. She's innocent, believes the best about people. The club would have chewed her up and spit her out. I didn't want to take the chance that she'd follow me back to California."

"How did you know her car was in the shop?"

"I put a tracker on it."

"You're keeping tabs on her?"

"She may not be mine anymore, but she's my responsibility."

"What about Ellie?"

Duke's eyes clouded, and he looked out the window into the parking lot.

"Have you met her?" he asked softly.

"For a couple of minutes. She's a mini version of Sheridan."

He half-smiled at that.

"I bet she's a handful," he chuckled. "Her mother sure was."

"Watch it," I warned.

"That's not what I meant. Sheridan was full of life. Always saw the bright side of every situation. She wasn't scared to try something new or put herself out there." He looked down at the coffee cup in his hands. "She brought out a side of me I thought had died years ago," he admitted.

"You've never seen your daughter?"

"Only from a distance."

"Sheridan seems to do a good job raising her."

"When she moved here, it was a relief. Knowing that her parents were here to help her out. Knowing that she wasn't doing it all alone."

"You're helping her pay for her house, aren't you?"

"How'd you figure that out?"

"A guess."

"It's my house. I bought it for her, so she'd have a decent place to live with Ellie."

"What are you doing with the rent?" I smiled at his look.

"College fund for Ellie."

"Are you ever going to be in Ellie's life?"

"No. I've made too many enemies over the years. I couldn't stand it if something happened to either of them because of me."

"Are you still in love with Sheridan?"

Duke looked down and spun the mug around, pondering his answer.

"I'm not sure I was in love with her," he answered. "I cared about her a lot and maybe I would have fallen in love with her. But I'm the reason she's raising my daughter alone and had to give up her dreams. I'll do anything to keep them safe." His gaze hardened.

"You trying to warn me off?"

"Do I need to?"

"You're right. Sheridan is special. I will not hurt her. She's pretty standoffish. She may not let me even try. But I'll warn you. If I have my way, I'm going to be in her life, and that includes Ellie."

"As long as you know I don't have issues with putting you six feet under if you fuck this up."

Duke clammed up as Verna sat two plates piled high with country-fried steak, mashed potatoes, and green beans in front of us. "Everything look okay?" She asked, eyes darting between the two of us.

"Looks delicious," Duke answered with a wink. "We'll let you know if we need anything else. Thanks."

I waited until she was out of hearing distance before answering.

"You know Cobra has a hard-on for me and my club, right?"

His dark eyes narrowed. "How so?

"Were you around when his son died?"

He looked at me, then his eyes widened with realization.

"Mother fucker," he hissed. "I didn't put two and two together."

He leaned back in the booth.

"It shouldn't be a problem. You don't normally come this far east."

"No, New Mexico is about as far as we come out this way. This is the first time I've been in Texas in a decade."

"Until the fight," I reminded him.

"Fuck. I wasn't even thinking about that. I guess we'll cross that bridge when it gets here. It's a couple of months away. Maybe you can get her out of town that weekend."

"If Cobra gets a whiff of you spending time out here, he's going to wonder why."

"You're right." Duke drummed his fingers on the tabletop. "I can't fucking believe I'm saying this, but I'm trusting you with them."

I knew what it meant for him to say those words. To entrust a stranger with the safety of your family. It would have been hard for me to do.

"I will protect them with everything I have."

He reached over and pulled a napkin out of the metal container. After he patted his pocket, he motioned to the waitress.

"Darlin', could I bother you for a pen and piece of paper?" He smiled at her, and I swore she was going to faint at his feet.

"Sure," she breathed out.

She reached into her pocket and pulled out a pen, then tore a sheet off her pad lying them on the table in front of him.

"Thanks."

"Can I get you a refill?"

"No, I think we're good."

He wrote something on the paper and slid it in front of me.

"My number. I'm going to stay scarce, but you will call me if she needs anything."

"If she does, I'll take care of it."

"You better."

"Then we understand each other. Eat up before it gets cold."

CHAPTER 10
SHERIDAN

MY SECOND SATURDAY of work went much like the first. From the time I walked in the back door until I sat down for my break, I was going nonstop.

The crowd was rowdy as the country band that Shooter had booked played. The alcohol flowed, but nothing was getting out of hand. Kenna had told me that Shooter had hired another bouncer to keep an eye on things.

"Hey, Sheridan, can you run these beers into the back room?" Dave asked as I walked up to the bar.

"Where's Nessa?" There was no way I wanted to get on the she-devil's bad side. She already had it out for me.

"Probably out back. Just drop them off on the table and the guys can sort them out."

He pushed the tray toward me that held several bottles of beer and two orders of hot wings.

"Sure thing."

I made my way toward the back room. Several of the bikers were playing pool and looked me over as I made my way past them. None of these guys I recognized. The first table was empty, and I placed the tray on it.

"Here you go, guys." I smiled and backed up.

"Hold up there. I haven't seen you around here before," one of the older men called out. He was handsome in a rugged way, with striking silver hair on his head and face. He hadn't lost any bulk at his age and was rather intimidating as he stood up.

"It's my second night," I responded, my voice shaking.

"What happened to Nessa?"

"Dave said she was out back. He didn't want your wings to get cold, so he told me to bring them."

"Yeah, she's out back on her knees," another called out and the others laughed.

My face heated.

"Thank you for bringing them, then. I'm Brass." He reached out his hand to shake mine.

"Sheridan," I replied placing my hand in his but he didn't let go.

"Why don't you join us?"

"I need to get back to work, but thanks for the offer." I stepped back pulling my hand out of his. Straight into someone else.

"Easy, Sheridan," Levi's voice washed over me. My knees wanted to buckle with my relief that it was him.

"What the hell are you doing in here?" a feminine voice hissed out.

"Your job," Brass bit out. "Deliver our food next time before you go suck a cock, okay?"

I pushed myself closer to Levi.

"Come on, let's get a drink," he murmured in my ear.

Not looking up, I moved around his other side, away from Nessa, and hightailed it to the bar.

"I'm taking my break now," I told Dave as I walked past him.

I needed air. Was it Levi who was out back with Nessa? The thought made me sick to my stomach.

"Slow down, would you?" Levi called out from behind me. His hand wrapped around my arm, drawing me to a stop.

"Where are you off to in such a hurry?"

"It's my break time. I only get fifteen minutes."

"That'll give us a few minutes to talk."

"Oh, did you find some used parts for my car?" I asked, hopefully only because any other conversation may have caused me to break down.

What the hell was wrong with me?

Maybe it was getting close to my period? It makes me super emotional around that time of the month. Please let that be what was happening.

"I did, but I wanted to see how you were doing?"

"I'm fine. Everything's fine." The smile on my face was as fake as my words. Maybe he didn't notice.

His eyes narrowed.

Nope. He saw right through my bullshit.

"What's wrong?" His hand ran up and down my arm. Goosebumps pebbled in its wake.

"Nothing. Why would you think something's wrong?"

"Come on," he said, ushering me into Shooter's empty office. He shut the door behind us.

"Talk to me." He leaned against the desk.

"About what?"

"What's bothering you? Did the guys scare you? They can be a rough bunch, but they'd never hurt you."

"Maybe a little," I confessed.

"I'm sorry." He caught my hand with his and pulled me closer. He smelled like leather and sandalwood. Not Nessa's overwhelming perfume.

"It's not your fault." He twined our fingers together, his hand swallowing mine.

"How about taking a ride with me sometime?"

"A ride?" I squeaked.

"On my motorcycle," he chuckled. "Have you ever been on one?"

"No," I hesitated, "but I'm not sure that's a good idea."

"I'll keep you safe, Sheridan."

"That's not what I meant."

"It's only a ride. Maybe we can stop and get some dinner somewhere."

"It's not a good idea."

"Why not?"

"Levi, I'm not looking for anything."

"It's just a ride and dinner. Not marriage," he teased.

"You scare me," I breathed out.

"I do?" His beautiful eyes widened. "I don't want to scare you."

He leaned in closer, his breath wafting over my lips.

"Truth is, you scare me, too."

His lips touched mine, and I was lost to his touch, his taste. My lips parted, and he deepened the kiss. My hands clutched his vest tight as I raised up on my tip toes. His hand burrowed under my hair, wrapping around my nape as he pulled me closer. His tongue found mine. The intimacy made me moan in the back of my throat. His knees bent and his arm came under my ass, lifting me up. My legs wrapped around his hips, arms around his neck. Why did this seem so familiar? The thought fleeted when he squeezed my ass. As lost as I was in the heat of his kiss, I didn't hear the door open.

"The only person who gets to have sex in my office is me," Shooter barked out.

In shock, I dropped my legs from Levi's waist as he raised his head. His breath was coming as fast as mine. I licked my lips, his taste lingering there. He swiped his thumb across the wetness on my bottom lip before looking at Shooter.

"Sorry, man, we just came in here to talk, and things got a little out of hand."

"I need to get back out there anyway," I added, shaking with lust and embarrassment. "I'm sure my break is over."

Breaking eye contact with Levi, I rushed out of the room.

CHAPTER 11
SHERIDAN

I WAS a nervous wreck all day. Ellie being sick was not what I needed right now. I panicked when I couldn't get in touch with Mom, Ray, or Kenna. Calling Levi was an act of desperation.

Mom had called back two hours after Levi had picked up Ellie. She and Ray had been out of cell range and hadn't gotten my call. Kenna had been at school and wasn't able to answer her phone.

Mom had gone over to the house and called when she left.

"He has everything under control and said that he'd stay until you got home."

"Ellie's okay?"

"She was on the couch watching cartoons."

"And he said he'd stay?" That surprised me. I expected him to bolt as soon as she arrived.

"He said there wasn't any point in exposing me if Ellie's contagious."

I hadn't even thought of that. Now he'd been in Ellie's germy presence. And if she was sick, I'd get sick.

Gladys waved me out the door as soon as the last animal left. The ride home was quick despite it being rush hour. Maybe luck was on my side for once.

Levi's black truck was parked in the driveway, and I pulled in beside him.

The mess I expected to find when I opened the back door wasn't there. Everything was spotless. I heard Elsa singing *Let It Go* from the living room and walked that way. The sight I saw made my heart swell. Levi was sitting on the couch with Ellie curled up beside him. Ripper lay at their feet, eyes on me. I could tell my baby didn't feel like herself because she wasn't acting out the scenes in the movie as she usually did. Ripper let out a whine and Levi looked over at me.

"Hey," he whispered.

"Hi. I'm going to change."

He gave me a chin lift and went back to the movie. One of his large hands ran over Ellie's silky, dark hair.

Once in my room, I stripped out of my scrubs and pulled on a pair of black shorts and a pink tank top. I shook my hair out of the messy bun that I had it in and went back to the living room.

Once Levi spotted me, he lifted Ellie away from him and stood up. Ellie saw me there and waved before focusing back on the television.

"She got sick a couple more times after we got home, but nothing since. She drank some watered-down Gatorade but didn't want to eat anything."

I nodded.

"I washed her clothes, and the dryer will be done in a few minutes."

"You didn't have to do that."

He shrugged it off.

"Thank you for taking care of her."

"I told you whatever you need. I'm going to head out."

He was almost out the back door before I found my tongue.

"Do you want to stay for dinner?"

His hand stilled on the doorknob as he glanced back over his shoulder at me.

"It's the least I can do."

"I'd love to."

He sat down on the stool on the other side of the counter.

"Is your boss always like that?"

"An asshole?"

"Yeah."

"He is, but only when Dr. Collins isn't there."

"I wanted to kick his ass for talking to you like he did."

"Thank you for refraining. Despite Dr. Lansky, I like my job."

"Will you be able to stay with Ellie tomorrow? Dragon Lady at the daycare said she couldn't come back until after twenty-four hours. She'll need more spare clothes, too."

"Mom said she would stay with her."

"What are we having for dinner?" He leaned against the counter.

"Good question."

I turned and opened the refrigerator door. Mom had sent home a large pan of lasagna on Sunday.

"Leftover lasagna?"

"Homemade?"

"My mom's recipe. She's an amazing cook." Pushing the buttons on the oven, I set it to preheat. "Salad okay?"

"Don't go to any trouble."

"It's not. I need to use it up before it goes bad."

Levi's breath caught as I hopped up on the counter and opened the cabinet door. I grabbed the red bowl from the shelf and set it down on the counter.

"Jesus, woman. I could have gotten that for you."

He came up behind me and placed his hands on my hips. My skin heated. He tightened his grip and lifted me off the counter.

"I've been short my whole life, Levi. If I waited for someone tall every time I needed something, I'd get nothing done." I looked up at him and smiled.

He placed a kiss on my forehead and backed away.

"Does your mom do that, too?"

"Who do you think I learned it from?" I laughed. "Will you grab the bag of salad mix from the drawer at the bottom?"

The oven beeped, and I placed the lasagna on the rack.

"It'll be about thirty minutes for it to warm up. You want something to drink? I've got Dr. Pepper and sweet tea."

"Sweet tea, please."

I poured us both a glass and sat down on the stool next to him.

"How's work?"

"We've been busy," he replied.

"Is your dad mad you left today?"

"No, he knows it was important."

"I can't thank you enough for today."

"You don't have to. You and Ellie are a package deal."

"Levi," I sighed. "You're right. We are, and that girl is the most important thing in my life."

"I get that. I wouldn't expect anything else. You've given up a lot for her to have a good life. You're a great mom, Sheridan."

"I felt like a horrible one today," I confessed.

"It's okay to need help. I'm glad I could be there for the both of you."

He reached up, placing his hand on the nape of my neck, and kneaded. My head fell forward at the pressure. He chuckled when I groaned.

"Feel good?"

"God, yes," I sighed.

"How is it that she hasn't noticed that you're home?"

"She did, but Elsa's on. Ellie's a little obsessed with her."

"No kidding," he snorted. "We've watched it twice."

"She'd have it on all the time if I'd let her."

A buzzer sounded.

"Dryers done. I'll get her clothes out." Levi stood up.

"You don't have to. You've done enough."

"It's no problem. They'll wrinkle."

Who the hell was this man?

"What's that look for?"

"Most men wouldn't care if they wrinkled."

"My mom was a stickler. She had my brother and me cleaning our rooms and doing our laundry. We even took turns cooking dinner during the week. She told Dad she wasn't sending us out into the world without being able to take care of ourselves."

He went into the laundry room, and I put the salad together. He came back with a pink laundry basket.

"Does that mean your home is clean?" I cocked an eyebrow.

"Most of the time. It depends on how many hours I'm working at the garage." He pulled out a shirt and folded it.

"Did you always want to work with your dad?"

"I've been obsessed with cars since I was little. If Dad was home and working on something in our garage, I was there bugging the shit out of him."

"You said you have a brother? Is he older or younger?"

"He's two years older. He's stationed in Germany."

"That has to suck, not being able to see him."

"We FaceTime when we can, but it's been a few years since he's been home. Mom and Dad flew over there last year and saw him."

"He didn't want to work with you two?"

"Cars weren't his thing. I could spend hours working on one and he'd be bored within twenty minutes. He was more into sports."

"What was your first car?"

He smiled. "Dad and I fixed up a sixty-six Chevy Chevelle that he had found. It was in terrible shape. We spent hours on that thing after he got off work."

"Oh, you were the bad boy with the hot car, huh? I bet you had to beat the girls off with a stick."

"I wasn't that guy. I was scrawny."

I looked him up and down. I couldn't picture it. He was tall, dwarfing my five foot one inch. His biceps stretched the limits of his shirt sleeves when he bent his arms. His hands looked massive as they folded my daughter's clothes.

"Did you play sports, too? Or was that your brother's thing?"

"I wasn't coordinated enough. I tripped over my own feet back then."

"I can trip over air," I laughed. "I played basketball, though. I'm quick."

"Mommy?" Ellie came into the kitchen, dragging her blanket behind her.

"Hey, Sweetie. How does your tummy feel?"

"Okay."

"Are you hungry?"

"No,"

"Thirsty?"

"Can I have some gater-cade?"

Levi laughed when she mispronounced Gatorade.

"I'll get you some."

Levi picked her up and sat her on the stool while I pulled a cup out of the cabinet. After pouring the drink into the cup, I screwed on the lid and handed it to her.

"Do you want some Cheerios?"

She nodded as she drank.

"What about a banana?" Levi asked.

"I don't have any."

He winked and pulled a grocery sack from the counter.

"I had some dropped off earlier with the Gatorade. Bland foods are good for upset stomachs. I got some applesauce in here, too."

I looked at him, mouth gaping.

"I told you I had this." He winked and I almost freaking swooned.

Ellie munched on her banana slices and cheerios while we ate lasagna and salad. It was strange to have a man in the house that wasn't Ray. Ripper, who didn't tolerate many people, laid at Levi's feet. It wasn't awkward, it was nice. As Levi helped himself to a second helping of lasagna, I noticed Ellie's eyes drooping.

"Ellie, it's bath time."

"Okay," she whispered and slid off the stool.

"It'll be a few minutes if you want to hang around."

Levi nodded around a bite of food.

I knew my baby didn't feel like herself as she let me wash her hair without a fuss. As soon as her head hit the pillow, she snuggled her stuffed dog and fell asleep.

"She asleep?" Levi asked, tossing one of the kitchen towels over his shoulder.

"Out like a light." My eyes widened as I glanced around the

kitchen. Everything was cleaned up. He'd even finished folding the laundry and had placed it back in the basket.

"I wasn't sure where it went, so I left it in there." He nodded at the basket.

Emotions overwhelmed me and my eyes stung with the tears I held back.

His smile dropped with my struggle. "What? What's wrong?"

There went the waterworks. I'm not what you'd call a pretty crier. My nose ran, my eyes swelled up and my skin got blotchy. Levi gathered me close despite all the messiness. He rubbed his hand up and down my back and murmured words I didn't understand.

Everything poured out of me in those minutes. The frustration of doing everything myself, depending on others to help care for my daughter, the loneliness I denied to everyone. Myself included.

I needed this.

His touch, his comfort.

I soaked it up like the ground did rain after a three-month drought.

How long we stood there I didn't know.

Embarrassment made me want to stay pressed to his chest. I inhaled, smelling his laundry detergent and him. The slight smell of motor oil, musk, and sandalwood. His heartbeat was a steady rhythm to my ear, lulling me into a sense of peace.

"Better?" His chest rumbled with the word.

I nodded, afraid to speak.

"Want to talk about it?"

Shaking my head, he hugged me tighter.

"I think you needed that," he murmured.

I moved out of his arms and turned away from him, rubbing my hands over my damp cheeks.

"Damn, I can't believe I broke down like that," I uttered. "You probably think I'm a crybaby."

"Why would I think that? You've had a lot of shit thrown at you."

"I hate crying," I let out a watery laugh wiping under my eye. My mascara had more than likely smudged, leaving me looking like a raccoon.

"Nothing wrong with a good cry now and then."

He came up behind me. His arms wrapped around my waist, pulling me back, and his chin rested on my head.

"Cry a lot, do you?"

"Not so much," he chuckled. "When I needed to let all that emotion out, I beat the hell out of the heavy bag."

"I'll try that next time."

"Crying doesn't make you weak."

"It feels that way."

"Giving up is weak. You might be one of the strongest people I know. You've sacrificed to give your daughter a good life. You work your ass off to make sure you don't owe anyone. Weak is the last thing that applies to you."

"You don't know me," I argued.

"That's what I've seen. I want to get to know you. Your dreams, your fears, your desires. I want it all. I need it. I need you."

He turned me in his arms and lowered his head. His lips brushed mine tenderly, his beard tickling my face. I sagged against him, parting my lips. No further invitation was needed. He deepened the kiss, tongue seeking mine. He splayed his hand against the bare skin of my lower back, pressing me harder against him. He was hard everywhere. I felt bereft when his lips left mine. Resting his forehead against mine, he murmured, "Take a ride with me next weekend."

"I have to work."

"We can go early. I'll get back you back in time."

"I don't know."

"Please?"

"I'd like to, but I don't want to miss any time with Ellie. I already feel like I'm missing half her life."

"Take a ride with me Saturday and we'll take Ellie somewhere on Sunday to make up for it."

"Can I think about it?"

I sensed his frustration, but he nodded.

"I don't want to leave you." His eyes filled with heated promise.

I didn't know what to say. I wasn't ready for this to go any further, but I didn't want him to leave either. My body craved more of him. His touch, his kiss.

Sensing my hesitation, he kissed my forehead.

"I've got to be at work early in the morning. I'll call you."

With one last kiss, he left.

I wanted nothing more than to call him back.

CHAPTER 12
TRIGGER

I SHUT the hood of Sheridan's car with a thud. The last part had arrived and was installed. Between Duke and I, her car was as good as it was going to get. I'd given the car a tune-up, replaced parts that needed to be replaced, added coolant to her air conditioner, and put on new brake pads and tires.

I knew she'd be relieved to have it back, even if it was a piece of shit. She wouldn't have to worry about breaking down anytime soon.

"Why the hell does this car have two different invoices?" Dad said from behind me.

I bit back a groan. Damn, his nosy fucking nature.

"Someone donated to fix her car. Sheridan doesn't like charity. One is the real invoice for the office and the other is for her."

"Someone donated, huh?"

"Something like that," I hedged.

"Is this shit going to come back and bite us in the ass?"

"No. She's not going to know anything about it."

"Who was this generous person?"

"No one you know."

"Quit fucking with me, Trigger," he barked out.

"It was her ex."

"Well, that's a new one. I didn't think he was in the picture."

"He's not. He didn't want her to know he did it."

"Why the fuck not?"

"He's not a good guy. Said she's better off without him being in her life. He's looking out for her the only way he can and keep her safe."

"What the hell is he into?"

"He's a Devil's Reign member."

Dad's eyes widened at the name.

"How the hell did she get messed up with them?'

"She didn't. She met Duke when he was visiting his mother in Colorado. She has no clue who he really is."

"What a cluster fuck." He rubbed a hand across his head. "What the hell are the odds he'd belong to that club?"

"If I hadn't seen the tattoo, I wouldn't have known. He wasn't wearing his colors or riding his bike when he came here."

"At least when this car is gone, that connection is gone."

My eyes darted away. Why the fuck did I mention any of this?

"What?"

"She's working at Shooters on the weekend."

In for a penny, in for a pound.

"And I asked her to go for a ride with me next weekend."

"Fuck me. You like this girl." It wasn't a question.

"Yeah, I do."

"Did his club know about her?"

"No. when he found out she was pregnant, he bailed. He didn't want them finding out, said his Prez is a real bastard if he has something he can hold over their heads."

"He's a bastard all right. Heard that he killed a member's old lady when he was short twenty bucks after a run."

"Duke went back to California, and she ended up moving here. There shouldn't be any kind of connection between them."

"Except that he showed up here to help her out."

"I think he covered his tracks. It's not the first time he's done something like this."

"I've got a bad feeling," he cautioned.

"You're the one who let them enter the tournament," I argued. "This wouldn't even be a concern if they weren't coming here."

"Watch it," he warned.

"Sorry," I ran a hand over the back of my neck, "Look, it's going to be fine."

"Did she take you up on the ride?"

"She said she'd think about it."

"What's to think about?"

"Her kid for one. She's working two jobs to cover her bills and the repairs for the car. She said she's not spending enough time with her."

"It sounds like she's a wonderful mother."

"She is. Everything she does is for that little girl."

"Remember, they're a package deal. Think about that before you decide to get serious. A readymade family is a big deal."

With that, he returned to his office.

Pulling out my phone, I called Sheridan.

"Hey, there," she answered.

"Hi. How's your day going?"

"I will not use the 's' word, but it's been good. How about you?"

"Got your car all fixed up," I told her.

"How much did it end up costing me?" I pictured her biting her lip in worry and chubbed up a little. Thankfully the coveralls covered my groin, and it wasn't noticeable.

"Six twenty-three."

"That's a lot less than you told me."

"I found a lot of used parts and since I did all the work, I discounted the labor."

"That's not fair, Levi."

"Deal with it."

"Stubborn ass," she whispered.

"Absolutely. Do you want me to bring it over tonight?"

"I can come pick it up. There's no use in making you work later than necessary."

"I'll bring it over. You two like pizza?"

"Who doesn't?"

"Anything you don't like?"

"I'm good with anything. Ellie only likes cheese or pepperoni, but you don't have to do that."

"I want to. I'll be over about six thirty."

Not giving her the chance to argue, I hung up.

I pulled into Sheridan's driveway and parked bedside her loaner car. Walking up the front sidewalk, I noticed chalk drawings I made a point to step over. The scribbles were cute, and I pictured Ellie out here having fun with Sheridan, keeping a close eye on her. The flower beds were damp, the vibrant colored petals glistening in the sunlight.

Ripper's deep bark greeted me when I rang the doorbell.

"I get it," a little voice yelled. "Who is it?"

"It's Levi."

"It's Levi, Mommy." She yelled. Sheridan said something I couldn't make out, and the lock slid open. Ellie pulled the door open wide and smiled up at me. Ripper didn't pull a runner like I expected but sat sentry behind her.

"Please come in."

"Thank you."

Ripper's eyes followed me as I entered, and Ellie shut the door behind me. I let her lead the way and Ripper kept himself between the two of us. We walked into the kitchen, and I sat the three pizza boxes down on the counter.

Sheridan turned from stirring the pitcher of tea and her eyes widened.

"Goodness, did you think you were feeding an army?" She laughed.

"No, but I can eat a whole one by myself."

"A whole pizza?" Ellie asked from beside me.

"The whole thing," I confirmed.

"I want a whole one," she told her mother.

"Start with one piece, then we'll see," Sheridan compromised with her.

Sheridan passed me a plate and placed a slice of pizza on a smaller, pink plate for Ellie.

"Do you want some tea? Or I have Dr. Pepper and milk." Sheridan turned to the cabinet and took down two glasses and a pink cup.

"Tea is fine."

"I want tea, too," Ellie piped up.

Filling the glasses up with ice, she poured us tea.

"You're getting milk. No tea this late." She pulled the gallon of milk out of the refrigerator.

Her little lip puffed out as she glared. Sheridan filled up her cup and screwed the lid on.

"Would you like pepperoni or BBQ chicken?" I gestured to the boxes.

"I've never had BBQ chicken on pizza before," Sheridan replied. "I'll try that one, please."

"It's my favorite."

I placed a slice on her plate as she sat down. I planted myself on the last stool and waited. Her beautiful eyes widened in pleasure at the first bite.

"Good, isn't it?" I asked.

She nodded her head, chewing.

"Have you thought about this weekend?"

"Mom wants Ellie to stay with her until Sunday. They're going up to see my aunt in Dallas. I think mom wants to show Ellie off."

"That's a yes, then?"

"As long as you have me back for work before three, that's a yes."

Mentally I was throwing my hand up in the air screaming yes, but I just smiled at her.

"I'll pick you up at ten. Wear jeans and boots if you have them."

She nodded and took another bite of pizza.

"Levi, wanna watch a movie with me?" Ellie asked in her sweet little voice.

I looked at Sheridan as she gave me a shrug and a nod, which I interpreted as you're more than welcome if you want to, but it's at your own risk. Don't think I wasn't staying.

"What are we gonna watch?"

"Elsa!"

"How about we watch something besides Elsa? How about Lilo and Stitch?" Sheridan offered, and I wanted to kiss her for it.

Ellie put her elbow on the counter and tapped her finger on her cheek like it was a hard choice for her to make. It was the cutest damn thing I'd ever seen.

"Ok," she chirped.

We finished our pizza and curled up on the couch to watch the movie. Never in a million years would I have imagined myself doing this and having the damn time of my life.

Halfway through the movie, Ellie's eyes drooped as she leaned against me. It pleased me to no end that she felt comfortable with me. I knew that would be one thing to win her mom over.

"Ellie, let's go get a bath and get ready for bed," Sheridan told her as she stood from the couch.

"But the movie is not over," she whined, rubbing a fist on her eye.

"We can finish it tomorrow. Tell Levi goodnight."

Ellie climbed on her knees next to me and planted a wet kiss on my cheek.

"Goodnight, Levi. Your face tickles," she giggled, climbing off the couch.

"Goodnight, sweetheart."

Sheridan looked at me, hopeful and tired at the same time. It didn't escape me that she was nodding off during the movie, too.

"I think both my girls need to get some rest tonight."

Sheridan's eyebrows shot up to her hairline. "Your girls?"

"If I get my way, yes."

With her mouth still open in shock, I gave her a small kiss and walked out of the living room.

It was one of the hardest things I've done.

CHAPTER 13
TRIGGER

THE WEEKEND ROLLED AROUND at an excruciatingly slow pace. No matter how busy I had been at work, the clock refused to speed up. I pulled into Sheridan's driveway at ten minutes until ten and I was proud of myself for holding out that long. Her neighborhood was quite busy with kids playing in front yards and people mowing before the heat of the day forced them inside. The roar of my bike drew the attention of a few, including Michael's dad. Erik came out of the garage and waved when he realized it wasn't his son, Hammer, coming for a visit.

I killed the engine and removed my helmet as Sheridan came out of the back gate. I wanted to haul her ass back into the house and strip her down. Faded jeans encased her legs. A blue tank top left her arms bare but skimmed over her curves. My hands itched to cup those breasts. A pair of aviator sunglasses hid her eyes. In her hands, she carried a small backpack and another shirt.

"Am I dressed okay? I wasn't sure." She gestured to her outfit.

"It's fine."

"I brought a long-sleeved shirt just in case."

"It may be too hot for it, but you can always take it off later."

She nodded but didn't move closer. I got off the bike and walked up to her. Picking up her hand, I felt the slight tremor that ran through her.

"Nervous?"

"Is it that obvious?" She breathed out.

"Only a little," I chuckled. "We don't have to ride today. We can do something else." The last thing I wanted was to scare her off, but riding was a big part of my life.

"No, I want to," she rushed out. With a deep breath, she maneuvered around me and stomped toward my bike.

"Do you want to wear the shirt?"

"I guess not. It's already getting hot."

Taking the shirt and bag from her, I tucked them into the saddlebag and pulled out her helmet.

"Let's get this on you."

Placing the black helmet on top of her braided hair, I made sure it fit before buckling the straps underneath her chin. I climbed on the bike.

"Just put your foot on the peg," I gestured to the metal sticking out, "and swing over."

Sheridan did as I instructed and sat as far back on the seat as possible without falling off.

"Sheridan, you're gonna have to get closer to me than that. All the way up and put your arms around me."

She scooted closer and wrapped her arms around my stomach. The heat of her body pressing into mine was both pleasure and torture.

"Are you ready?"

"Yes."

Starting the engine, the sound reverberated off her house. Drawing a gasp from her, I smiled as her arms clutched me tighter. Letting the familiar vibration flow through me, I pushed the bike backward until we were facing the street. I patted her hands where they locked together on my stomach, telling her to keep them there, and pulled out onto the street.

After about twenty minutes, we made it out of the city and its traffic. Sheridan had her head buried against me the whole time. Now that we were out on the open road, I could tell she was enjoying it. Her death grip around my waist had lessened and her helmet no longer pressed into my back. The familiar rush of freedom came over me as it did every time I rode my bike.

After about an hour on the road, I turned into the parking lot of a café my brothers and I like to stop at for a quick bite to eat. Only a couple of old pickup trucks were parked as I pulled into a spot. After killing the engine, I pulled off my helmet and felt Sheridan do the same.

"When you get off," I warned her, "your legs are going to be wobbly. You can hold on to me if you need to."

Her hands gripped my shoulders as she swung her leg over and stepped down. She gripped my arm when she realized I wasn't lying.

"Is the feeling ever gonna come back into my legs?" she laughed.

"Give it a few minutes and the shaking will stop."

Once she was stable, I led her into the café with my arm wrapped around her waist. She felt perfect against me. It made me visualize how perfect she'd feel underneath me or on top of me. Basically, any way I could get her. Opening the glass door, old country music floated in the air. The scent of grilling meat hit me hard, and I realized how hungry I was. An older woman opened the swinging door into the dining room from the kitchen.

"Trigger, I'll be damned." She smiled at the two of us and rushed over.

"It's good to see you, Ronnie. Sheridan, this is Ronnie. She owns the Middle of Nowhere cafe with her husband. Ronnie, this is Sheridan."

"It's good to meet you, sugar." She looked out the front window. "Where are the rest of the boys?"

"It's just us today. I thought I'd take Sheridan for a quick ride since she'd never been on a bike before."

"I remember my first time. I didn't think I'd ever get the feeling back in my legs." Ronnie laughed.

"It's starting to come back," Sheridan chimed in. "Where's your restroom?"

"Right down that hallway. First door on your right."

"Thank you. I'll be right back."

"Do you want sweet tea or a Dr. Pepper?" I asked as she walked away.

"Sweet tea, please."

Ronnie and I both watched as she walked to the restroom, her leg still a little wobbly.

"That's a beautiful girl there, Trigger. What the hell she is doing with you?"

"You wound me, Ronnie." I clutched a hand on my chest with mock pain.

"Ok, you smartass," Ronnie laughed. "Take a seat wherever and I'll get your drinks."

I picked a booth that faced out into the parking lot where I could monitor my bike. Ronnie came back with four glasses, two ice waters, and two sweet teas.

"You want your usual fried pickles?"

"Yes, ma'am."

"I'll get those started and I'll be back in a few minutes to get the rest of your order."

"Thanks, Ronnie."

After a few minutes, Sheridan emerged from the hallway and made her way to the booth. I couldn't take my eyes off her. The innate grace in her movements drew me like a magnet. As soon as she sat down, she picked up the glass of water and gulped it down.

"I didn't realize I was so thirsty," she remarked when she sat the empty glass down.

"How did you like your first ride?"

She ran the rim of her finger around the edge of the glass, avoiding eye contact with me. My heart stopped. I needed her to like it. She felt right on the back of my bike.

One corner of her lips kicked and then she was grinning, eyes twinkling with delight.

"I loved it. At least after we got off the highway."

I released the breath I had been holding.

"Highways are scary when you're not used to it."

"Scary is an understatement. Terrified is more like it. Don't those people look where they're going?"

"It's one thing that makes riding a motorcycle dangerous. Since it's small, it's harder to see."

"I wanted to hit that woman who was looking at her phone," Sheridan fumed.

I didn't blame her as the woman damn near sideswiped us. Luckily, I swerved out of the way, and she missed us by a couple of inches. Damn woman never looked up from her phone.

"People are idiots," I agreed, looking over to see Ronnie walking our way.

"Here you go. Fried pickles and extra ranch." She placed the red basket on the table between us along with two bowls of ranch and plates.

"Thanks, Ronnie."

"Are you ready to order?"

Both of us ordered cheeseburgers and fries and Ronnie went to put our orders in.

"How'd you know?" Sheridan asked, picking up a pickle.

"Know what?"

"That I love fried pickles?"

"Lucky guess," I laughed. "I always order them when I come here. They're the best I've ever had."

She popped one in her mouth and chewed. I could tell when the kick of spice hit her. Her eyes opened wide.

"Damn, that is good."

"Ronnie's secret recipe. The heat builds with each one," I added as I picked up my own.

We talked about everyday things as we waited for our food to arrive, our favorite foods, BBQ chicken pizza for me, sushi for her, movies, any of the Marvel franchise, Fools Rush In, and Sleepless in Seattle for her.

We both agreed that Die Hard was a Christmas movie.

"I want to do a Die Hard Christmas Tree one year when Ellie is older," Sheridan commented.

"That would be amazing," I agreed. "Favorite author?"

"That you've heard of? Dean Koontz. You?"

"Stephen King and Lee Child. Who would I not have heard of?"

"Suzanne Wright, Marie James, R.L. Mathewson., Sierra Simone, Winter Travers," she ticked each name off on her fingers before I cut her off.

"Why would I not know them?" I asked, not that I had a clue who these people were.

"Read a lot of romance, do you?" She chuckled.

"Okay, you got me. I don't know any of them."

"That's what I figured."

"Here you go, kids," Ronnie said as she walked up to the table and put down the plates of food in front of us. She fished out a bottle of ketchup from her apron pocket and plunked it on the table. "Do you need any refills?"

We both declined, and she went to the next table that had seated a couple of booths down from us.

I had just taken my first bite of the juicy burger when the sound of engines filled the air. One after the other, motorcycles filled the opposite side of the parking lot from where I parked. From where we were sitting, I couldn't decipher the markings on their cuts.

"What is it?" Sheridan asked and looked out the window.

"Nothing. How's the burger?"

"Fantastic. You're going to bring me back here again."

"I am, am I?"

"Mm-hmm," she mumbled with her mouth full.

The door opened and a clamor of loud voices entered the otherwise quiet room. The group of men barged into the café with Ronnie, heading them off. She directed them to the tables on the opposite side of the room from us. None of them looked familiar until the last guy sat down.

Duke.

What the hell was he doing back in town? Then it hit me. These men were the Devil's Reign MC. The people Duke hid Sheridan from. The one whose president had vowed to make me pay for the death of his son. And they were sitting less than fifty feet away from us.

Fuck.

What the hell were they doing so far from their turf? None of the men seemed to have noticed us sitting there or didn't care about the other patrons. Sheridan happily munched away on her fries, but my appetite vanished as my apprehension grew. If my club had been here, I wouldn't have been worried. I'd have had more than enough backup to keep Sheridan safe.

"Something wrong?" Sheridan asked when she noticed I wasn't eating.

"No, sorry. Thought I saw someone I recognized." To appease her worry, I took a bite of my burger. It tasted like sawdust in my mouth. Taking a drink of tea, I washed it down. Satisfied, she continued to eat.

As we finished, Ronnie came by and dropped off the check.

"How was everything?"

"It was delicious," Sheridan answered. "If you ever decide to part with the pickle recipe, let me know. They were the best ones I've ever had."

Ronnie laughed. "You're not the first one who asked for that recipe. I told Joey, my husband, that I'll have it published in the paper when I die. That's the only way I'll ever let it go."

"I don't want it that badly," Sheridan quipped.

"Trigger will have to bring you back for some more."

"She already told me I was," I added.

"Good," Ronnie remarked. She looked over at me. "You've got a good one here. Make sure you don't screw it up," she warned me with a look.

"I'll do my best," I promised, "but I can't guarantee that I won't mess it up. I'll just have to make it up to her." I winked at Sheridan, and she blushed.

Picking up the check, I reached back and pulled out my wallet.

"How much for mine?"

"Woman, don't insult me that way."

"I thought I'd offer. I'm going to run to the restroom before we leave."

Fuck.

The restrooms were down the hall that was between where we were sitting and the Devil's Reign MC. My heart rate sped up as she scooted out of the booth. The only good thing was Duke sat with his back to her. When she passed by him and went down the hall, I released the breath I held. A few of the men had noticed her and stared until she disappeared from their sight.

The men made a few ribald comments, but they quieted when Ronnie appeared with a tray laden with food. As she placed a plate in front of Duke, he dropped his napkin, bent down to pick it up, and looked in my direction. His eyes narrowed on me. I acknowledged him with a lift of my chin and looked back at the hall, then back at him. His eyes widened when he realized the woman the men were commenting about was Sheridan.

The group all started eating when Sheridan emerged. A couple of them glanced up but said nothing. As she approached the table, I threw down some bills on the table.

"You ready to go?"

"Sure," she replied, but she frowned. "Something wrong?"

"No, just ready to get on the road." It wasn't a lie. I wanted to get her the hell away from these guys.

There wasn't any way to avoid being seen by the group if they looked up as we exited. We were a mere foot away from the door when I felt it. The heat of a stare. I looked over my shoulder and Cobra stood from the table. The look of pure hatred on the man's face sent a shiver through me, but I kept my face impassive. We needed to get the hell out of here.

Sheridan opened the door, unaware of the danger staring me down. I hurried her toward my bike and climbed on. She situated herself behind me and we put our helmets on. Starting the engine, I looked back at the door.

Cobra stood there, looking at the two of us. He stared at Sheridan with a wicked gleam in his eyes. He looked back at me and smiled. It chilled me to the bone. I backed up the bike and tore out of the parking lot with Sheridan clinging to me.

What the hell had I done?

CHAPTER 14
SHERIDAN

THE PAST COUPLE of weeks had been, I didn't want to jinx it, but they had been wonderful. Levi had been spending a lot of time at the house with Ellie and me. He was still training Michael for some fight that he was tightlipped about, but I didn't care. I was over the moon. Ellie was crazy about him. That worried me, though. What if we didn't work out? It wasn't just my heart that would break.

The only downfall was that if Levi was at the house, one of his friends would stop by. We spent little time alone. Maybe it was a blessing. I wasn't sure if I was ready to take the next step with him. The last time I let a man into my bed, I had ended up pregnant and alone.

Not that I worried Levi would do that. No longer was I that naïve girl that thought I'd met my prince charming, and we would ride off into the sunset. I was a lot smarter these days. At my last checkup, I had requested birth control, something I hadn't had to have since I'd given birth to Ellie. This time I wasn't leaving anything to chance.

I heard the engine coming down the road and Ellie sat up from where she was lying on the couch and an excited look on her face.

A knock at the back door preceded Levi and Wrench coming in. Ellie was ready for bed, but she refused to go to sleep until Levi read to her if she knew he was coming over. Her face lit up when she saw him, and she ran to him. Levi scooped her up.

"You ready for your story?"

"Uh-huh," she nodded.

He carried her over to me and gave me a kiss.

"Be right back," he told me.

"Night, Mommy." She kissed my cheek.

Leaving me alone with Wrench, he took Ellie to her room.

"Can I get you something to drink?" I asked Wrench, walking into the kitchen.

"You got a Dr. Pepper in there?"

He laughed when I gave him the 'are you crazy' look. Opening the door, I pulled out two cans and handed him one.

"How's everything at work?" he asked as he popped the top. "You work at the vet clinic on Miller, right?"

"That's the one. It's been good." I sat on the couch and curled my legs underneath me.

"And Shooter's?"

That was a sore subject. Nessa had been a pain in my ass the past few shifts I had worked.

"That bad, huh?"

"It hasn't been pleasant, that's for sure."

"Nessa is a bitch."

"I won't argue with you about that. I'll only need a few more shifts and I'll be able to quit."

Kenna had been right. The tips were substantial at Shooters. I'd never worked at a place where a table or two didn't shortchange me. It was as if it terrified people to piss off the staff. Given that the owner was part of an MC, maybe they were. I didn't complain. I had paid off my car repairs, replenished my savings from repairing my transmission, and put money back for Ellie's Christmas presents. Not too shabby at all.

"Don't let Shooter hear that," Wrench warned.

"He knew this was short-term when he hired me."

"Yeah, but I don't think he realized how hard you would work. You put the others to shame. I don't think he'll let you go that easily."

"He can try."

Shooter had mentioned a few days ago that he wanted me to come on full-time. As flattering as it was, I declined. I loved my job at the clinic and Shooters took up my time with Ellie. Nessa, spilling a plate of wings on me later that night, had sealed the deal.

"How's work for you?"

"Busy as hell."

"Still having issues with your brother?"

He nodded; eyes clouded with regret.

"Have you thought about hiring someone else?" I asked softly.

"I've put some feelers out. It pisses me off that I'm having to."

I didn't know what to say as he took a drink. Getting in the middle of his problem wasn't a good idea. He didn't know me.

"She's out," Levi spoke as he came into the kitchen. He nabbed a drink out of the fridge and sat beside me on the couch. Wrapping an arm around my shoulder, he pulled me to his side. He picked up the remote from the side table and turned the channel to a rerun of NCIS: New Orleans. It wasn't long before my eyelids started getting heavy as he and Wrench talked about cars.

"I'm going to head home." Wrench's voice yanked me back out of my doze. A different episode was on the television, making me realize I had gone to sleep. Talk about embarrassing.

Wrench shook Levi's hand and went out the front door. His bike roared to life, more than likely waking the neighbors.

"You awake?" he murmured against my head.

"If I say no, can I stay right here?" I mumbled, burrowing closer to him.

"You can stay there as long as you want." He ran his fingers through my hair. I snuggled in closer and closed my eyes.

"I need to get a shower," I yawned.

"Up you go then."

Half awake, I walked to the bathroom and stepped inside, half tempted to ask him to join me.

CHAPTER 15
TRIGGER

WHEN THE BATHROOM DOOR OPENED, steam poured out smelling like Sheridan's soap. Vanilla and jasmine had become some of my favorite smells. Her hair was still pulled up on top of her head, but some tendrils had escaped and dripped onto her bare shoulders. My eyes tracked the drops as they moved down her chest to where the towel wrapped around her breasts. Suddenly, I was thirsty.

"Levi?"

"Hmm?"

"Do you want me?"

"More than anything," I vowed.

"Then why . . ." she hesitated, biting her bottom lip.

"Haven't I done anything about it?"

She nodded and looked away.

I walked to her and put a finger under her chin, forcing her to look up at me. When her eyes met mine, I could see the fear and wariness in them.

"I've never done relationships. I want to do this right, but I don't know what the fuck I'm doing. I don't want this to end because I pushed you before you were ready."

"But—"

"It won't hurt either of us to take this slow. My hand is getting more of a workout, but it'll be worth it."

Her eyes opened wide when she caught the implication of what I said and red creeped up her chest into her cheeks.

"Do you picture me when you're getting that workout?" she whispered.

"Every fucking time."

"How?"

"What?"

"How do you picture me?"

She treaded in very dangerous waters. One little pull on the corner of that towel and I would show her all the ways I'd pictured her.

"Do you really want to know?" I whispered, trailing a finger down the soft skin of her arm.

"Yes," she breathed out. "I need to know if what you see matches what I dream you do to me."

Damn, the little witch killed me.

"You dream of me? Do you use that vibrator in your drawer to bring you relief or do you put a finger on your clit and rub until you come all over your hand?"

"Both," she confessed.

My cock went from semi-hard to rock fucking solid in a second.

Without hesitation, I picked her up and took her to the couch. No way could I take her to her bed and not bury myself inside her. I positioned her to straddle me but kept the towel covering her. If I saw an inch more of skin, it would be game over for the both of us.

"The first thing I do is take off your shirt to see what color bra you have on and if I can see your pretty little nipples through it."

I trailed a hand over the terry cloth covering them— she whimpered.

"I suck on them through the lace, getting them good and hard until you are writhing against me." I cupped her breasts through the towel.

"Then I pulled the bra down until there was nothing between you and my mouth. I'd lick and suck and bite until you're begging me for more. I'd wonder if I could make you come just from playing with your sweet little nipples."

Her hands clenched on my knees where she leaned back.

"Once you begged, I'd kiss my way down all the soft skin until I'd get to your pussy. Your thighs would be wet from how much you want me. I'd spread you open wide so I could see it all. Would you be wet for me?"

I trailed my hands down as I told her what I would do. Her thighs squeezed mine.

"Yes," she moaned.

"I'd lick up all those juices from your thighs to your clit."

She whimpered and my cock pulsed behind my zipper.

"While my tongue was on your clit, I'd slip one of my fingers up your pussy to see how tight you'd grip my cock."

"Please," she begged.

Fuck me.

"I'd let your juices coat my hand before adding another finger and stretching you. You're dying for it, aren't you?"

"Yes," she groaned.

I moved my thumbs up to the crease of her thighs and rubbed the material.

"I'd pull my hand away and lick all the juice from my fingers while you looked up at me, wanting more. Wanting my cock to fill you up. You want that?"

"Levi." Her hips pressed against my thighs.

"I'd push inside of you slowly, letting you feel all of me before I slammed all the way home. Would you scream for me?"

"God, yes," she whined.

"I'd rub against your clit with every thrust until you couldn't take it anymore."

My hand worked between the towel and her thigh. She was soaked. When she didn't pull away, I inched between her thighs. My thumb found her hard little nub, and I stroked it. Her hips jerked.

"Please, please," she pleaded.

"You want me to make you come? Do you need it?"

"Yes!" She screamed and lifted her hips, allowing me to slide my fingers lower. I pressed on her clit and slammed two fingers inside her. It felt better than I ever dreamed— tight, hot, and wet. With two thrusts, she clamped down and screamed my name. She trembled in my arms as I drew her to me.

Fuck.

If this was just foreplay, the act was going to kill me.

I stood, shelving her ass with my arm, and hurried down the hallway to her room. She looked up at me with her eyes glazed with desire. As we reached her bed, I had to be sure.

"Are you ready for this? If not, tell me now."

"Levi, please."

I eased her back onto the bed. So much soft skin on display as her towel fell open.

"Damn, you're beautiful," I ground out, running my hand from her neck down her sternum to the juncture of her thighs. She trembled beneath my touch.

"The picture I've had in my mind doesn't come close to reality," I confessed.

"Levi," she moaned, arching into my touch.

Her pale thighs were silky against my palms as I spread them apart. The thin strip of hair on her mound pointed right to the promised land. Her pink flesh glistened with her juices. Using my thumbs to open her wider, I ran my tongue through her folds. Her hand clenches my hair as she gasped. I worked her over until she was writhing under my tongue and the sweetest moans were pouring from her lips. Sucking on her plump clit, I plunged two fingers inside her wet pussy. She arched off the bed, thighs clenching my head, and cried out as she milked my fingers.

Unable to hold back any longer, I kissed the inside of her thigh and stood. Luminous hazel eyes peered up at me as I pulled my shirt over my head. Her breath hitched when I popped the button on my jeans and slid the zipper down. Her eyes were glued to the motion. The denim slid to the floor, leaving me only in my black boxer briefs. I placed my thumbs under the elastic and gave her one last chance to change her mind because as soon as the barrier was gone, it would be hard as hell for me to hold back.

"Look at me, pretty girl," I ordered.

Her eyes caught mine. Arousal darkened hers until the emerald shards outshone the brown. Her pink tongue swept across her bottom lip.

"Are you sure?"

"Yes. Please, Levi. I need it. You. I need you."

Fuck if that didn't make me feel ten feet tall.

Pushing down the fabric, my dick bounced, and I watched her swallow hard. My hand wrapped around the shaft, and I stroked it. Clear liquid dripped from the tip, and I knew I was close to blowing my load and I hadn't even gotten inside of her yet. Her beautiful eyes followed the motion of my hand. Her breathing picked up, and I watched her nipples tighten even further.

I leaned down and meshed my lips to hers, letting her taste herself. Tongues dueled as passion flared higher than I'd ever dreamed possible. Wrapping my arms around her, I picked her up, placed her higher on the bed, and lay between her splayed thighs. The heat of her pussy seared my stomach, and I couldn't wait to feel it hold my cock.

Notching the sensitive head at her wet opening, I bit my lips to hold back from shoving my way in.

"Wait, wait, wait," she screeched.

I squeezed my eyes shut and held still.

"Condom," she whispered.

My eyes popped open in relief. She wasn't telling me to stop.

How could I have been so stupid? I'd never had sex without being gloved up. My mind raced to remember if I had one with me.

"Drawer," she whispered, nodding to the nightstand.

I reached over and pulled it open. On top was a brand-new box sitting there. I grinned.

"Someone was prepared," I chuckled.

"Kenna," she said as she flushed bright red.

"Tell me to thank her later."

I made quick work of opening the box and pulled out a length of packages. Leaving the comfort of her body, I rolled the latex down my shaft. Her whimper caught my attention.

Wrapping my hands around her thighs, I pulled her closer until they rested on top of mine. There she was at my mercy, splayed open like an offering, and I felt like a beast. I ran my hands up her body until I reached her chest. Her fleshed pebbled under my hands. I pinched each nipple and tugged them gently. Her knees squeezed my side. I reared back and placed the head of my cock at her opening. She looked too small to take me. My thumbs parted her lips as I pushed into her. My eyes were riveted to where I joined her. Wet heat bathed the head and shaft as I pushed forward. Her hips squirmed and I dragged my gaze to hers to make sure she was okay.

"You okay?"

"Yes," she panted. "Please, Levi. I need you."

The begging did it. I pushed all the way in until I buried myself to the root. I paused, catching my breath as my release threatened to come too soon.

"Levi," she breathed out, and her hips twitched in encouragement.

Leaning over her, I blanketed her body with mine, marveling at how small she was beneath me. Kissing her hard, I pulled back and plunged back in. I caught her gasp in my mouth.

With each thrust, we chased our orgasms. I rubbed against her clit and felt her milking me. Her fingers dug into my shoulder as her eyes slammed closed. A keening cry left her lips as she clamped down on me. Moving faster, I slammed into her as she crossed her legs across my back. I bit back the yell that attempted to escape my lips as I emptied myself into the condom.

Unable to leave the warmth of her body, I rested my forehead on hers and our breaths mingled.

Her eyes slowly opened, and she smiled.

I opened my mouth to say something, but the words wouldn't come. How did you tell someone that you'd never come so hard in your life? That it was unlike anything you'd ever had before.

"Hi," I managed to breathe out like an idiot.

But she smiled wider.

"Hi," she whispered back. "That was amazing."

Yep, ten feet tall and bulletproof.

Not able to resist the temptation, I kissed her again. Slow and tender, I poured my feelings into the kiss. With reluctance, I pulled away from her.

"Be right back."

In the bathroom, I threw away the used condom and looked at myself in the mirror. Small red scratches dotted the tops of my shoulders. I couldn't hold back a smile at my souvenirs. I turned off the light as I walked back out.

She was still lying in the same place I left her, but she had caught her breath. I reached down beside the bed and picked up my underwear. As I slid them on, she jumped up and went into the bathroom like her ass was on fire.

This was normally when I was hightailing home, but I didn't want to leave. I sat on the edge of the bed and waited for her to appear. I heard the toilet flush and the water running in the sink. The door opened, and she seemed hesitant to come back into the room.

"Sher, what's wrong?"

"Nothing," she blurted.

"Sher," I warned.

"I'm not sure what to do now," she admitted, looking at the floor.

I walked over to her and placed my finger under her chin, forcing her to look up at me.

"Do you want me to leave?"

"No."

"Good. I don't want to leave."

And I didn't. I wanted to feel her sleeping next to me.

"Is there anything we need to do before we go to bed?"

"Just make sure everything is locked up and set the alarm."

"Do you want me to do it, or would you feel more comfortable doing it yourself?"

"You can."

She rattled off the code for the alarm system. I kissed her lips and went out into the hallway. Taking my time, I made sure each door was locked, and the alarm set, giving her time to do whatever women did before sleeping. It wasn't something I'd experienced before. When I returned to her room, she sat on the edge of the bed in a black shirt that dwarfed her slender frame, securing the end of her braided hair.

It stopped me in my tracks.

I shouldn't have thought it was one of the sexiest things I'd ever seen, but it was.

"All locked up."

"I'm going to check on Ellie," she blurted out as she fiddled with the end of her hair.

"All right."

She hurried out of the room, and I listened as she opened the door to Ellie's room.

Was she as nervous as I was? It was the first time I'd spent the night with a woman. Was there a rule for this? Protocol?

Fuck if I knew.

I straightened the covers and tucked into the side opposite where she slept. I placed my phone on the table and double-checked the alarm was set early enough for me to get home and ready for work.

She paused when she came to the doorway.

"She okay?"

"Sound asleep."

"Come to bed, Sheridan."

I pulled back the covers as she came to her side. She slid between the sheets and faced me.

"I've never done this before," she murmured.

"What?"

"Spent the night with someone."

"Me either," I confessed.

Pulling her to me, she rested her head on my chest and laid her leg over mine. I reached over and turned off the only light left on in the room, plunging us into darkness except for the sliver of moonlight let in by the curtains. After a few minutes, her breathing evened out and I knew she was asleep. I placed my hand on her calf and pulled her closer to me.

My only thought was I could get used to this.

CHAPTER 16
SHERIDAN

THE NEXT MORNING, I woke up in my bed alone. Had I dreamed last night? I ran my hand over the other side of the bed, touching the cool surface. Maybe I had. Sitting up on the side of the bed, I felt a twinge between my legs and knew it hadn't been a dream. But where the hell was he?

Turning off my alarm, I got up and got ready for the day. I wrapped a towel around myself as I got out of the shower. Smelling coffee drew me to the kitchen, and I stopped short when I got to the threshold. Levi sat at the counter with a white bakery box in front of him. He looked up and a wicked grin spread across his face.

"I'm glad you didn't get dressed for me," he muttered, ogling me.

"For heaven's sake," I scolded him. "I smelled the coffee."

"Come here and give me a kiss and I'll pour you some," he tempted me.

As not to dislodge the towel that was the only thing keeping me somewhat modest, I walked to him. He pulled me closer and kissed me. A mere brush of his lips and I was ready to drag him to the floor.

"That's one way to say good morning."

"I didn't think you were still here."

"I woke up earlier and went home to shower and change. I needed to see you this morning before I went to work. I thought I might make it back before you got up, but you were in the shower. I even brought doughnuts to sweeten the deal."

"That is sweet."

He handed me a steaming mug of coffee and directed me to my room.

"Go get that cute ass dressed before I forget your daughter could wake up any minute. I don't want her to see me ravishing her mother." He patted me on the ass.

Damn that man. Didn't he realize he was getting me all worked up?

After I threw on a pair of dark pink scrubs, I pulled my hair up into a messy bun. I crossed the hall to wake up Ellie. Ripper poked his head up when I walked in. His bushy tail brushed across the blanket covering Ellie's bed. Giving a quick head scratch, I moved up to where Ellie lay, legs tucked underneath her torso and hair a tangled mess around her face.

"Good morning, Sunshine. Time to get up."

I smoothed her hair away from her face, and her eyelids fluttered open.

"Morning, Mommy," she whispered.

Ripper whined at the sounds of her voice, crawled toward the head of the bed, and laid his head on her chest. I realized Ripper hadn't raised hell when Levi came into the house with us sleeping.

"Guess who's here and brought doughnuts?"

"Gigi?"

"Try again?"

Her hazel eyes lit up. "Levi?"

"He's in the kitchen. Go to the bathroom and wash your hands first," I ordered as she jumped out of the bed and rushed out the door with her hair flying out behind her. Ripper looked at me with his head cocked to the side.

"I think she has a new favorite," I told him with a scratch behind his ears as Ellie squealed. Ripper whined in response and looked at me with sad brown eyes.

"Outside," I muttered, and he jumped off the bed, nails clicking down the hallway.

I made my way down the hall to find my daughter sitting on Levi's lap, a doughnut frosted with chocolate and sprinkles in her hand and chocolate milk in the other. Daycare was going to love her today.

Ellie smiled at me, frosting on her face.

"You know that she's going to be h-e-l-l today, right?"

Levi looked at me, his brow furrowed.

"Sugar," I informed him.

"Shi-oot, I'm sorry, I wasn't thinking," he apologized.

"It's okay. She doesn't get to indulge in doughnuts very often. I'll make her a scrambled egg to even it out. You want some?"

"Sure."

I whipped up a pan of scrambled eggs and dished it up for the three of us. It felt natural sitting here, eating together like a family.

After we finished eating, I cleaned Ellie up and got her ready for daycare. When we walked back to the kitchen to grab her backpack, Levi was drying the dishes.

"You didn't have to do that," I chastised.

"No, I didn't, but why wouldn't I?" He arched a brow as he put down the clean skillet.

"Thank you," I whispered, placing a quick kiss on his cheek.

"Ellie, please get Ripper his food."

"Yes, ma'am."

Ripper's ears perked up and watched Ellie as she scooped out his food and poured it into his bowl. Only after she moved away did he approach and start eating,

"That is an amazing dog," Levi remarked.

"He's a retired police dog."

"Retired? He doesn't look that old. Did something happen to him?"

"His sense of smell got messed up, and it was enough to retire him."

"How did he end up with you?"

"His handler, Larry, is good friends with Ray. He'd bring Ripper over to my parents when he visited. Ripper wouldn't leave Ellie's side, so when he had to retire, Ray talked Larry into letting Ripper live with us since he got a new canine partner."

"We need to get a move on before it gets too late," Levi said, looking at his watch.

"You ready to go, Ellie?"

"Can Levi take me?" Ellie looked up at me.

"Ellie, I'd love to, but I can't take you on my bike," he replied, crouching down beside her. Her little lip pooched out and Levi looked up at me at a loss.

"Ellie, get your backpack. We need to leave before we're late."

She continued to pout as she picked up her sparkly pink bag from the chair.

"It's not going to work, kid. Give it up," I warned.

She turned with a sly grin and ran over to Levi, who was still crouched down and launched herself at him. He caught her with a humph and fell on his butt, making her giggle. He tickled her until peals of laughter bounced off the walls. Ripper circled around them, barking in excitement.

"Okay, you guys, we need to get on the road."

Levi stood with Ellie in his arms and my ovaries pulsed. Was that even possible? Damn, I had lost it.

Levi buckled Ellie into her car seat and turned to me.

"Be safe," he whispered as he drew me into his arms and pressed his lips to mine.

"I will," I promised. "Watch out for the crazy drivers."

He kissed me again, reluctant to leave. With a groan, he tore himself away and got on his bike. With a flick of his fingers, he drove off. I rounded the front of the car and my gaze settled on a beige sedan sitting in front of an empty house. A lone person sat in the car. Shadows obscured his face, but I knew he was staring at me. Shivers raced down my spine and I hurried inside the car. As soon as the door shut behind me, I locked the doors. My eyes moved back to the car. Why was it freaking me out? It was just a run-of-the-mill car. Maybe they were there to see the house since it was for sale.

"Mommy, let's go," Ellie called out from the back seat.

My attention jerked back to her. Shaking off the weirdness, I started the car. It cranked on the first try just like it had every time since I got it back from Levi's shop.

I backed out of the driveway and eased onto the street. When I started forward, I couldn't resist glancing back in the mirror at that car.

The eerie sensation didn't leave me until I'd turned off our street and out of the view of that man.

The next night, Levi, Wrench, Sully, and Michael came by after they were done at the gym. Levi grilled us burgers while we swam. I hadn't realized how lonely I had been until my house was overflowing with conversation and laughter. Let's be real. My daughter wasn't the greatest conversationalist at three years old.

These men blew every misconception I had away. They were polite and funny. They included Ellie. Only one or two curse words slipped out, and they were apologetic when it happened.

The next couple of weeks were the same. Levi would come by with one or more of his brothers and stay a few hours.

As much as I enjoyed having the company, I craved alone time with Levi. He spent the night almost every night and would make love to me until I passed out from exhaustion. I couldn't complain about that, but it felt more like I was a booty call for him than, well, whatever the hell we were to each other. At my age, did you call someone your boyfriend? That seemed so high school. I didn't even know what the heck our relationship was. It wasn't something I'd asked.

Was I afraid of the answer?

God, yes.

What if this meant more to me than him? He said he'd never been in a relationship before or spent the night with a woman and now he was doing it on a near-daily basis.

Friday morning when I walked outside with Ellie, I noticed the same car parked on the street. The man sitting in the driver's seat seemed to stare straight at me. Cigarette smoke curled out of the cracked window. The burning tip of his cigarette reminded me of a movie with a demon who had glowing red eyes.

Despite the heat of the summer morning, chills raced over my spine. I couldn't get into the car quick enough. I needed to get away from the evil. Backing out of the driveway too fast, I prayed there wasn't any other car coming down the street. My heart pounded as I jammed my foot on the accelerator and put as much distance between me and that man as I could.

By the time I dropped Ellie off at daycare, I felt foolish for letting my imagination get the better of me. No more reading scary stories before bedtime, I warned myself. The man in the car probably thought I was crazy. Levi texted me later in the morning, but I didn't mention my freak-out to him. I was embarrassed enough for both of us. I didn't need him thinking I was a hysterical woman.

Once it was time for my lunch break, I rang Kenna up.

"Hey, what's up?" she yawned.

"Not much. It's my lunch break. I thought I'd call you."

"How's work?"

"Same old thing. Lots of cute fur babies that are terrified of being here. The puppies are sweet, though. They don't associate us with anything yet."

"How are things with you and Levi?"

"Good," I muttered.

"What's wrong?"

I should have known she would have picked up on something, even from one word.

"I don't know," I admitted. "Things have been great. He comes over almost every night."

"But?"

"It's always with one of the guys. Or a bunch of the guys. It's never just him."

"Are the guys assholes or something?"

"No, they're fine. They bring over food to grill out. They pick up after themselves and they're sweet to me and Ellie."

"But you're not getting any alone time with Levi," she concluded.

"It's driving me crazy!"

"Are you at least getting a little something-something?"

I could see her wagging her brows and laughed.

"That's a yes. Is he any good?"

"Kenna!"

"What? I need to live vicariously through you," she grumbled.

"Please," I scoffed.

"I don't have anyone right now. I don't want to do the one-night stand thing," she argued. "I may have too, though. I swear my va-jay-jay has cobwebs growing."

"I bet if you let Shooter know, he'd knock those cobwebs out," I teased.

"Don't go there!" she snapped.

"Uh oh, what happened?"

"Nothing I want to humiliate myself by repeating."

"Come on, if you can't tell me, who can you tell?"

"I kissed him the other night," she admitted.

"Holy shit! How was it?"

"Better than I had imagined. If he fucks like he kisses, no wonder he has women all over him all the time," she griped.

"And?"

"Nothing. He told me nothing would ever happen between the two of us. I'm too young and innocent for him," she mocked.

"That's bullshit," I blurted out.

"It is, but he hasn't spoken to me since unless it was work stuff."

"I'm sorry."

"It is what it is. I'm not chasing after some man who doesn't see what a great catch I am."

"And modest, too," I laughed. "But you're right. it's his loss. You're awesomesauce."

"Thanks," she laughed.

"Let me tell you what I did this morning."

"Is it good?"

"I was a dork. I've been reading and I guess it freaked me out more than I realized. Ellie and I were getting in the car this morning and, you know, that house that's for sale a couple of houses down from mine?"

"That cute one? Sure."

"There's been a car parked in front of it a few times I haven't seen around the neighborhood. Anyway, the driver was smoking a cigarette, and I convinced myself that it was demonic glowing eyes. Freaked the hell out of myself. I drove off like a crazy person. I'm lucky I didn't have a freaking wreck."

"No more Stephen King for you," she teased.

"It was Dean Koontz, but whatever. I feel so stupid, but it gave me the heebie-jeebies."

"The guy was just sitting in the car?"

"Yeah."

"Maybe it's your mom-instincts kicking in. You know a stranger in the neighborhood. Who knows what he could be there for?"

"Great, now I'm going to be more paranoid."

"It's not paranoia, it's being aware. Watch out for yourself and Ellie. Get the license plate next time. I bet you could get Ray to check it out and see if the guy is legit."

"No, I'm not bringing Ray into this. He'll start patrolling the neighborhood and I won't have any privacy. He'll have my mom calling every morning about the motorcycle in my drive."

"On the bright side, the guy won't be there for long if he has nefarious intentions," she remarked. "Hey, did I tell you I got my acceptance letter from Lola's Cosmetology College?"

"No, but hell yeah! I knew you'd get in."

"I start next semester."

"Are you still going to work at Shooters?"

"I may have to cut back a few hours, but I won't be able to afford much more. I've saved up most of the tuition and fees for the classes, but I'll still have bills to pay."

"I told you before you can move in with Ellie and me to save money."

"Honey, you want to get laid, not add another obstacle to it," she teased. "I appreciate the offer, though."

"It's always there. Sisters before misters."

"I still think that's a stupid saying," she laughed.

"It doesn't have the same ring as bros before hoes, does it?" I looked at the clock on the dash. "I've got to go. I've got five minutes left before my break is over."

"Talk to you later."

"Bye."

I scarfed down the rest of my sandwich in record time and went back to work.

Levi texted me on my next break and I smiled.

"Get off your phone, Sheridan," Dr. Lansky snapped when he walked into the room.

"I'm on my break," I told him.

"I don't care. Get off your phone."

What the hell was his deal? I finished my reply text and slid my phone into my pocket.

"I'm sorry. I thought it was allowed since I'm on break."

He stalked over to me, and I backed up. The breakroom was small and in the back part of the building. The room seemed to shrink in on itself as he came closer. His lip drew up in a sneer.

"Think you can do whatever you want because you're pretty?"

"What? No," I argued.

"You bitches are all alike."

"I'm sorry?" My back hit the wall. Panic rose swiftly and my heart threatened to beat out of my chest as I realized I was trapped. What the hell was going on?

"Of course you are," he barked out. "How are you going to make it up to me?"

His nasty breath wafted over my face as he ran a finger down my face. I jerked away, and he grabbed my jaw and forced me to face him. I winced at the pain, and he smiled, pressing harder.

"Why don't you get on your knees and show me how sorry you are?" He licked his lips, and I shut my eyes in revulsion.

"Get away from me," I mumbled, the words unclear from the pressure he applied.

"What was that?"

"I said get the hell away from me!" I raised my knee and aimed for his groin. His face went white when I made contact with his balls. As he bent over to cup himself, I hit his nose, palm side up with everything I had, and shoved him away. As soon as he swayed, I sidestepped him and ran out of the room. The first person I saw was Tonya as she stared at me, slack-jawed. The next was Dr. Collins as he stepped out of one of the exam rooms.

"Sheridan, what happened? Are you all right?"

Only then did I realize the tears running down my face.

Dr. Collins grabbed my hand and dragged me into the room he had vacated. My breaths came in short pants, my vision blurred.

"Breathe, Sheridan. In and out," he murmured, rubbing my hand. "Breathe with me."

After a few minutes, the shock of what happened wore off.

"There, there, that's better," he whispered. "Now what happened?"

"Dr. Lansky," I began, but the words lodged in my throat.

"What about Dr. Lansky?"

"He cornered me in the breakroom room. Called me names and told me to get on my knees to apologize for being on my phone," I rushed out. "I was on my break. I didn't think that was against the rules." My last words ended with a sob as I sank to the floor.

"It's not, my dear. You stay right here. Gladys will stay with you."

Another hand touched my shoulder, and I leaned into it.

"Sheridan, did he touch you?" Gladys asked as Dr. Collins shut the door behind him.

"He, he, he grabbed m-m-m-my face," I stuttered.

"Yes, he did. I can see the redness on your jaw. Can I take a picture?"

"Why?"

"Evidence, Sheridan. That bastard can't get away with this."

"I don't want to lose my job."

"Sheridan, that will never happen."

Shouting sounded from the hallway. I clutched Gladys to me as she sat down. Fear made it hard to breathe.

"The door is locked. He can't get in here," she reassured me.

A few minutes later, muted sirens penetrated the walls of the room.

"What's going on?"

"I'm sure Dr. Collins called the police. Dr. Lansky assaulted you."

"The police?" I asked, confused.

"It's okay, Sheridan. Just sit here with me and let Dr. Collins take care of it."

I lost track of time as we sat there. Finally, a knock sounded on the door and Gladys rose to answer it. Dr. Collins stood there with a female uniformed officer.

"Sheridan, do you feel up to talking to Officer Paget about what happened? Dr. Lansky isn't here and nothing else will happen to you."

"I guess," I answered. "Can Gladys stay with me?"

"Yes, she can," Officer Paget remarked, coming into the room. "I know this can be difficult, but can you tell me what happened?"

I retold the events that happened while Gladys held my hand, offering me silent support. Officer Paget documented my bruises that I didn't know had started to appear in the shape of Dr. Lansky's fingers. The longer I spoke, the sorer my jaw became.

"I think that's all I need for now. Ms. Taylor. Dr. Collins is getting the footage from the camera, and we will review it. I'm sorry this happened to you." With a kind smile, she left the room.

"Sheridan, I want you to take the rest of the week off."

"No, I—"

"No, I insist. It will be a paid leave and if you need more time than that, you let me know," Dr. Collins warned. "Is there someone I can call for you?"

Levi was the first person to pop into my head, but I dismissed it immediately. I didn't want to think of what he would do when he found out this had happened. Dr. Lanksy better pray he'd still be in jail when Levi found out.

"Kenna. I don't remember her number."

Gladys took the phone from my hand. "I will handle it, Dr. Collins."

"Thank you, Gladys."

"Sheridan, I need you to unlock your phone," Gladys said, handing it back to me.

I sat there staring at the puppy poster on the wall, and Gladys spoke with Kenna. Her shriek of outrage could be heard as Gladys moved the phone away from her ear.

"Your friend has a healthy set of lungs," Gladys remarked, handing me back the phone. "She's on her way."

"He's really not here?"

"No, dear. He's not. You're safe."

A torrent of emotion rolled through me, and I cried in her arms.

Everyone knew when Kenna made her way inside the building.

"Where the hell is she?"

"She's a little protective," I said with my first smile in what felt like an eternity.

"That's a good thing to have in a friend."

"She's the best."

The door opened and Kenna barged in. She was still wearing her sleep shorts and thin t-shirt, hair thrown up in a lopsided ponytail.

"Sheridan, are you okay?"

I nodded, and she sagged against the door frame.

"Where the fuck is he? I'll kill him."

"The police took him to the station," Gladys informed her.

"Fucker's lucky."

I barked out a laugh and Kenna smiled. "Come on. Let's get you home. Dr. Collins said you have the rest of the week off. I think this calls for ice cream."

My favorite form of therapy.

CHAPTER 17
TRIGGER

"WHOSE GOING with you to Sheridan's tonight?" Hammer asked as we finished up work on the heavy bag.

"Wrench and Savage."

"Savage complaining any about having to babysit?"

"No, he's a night owl, anyway."

When Sheridan and I had gotten back from our ride a few weeks ago, I had told my brothers about the Devil's Reign MC being so close to our territory and that they had seen Sheridan with me. Most of the members knew the history between Cobra and me and the threats. Not one of my brothers wanted to see an innocent woman hurt in an act of retaliation against me. As far as we knew, the Devils had left the area, but I remained uneasy. The look in Cobra's eyes, when he looked at Sheridan, had woken me from a deep sleep more times than I could count.

"Sheridan has no idea that you're having her place watched?"

"No."

"Dad noticed."

"That doesn't surprise me," I laughed.

"He wanted to know what was going on in case he needed to help."

"Just keeping an eye out helps."

"He noticed a car has parked at the empty house down from Sheridan a couple of mornings."

"The one that's for sale?"

"That's the one."

"Maybe he's checking out the house."

"Dad said he's not looking at the house. Never gets out of the car. Just sits there for a couple of hours then leaves."

"He must be getting there after Savage is gone because he hasn't mentioned it."

Hammer nodded in agreement.

"The car doesn't move until Sheridan goes to work," he dropped the bomb.

"Fuck," I breathed out. "She hasn't mentioned anything."

"She's noticed, though. Dad said she stared at the car for a few seconds, then hauled ass out of the driveway. She almost clipped the trash can at the end of the curb. That's not like her."

"No, it's not. She drives like a grandma with Ellie in the car. Did he get a plate number?"

"Partial. A few of the numbers are obscured. It's a Toyota Corolla."

"A common enough car not to draw much attention and blend in."

"I'm thinking it's a private investigator."

"That's not Cobra's style. He's balls to the wall."

"Maybe he wants to be sure before all hell breaks loose. He knows we'll retaliate if it's one of ours that is targeted."

"Fuck!" I ran a hand through my hair. "What the hell do I do, Hammer?"

"What you're doing. Keep alert and keep an eye out." He hesitated. "Maybe you should let Sheridan know what is going on."

"And scare her? Hi, Sheridan. I really like you, but this guy swore revenge against me for killing his son and now I think he's coming after you. Can you pass me the potatoes? That'll go over like a fart in church. "

Hammer winced. "Okay, I see your point."

"I'm fucked."

"Isn't she going to think it's strange that you never come over alone? You're supposed to be in the getting to know you phase and you're bringing us all over to her house."

"Trust me, I don't want you fuckers there," I laughed at his affronted look. "I don't know what the fuck I'm doing here."

"What do you mean?"

"What the hell do I know about being in a relationship? I usually just fuck and leave."

"Sheridan is definitely not like the club girls. They know the drill."

"I'm treading water here. I want more, but I don't know . . ."

"What?"

"How much more?"

"Are you talking about a ring and vows?

"Maybe?"

"I didn't realize you were that serious about her."

"She could be the one," I admitted.

"Shit. The girls aren't going to like that. Especially Nessa."

"Nessa fucks with Sheridan enough at work. There's no way I'm going to let that slip to make her go harder. Why Nessa thinks she has a shot at being my old lady beats the hell out of me."

"She's always gotten whatever she wants. The other club girls defer to her. Nessa thinks she owns all of us."

"Fuck that shit."

"Just saying," Hammer remarked. "Why do you think she went after Dagger so hard after he married Jen?"

"I didn't think about it. Dagger could have kept it in his pants."

"I'm not sure he didn't, but Nessa is a conniving bitch. Some pictures she sent Jen were from before they got together."

"How the hell is she still allowed in the club? Does Prez know?"

"Not unless Dagger said something. I overheard him confront Nessa about it."

"I didn't know. Fuck, that's messed up."

"Wanted to let you know what you're dealing with. Nessa will try to screw you over when it comes to Sheridan."

"I appreciate it. How are you feeling?" I asked when he rolled his shoulder and grimaced.

"Shoulder's a little tight, but not bad. Got hit with a four-by-four at the site today."

"Make sure you ice it up tonight."

"I will. Has the fight bracket been set yet?"

"Prez is still working on it. Lots of fighters this year."

Hammer grinned. "Just means more money."

"Don't get cocky," I warned.

"I'm not. I'm taking each fight one at a time. But it's still a lot of money on the line."

"Yeah," I agreed. "We're bumping up security. It's going to be our biggest turnout to date."

"That's good for the club."

"And a bigger headache."

"It'll be worth it."

"I think you're done for the night. Hit the showers."

"Sure thing, Coach," Hammer mocked.

"Fucker," I laughed and threw the towel I was holding at him.

"If you'll wait, I'll ride over with you. I need to check on Mom."

"Sure thing. Wrench should be here in a few minutes."

The sound of a motorcycle engine outside the building could be heard as if on cue.

"I'll be quick," Hammer remarked and headed for the locker room.

Wrench walked in and winked at the receptionist.

"Hey, brother," I said.

"Done already?" he asked, coming up beside me and watching two men spar in the ring.

"He's in the shower."

"How's he looking?"

"Like a fucking beast."

"Good. I plan on winning a lot of money when he wins." Wrench grinned.

"Don't tell him you're betting. He doesn't need the added pressure."

"I won't," Wrench agreed.

"He's going to ride with us."

"Alright. Is Sheridan okay with all of us coming over every night?"

"She hasn't said anything about it."

"I doubt she would, man. She wouldn't want to be rude. I could just hang out and keep an eye on things until Savage shows up. She might want some time alone with you."

"Hammer was saying the same thing."

"None of us have done the relationship thing besides Demon and he's fucking that up. I don't want you to do it, too."

"I don't know what the hell I'm doing," I confessed.

"Talk to her. Find out what she wants, but you need to spend time with her. Not her and your brothers. We'll keep an eye on things, and you focus on her."

"Maybe you're right."

"I'll hang with Hammer over at his parents and keep watch. You pay attention to your girl."

"Thanks, man."

"I'm glad one of us could talk some damn sense into you," Hammer quipped, coming up behind us and rubbing a towel on his hair.

"I think Mom was making baked ziti."

"Sweet," Wrench quipped. "Let's hit the road. My mouth is already watering."

"You going to bring me some?" I asked Hammer as we walked outside.

"Knowing Mom, she made enough for the entire block to eat."

"Hey, two o'clock," Wrench said as he lit a cigarette.

I glanced in that direction and noticed a Toyota Corolla parked in the corner of the lot. And wouldn't you know it? Some of the plate was obscured.

"What do you want to do?" Hammer asked as we walked toward our bikes.

"Nothing. Let's see what he does. Wrench, keep an eye out and see if drives by Sheridan's house."

"You got it."

I put on my helmet and started my bike. One by one, we filed out of the parking lot.

The car didn't follow.

I waved at the guys as I turned into Sheridan's drive, and they continued on. Kenna had parked her SUV in the garage where Sheridan's car usually was. Was she not home? She hadn't sent me any message like she did when something came up after work.

The back gate opened as I killed the engine. The grave look on Kenna's face has me jerking off my helmet and stomping toward her. Fuck, had they found her? Hurt her?

"What? What happened?" I barked out.

"Do not blow your top," Kenna warned. "Do not yell or blame her, you hear me?" She jabbed a finger into my chest.

"Jesus. Fuck okay. Is she okay?"

"Yes. She was assaulted at work today."

She confirmed my worst fear. My past had come back to haunt me and hurt Sheridan in my place.

Kenna took a step back from me.

I was at a loss for words. Red edged my vision as homicidal rage pumped through my veins.

"He grabbed her face and said some nasty stuff, but she fended him off. He's in jail right now, so you can't take that anger out on him."

Wait? Cobra would have done more than that. Maybe he sent one of his boys to send a message.

"I'd kill the mother fucker. Who was it?"

"One vet at her work."

My mind conjured the picture of that little fucker I'd met before.

"Oh, I know the one. He was giving her a hard time when Ellie was sick, and I dropped by to get the car seat."

"He's said some shit to her before, but she shrugged it off. Didn't want to rock the boat at her new job."

"Fuck the job."

"That's easy for you to say. Her boss gave her the rest of the week off with pay."

"No way is he getting out of pressing charges on that fucker."

"Her boss is the one who called the cops."

"Good. Fucker better be glad he's behind bars."

"I'm sure he'll make bail in the morning."

Kenna paled at the smile that I gave her.

"And we'll be waiting."

"Jesus. Don't tell me that shit. I don't want to have to testify against you."

"She's okay, though?"

"Some bruising on her jaw where he grabbed her. Ellie is staying with her mom tonight. We didn't want to get her upset. I need you to be calm when you go in there, okay?"

"Fine."

"It wasn't her fault."

"What? For fuck's sake, I know that."

"Just checking. I'm going to go. Can you help me get her car tomorrow? She was pretty shaken up, and I didn't want her to drive."

I nodded. "Thanks for being here with her."

"She's my best friend. Where the hell else would I be? I need to get to work, though. I told Shooter I'd come in as soon as you got here."

"Be careful and if Shooter gives you any shit, let me know."

"I can handle Shooter. Be good to my girl."

Kenna climbed into her car and backed out. I took several deep breaths and let the rage go. Sheridan didn't need to see that. As I opened the back gate, Ripper darted out of the doggie door with a bark. When he spotted me, his tail wagged.

"Good boy, Rip." I gave him a scratch before opening the back door.

The lights were off in the living room, the flicker of the television the only thing illuminating the space. Sheridan sat on the couch wrapped in the blue throw blanket she kept on the back of the couch. Her eyes weren't on the show playing, they were on me. Even from across the room, I could see the dark shading on her jaw. I bit back my rage.

"Hey, Sher," I said as I pulled off my boots.

"Hey," she whispered.

I put my boots by the door and removed my cut. laying it on the back of the chair as I walked to her. Her eyes never left mine. I pulled back the blanket and picked her up. Settling on the couch, I placed her sideways on my lap and curled an arm around her. Her head dropped to my shoulder as she melted into me.

"I'm sorry," I murmured against her hair.

"Nothing for you to be sorry for."

"You want to talk about it?"

She shook her head.

"If I'd kicked his ass for the way he talked to you the other day, he wouldn't have been able to do this to you."

"You didn't know. Hell, I didn't know. If I would have thought—"

"Not your fault. It's that fucker and he will regret ever putting his hands on you."

"Don't do anything stupid, Levi," she warned.

I pulled her closer and said nothing. Neither did she. I wasn't making a promise I wouldn't keep. Ripper curled up at my feet and stared up at us.

Maybe he felt the same helplessness that I did. But unlike Ripper, I would make up for not being there for my woman.

CHAPTER 18
TRIGGER

WE WATCHED a few episodes of home fixer-upper shows I pretended I wasn't interested in.

"Are you hungry?" I asked her.

"I've eaten about a pint of ice cream. I'll pop if I eat anything else."

My phone vibrated in my pocket, and I fished it out without displacing Sheridan.

I chuckled when I read the message.

"What?" She looked up at me with wide eyes.

"Hammer is bringing us food. His mom made two trays of baked ziti."

I texted him back the coast was clear, and he wouldn't be interrupting anything. A few minutes later, Ripper's ears perked up and a low growl erupted from his throat. Hammer knocked on the door. Ripper's bark echoed off the walls.

"Ripper, sit," Sheridan murmured. "Come in, Michael."

The door swung open, and he entered carrying a pan covered with aluminum foil.

"Hey, Sheridan. Mom wanted me to bring you dinner since she cooked like she's feeding an army. There's baked ziti, salad, and garlic bread."

"Thank you for bringing it over and tell her I appreciate it. I can't ever turn down her food."

"Hey, Trigger, can I talk to you for a second?"

I kissed Sheridan's head and picked her up off my lap. "Be right back."

Hammer and I walked into the backyard.

"What's up?"

"Wrench said the car drove by but didn't stop. He didn't want to follow and get caught."

"Okay. What the hell is going on?"

"I don't know. Did something else happen?"

"Fucker at her work attacked her today."

"You're shitting me," Hammer replied, rocking back on his heels.

"No. I wish I was."

"Where the fuck is he?"

"Kenna said he's still in jail, but will most likely be out on bail tomorrow."

"What do we know about him?"

"Just his name. Gerald Lansky."

"That's enough. Hawk should be able to get what we need. We're going to be paying him a little visit, right?"

"Damn right, we will. No one fucks with my woman and gets away with it."

"Get back in there to her. "

"Thanks, man."

When I walked back in, Sheridan was still sitting where I put her.

"You want some?" I gestured to the pan that Hammer had put down on the counter.

"Not right now. You go ahead." She threw back the blanket and stood.

Screw the food. She made my mouth water. She stretched, and it bared her stomach. I'd touched that silky smooth skin, but not enough. She yawned, then winced. Fuck the erection that was popping up. Tonight wasn't about taking her to bed and making her scream my name. Not after some douchebag with a tiny dick had assaulted her and made her hurt. I wanted her healthy and able to enjoy all the orgasms I was going to wring out of her tiny body. I pulled back the foil and the aroma of garlic, tomato, and spice filled the air.

"It sure smells good," she groaned.

"I'll leave you some."

"Promise?"

At my hesitation, her beautiful hazel eyes narrowed.

"I promise."

She gave me a look that said she'd believe it when she saw it and walked down the hall.

The shower turned on and I dug in. By the time the water turned off, I had devoured almost two-thirds of the food that Hammer had brought over. I sealed the rest up before I broke my word.

CHAPTER 19
SHERIDAN

"I CAN'T BELIEVE I fell asleep," I uttered, embarrassed that I had passed out after we started watching *Fools Rush In*. He swept me into his arms and sat me on his lap, towel and all, and started one of my favorite movies. The steady rhythm of his heart had lulled me to sleep.

His chest lifted beneath me when he laughed.

"I like you sleeping on me."

I reached down and pinched his stomach.

"How come the guys didn't come with you tonight?"

"They thought we needed some time alone."

"You didn't?" I regretted the words the second they came out of my mouth, and I tried to move away. He clamped his arms around me and held me to him.

"No, I wanted time alone with you. We needed some time with just us. Too bad Little Bit wasn't here. Did you want the guys here?"

Maybe she liked them as a buffer?

"No!" she nearly yelled.

"You don't like my brothers?"

"The guys are fine. It's just you never come around unless they're with you. At least until we go to bed."

"You think I keep them here until I fuck you?"

"Do you?"

"Hell no. That's not why."

"Then why?"

"I told you I was going to fuck this up," he huffed out, running a hand through his hair.

"You haven't messed anything up, but we're going to have to communicate better."

"Communicate. I think we've been doing very well," he teased.

He was right. We did, and I enjoyed every second.

"You know what I mean," I huffed out.

"Does it bother you that the guys come over?"

I hesitated for a second. A second too long for Levi.

"These guys are my family. If you accept me, you accept them," he warned.

"It's a little much sometimes," I confessed.

"I can understand that."

"Don't get me wrong, I like the guys, but I'd like to spend time just us."

"I'll work on that, but I can't guarantee that one or more of them will drop by if they know I'm here. We pretty much have an open-door policy with all the members."

"That's a little, um, invasive. What if one of them had come by when we were—?"

"I would have told them to leave."

"Maybe I have some boundary issues with that. I'm used to it being Ellie and me."

"Love me, love my club," he said, leaning back against the couch, away from me.

I wanted him to hold me and tell me he'd have them back off until we were more solid, but I guessed it wouldn't happen.

"Look, I know they're a big part of your life. I'm not trying to keep you away from them or them away from you. It's just how do you and I do this when they're always here?"

"Do what?"

"Be a couple. Have a relationship. Whatever the hell this is supposed to be?"

"I don't know," he confessed.

"Is this just about the sex for you?"

"No, it's not. If it was, I would have fucked you and been done."

"Thanks for that, I guess."

I climbed off his lap and clutched the towel tight, aware of how naked I was beneath it. I felt vulnerable for the first time with him. "I'm going to get dressed."

I threw on some clothes and came back out to find him slipping on his cut.

"You're leaving?" My voice wavered, and I hated it. I wasn't weak, damn it.

He heaved a sigh.

"No, I'm not."

"Then why are you putting that on?"

"Because I was going to leave."

"What changed in the last two seconds?"

"You."

"Me? I haven't changed—"

"You changed me. Any other woman, I would've walked out the door without a backward glance. But I can't leave you. I don't want to."

"I don't want you to leave either.

"Yeah, and you're right. We need to figure out what we want out of this and what we can compromise on. It's been a long day for both of us. Maybe we need to get some sleep and talk in the morning.

He walked over and kissed me softly before taking my hand. He led me into the bedroom and pulled out one of the large shirts I liked to sleep in and a pair of panties. Kneeling before me, he had me step into my panties and drew them up my legs, his touch gentle. He picked up the shirt and hesitated.

"What?"

"I don't want you to feel uncomfortable?"

"With you? I think you've seen everything," I murmured.

"You were attacked. I just, well, didn't know if you'd want to get naked with me right now, but I don't think I can get this shirt on otherwise."

"Levi, it's okay."

Pulling the towel loose, I let it drop to the floor.

Eyes locked with mine, he helped me put on the shirt. His hand feathered over the bruising that had blossomed into any ugly, purplish-blue.

"Levi," I murmured.

"Have you taken anything for the pain?"

"Some Tylenol earlier."

"You should take some before bed."

He turned and went into the bathroom. I sat on the side of the bed and wondered what was wrong? Did he look at me differently now? My stomach was tied in knots. I waited for him to come back out. It seemed an eternity before he came back out, but instead of looking at me, he walked out into the hallway with something in his hand. A cabinet door opened in the kitchen and then another. Then the ice maker rumbled to life, followed by the water filling a glass. A minute later, he armed the house alarm, and it beeped.

His footsteps sounded in the hall as he came towards the room. His tall frame filled the doorway as he came in with his hands full. A glass of water, a string cheese, and a bottle of painkillers. He handed me the glass and dropped the cheese on the bed. Opening the bottle of ibuprofen, he gestured to the snack.

"Don't want this to upset your stomach."

He shook out two bluish-green capsules and placed them in my upturned palm.

"Thank you," I said after clearing my throat. Tears burned my eyes as I blinked them away.

"What's wrong?" he asked, squatting in front of me.

The concern in his eyes and the soft way he said the words had the waterworks flowing. Taking the glass from me, he put it on the table, pulled me to his chest, and held me close. The comforting scent of his detergent and soap had me melting into his hard chest. His hand petted my hair, and he whispered to me.

"Sher, you're scaring me."

"I'm not meaning to," I sniffled.

"Do I need to take you to the hospital?"

"No, I'm not hurt. It's just been a shit day."

"It has," he agreed.

"I snotted all over your shirt, you know."

His laughter caused my head to bounce against his chest.

"I can think of worse things that could happen."

Placing a finger under my chin, he lifted my face to look at him. His thumb wiped the tears from under my eye.

"Take the pills."

He handed me the glass, and I popped the pills into my mouth. The cool water felt wonderful against my parched throat. The sound of a wrapper opening caught my attention as Levi opened the string cheese.

"Eat," he ordered.

After I took it from him, he crawled behind me on the bed and sat with his thighs on the outside of my hips. I jerked in surprise when the hairbrush touched my head, but I closed my eyes in appreciation as he made slow strokes through my long hair.

"A girl could get used to this," I purred.

"I'll keep that in mind."

He brought his hands to my hair and started plaiting it, to my shock.

"You know how to braid?"

"It'll make me sound like a pussy, but I watched some YouTube videos on how to do it."

"Why?"

"You braid Ellie's hair a lot of the time. If I needed to in a pinch, I wanted to be ready."

If I hadn't already been falling for him, that would have sealed the deal. For him to do that? I nearly cried again, but I wasn't sure he'd handle another round of waterworks tonight.

"That's sweet."

"It's not as good as when you do it, but it'll work." He secured the elastic around the end.

"I'm going to brush my teeth." I turned and kissed him. "Thank you."

"You're welcome."

When I came back out, he was under the covers and Ripper had made his way to the end of the bed. He looked at me with sad brown eyes. He didn't know what to do without Ellie here. Instead of leaving the door closed, I left it open a crack in case he needed out and climbed into bed. Levi drew me to him, and I curled into him. He clicked off the light, and I closed my eyes. His kiss on the top of my head was the last thing I felt before sleep claimed me.

The next morning, I woke in a rush, my internal clock telling me I'd slept too late. It took me a moment to remember what happened, and that I didn't have to be at work today.

Levi's side of the bed was empty. Disappointed, I got up and went into the bathroom. The mirror revealed the bruising that dotted my face and neck. The sight pissed me off.

"That asshole. I hope someone makes him their bitch while he's locked up."

Ripper whined from the doorway.

"Sorry, Rip. Let me take a shower and I'll get you fed."

He sat on his haunches and let out a soft woof.

"I'll take that as you agree."

The hot water felt luxurious, and I stayed in getting clean until the water turned cool. Having time to myself without a little girl clamoring for attention was an unfamiliar sensation.

The house was quiet, and it felt weird not hurrying to get ready for work when it wasn't the weekend. The coffee machine was on when I walked in, and the nectar of the Gods was dripping into the carafe. On the counter was a Styrofoam container. My stomach grumbled, reminding me I'd only had ice cream and cheese yesterday. I popped the top open to reveal a stack of pancakes and bacon. Even the little bottles of syrup were warm. He must have just left. I hurried out the back door to the gate. The smile dropped from my face when I saw my car parked there, but I couldn't see any sign of Levi. Damn.

Mom said she was going to take Ellie to daycare this morning, which left me with hours to myself, and I didn't want to be alone. It was too early to call Kenna since she worked last night. I texted Levi and told him thank you for breakfast and for getting my car.

I spent the next few hours cleaning the house without Tornado-Ellie messing it up behind me. Ripper got a bath. Laundry was done and put away. I still had hours before my daughter came home or Levi got off work.

I called Kenna as soon as I thought she wouldn't kill me for waking her up.

"Shouldn't you be sleeping in?" she grumbled into the phone.

"Like that was going to happen," I quipped.

"How are you this morning?"

"A little sore. My jaw's not hurting as much as I thought it would."

"Did Levi stay the night and take care of you?"

"Yes. He was very sweet."

"Sweet isn't the word I would use to describe him, but whatever."

"Well, he is," I defended.

"Excuse the hell outta me. It's not a side of him I get to see, but I'm not the one giving it up to him," she laughed.

"I thought we were going to have our first fight last night."

"What the hell? You got attacked, and he wants to start shit?"

"No. It was about having the guys over all the time and about how hard it is to get to know each other when they're here all the time. I don't want to reveal details of my life to a bunch of guys."

"That's a good point. Did he disagree?"

"No, not really. It was more of if I'm with him, I get the guys. too."

"Like a train?"

"Kenna, get your mind out of the gutter!"

"Just wondering. I've heard that some clubs do that."

"His better not because it's not happening."

"Hmmm."

"Quit picturing it, Kenna."

"I wasn't picturing you and them."

"No, you were picturing you and them making Shooter jealous."

"Think it would work?"

"No, because you wouldn't do that. That's more along the lines of something Nessa would do."

"Why did you have to bring that bitch up? You ruined my good morning vibe."

"You know I'm right."

"Whatever. I wouldn't do the train thing, but there are a couple of the guys I wouldn't mind hooking up with."

"Please don't tell me which ones. I don't want to be embarrassed in front of them."

She laughed into the phone. "Okay, I won't. I'll let you guess when you go to a club party."

"Club party?"

"Yeah, they have them every once in a while, and outsiders can come if they're invited. I've heard it gets crazy."

"You've never been to one?"

"I went once, but Shooter took me home before things got too wild," she pouted.

"Maybe I'll stay home," I hedged.

"If you're with Trigger, you'll have to at least make an appearance."

"I'm in over my head," I groaned and fell over face first into the couch cushion.

"You're fine. Trigger's a good guy. He wouldn't let anything happen to you and if it gets to be too much, he'll bring you home."

"I don't know about all of this. Am I ready?"

"Ready for what? A relationship? To open yourself up again?"

"Yes."

"Only you can decide that. I know that dirtbag broke your heart, but that's not a reason not to try again. What if Trigger is *the* one? Do you want to miss that chance?"

"When the hell did you get so wise about this?"

"Listen to me, Padawan. I know all."

"Give me a break," I laughed.

"Whatever. I need to get up and take a shower. When's your last night at Shooters?"

"This weekend. I've paid for the car repairs, put money up in savings, and for Christmas."

"It's going to suck having to deal with Nessa by myself. She left me alone when she was busy hating you."

"Get over it," I laughed. "Bye."

"Love you!"

I tossed the phone on the table. Kenna was right, though. I needed to decide if putting my heart on the line with Levi was worth the risk of having it broken again. I recalled the way he made me feel last night, and a shiver overtook me.

Yes, he was worth it.

CHAPTER 20
TRIGGER

I WAS in a grumpy ass mood all day. Everyone avoided me like the plague, afraid I would bite their heads off. How did shit go from amazing to shit so fast last night?

"Boy, get your ass in here," Dad barked from the office.

I put down the fuel filter I was replacing and washed my hands before heading in.

"What the hell is wrong with you today?" Dad asked as soon as I cleared his office door.

"Nothing. Why?"

"Watch your tone, boy," Dad warned.

"Sorry," I mumbled.

"Talk to me."

"I think I fucked up with Sheridan."

"It was going to happen." He shrugged.

"Geez, thanks for the vote of confidence," I quipped.

"It's not personal. You're a man. We fuck things up. The women forgive us, most of the time, and we move on with life."

"Sheridan said we needed to communicate and the first time she said something I wasn't comfortable with, I almost bailed."

"Almost bailed?"

"I had my cut on ready to walk out the door."

"Never took you as a coward. I sure as shit didn't raise you to be one."

"Thanks, Dad."

"What changed your mind?"

"She did. The way she looked at me. I couldn't leave her."

"Yeah, you've got it bad for this girl. Everything is fixable. Go talk it out. What was the problem?"

"The guys."

"She doesn't like them?" he asked in surprise.

"No, she does, but they're always over when I am. She doesn't realize it's because I'm worried about her."

"Ah, I see. Your mother had the same problem."

"You weren't in a club when you were dating, were you?"

"Worse. The army. Anytime we went somewhere that was close to base, we ran into someone I knew. It would go from the two of us to a group. She got tired of it after a while."

"Sheridan said it's hard for us to get to know each other with them around."

"She's right. You need to leave them at home."

"That happened last night. Wrench went with Hammer and hung out at Hammer's parents' house since they live next door."

"And? Was it awful?"

"It was nice. Missed Little Bit, though."

"Where was she?"

"With Sheridan's mom." I sat there for a minute with a million things on my mind, but one stood out. "How did you fix it with Mom?"

"Took her places the guys wouldn't be caught dead in."

"But that would be boring."

"It was. I had to put my foot down and tell them to leave us alone after a while."

"Did it work?"

"They took the hint to come over when invited."

"But I've been inviting them over with me."

"Let me ask you a question. Have you told Sheridan what is going on?"

"No. Hammer asked me the same thing last night. I don't want to scare her off."

"Ask yourself how she's going to feel when she finds out because she will. It may not be anytime soon, but women don't forget anything. Trust me on that one," he warned.

"I'll figure out how to tell her."

"You have to take the chance, son. She has the right to know that she may be in danger from something that happened years ago. She has more than herself to think about."

My stomach lurched at the thought of Ellie being hurt, maybe even more than Sheridan.

"Damn it."

"It's hard to do the right thing when you may not like the consequences," he advised.

"This is icing on the cake after what happened yesterday." I rubbed a hand over my face.

"Yesterday?"

"A vet where she works assaulted her."

"And I'm not bailing your ass out of jail. Why?"

"Because that's where he is or was. Figure he'll make bail today."

"This happened yesterday? And you wanted to leave last night?"

I nodded.

"What the fuck is wrong with you? Get your ass over there and make sure she's okay. I can't believe you even came to work today." He shook his head, then looked up. "Lord, I didn't think I raised an idiot."

"What the hell is that supposed to mean?"

"It means that you're a dumbass. You claim to care about this woman, but you were going to leave her alone after she was assaulted at work because you weren't ready to have an adult conversation?"

His eyes bored into mine. And then it hit me.

"Fuck, I am a dumbass."

"Get the hell out of here, go apologize, and take care of your woman."

"Thanks, Dad."

"And if you need bail money, let me know."

Within twenty minutes, I'd pulled into Sheridan's driveway. What the hell was I thinking last night? Boyfriend failure number two. All I could do was apologize and hope she forgave me because I was sure I'm going to screw up more in the future. When I shut off the engine, I could hear the music she had blaring in the house. Who knew my girl was a *Nothing More* fan? As soon as my hand touched the back gate, Ripper's barks came fast and furious. The music shut off.

"Someone there?" Sheridan called out when she opened the back door.

"It's just me."

Sheridan said something to Ripper, and he settled with a whine. I could tell she was getting closer each time her flip-flop hit the concrete. As soon as she pulled the gate open, I drew her into my arms.

"I'm so damn sorry," I rushed out.

"For what?" came her muffled voice, where I had her pressed against my chest.

"For making you feel you weren't important enough for me to spend time with by ourselves. There's shit going on that you don't know about, but most importantly, for last night."

"Um, Okay."

"Can I come in?"

She leaned back as far as she could while I still had her caged in my arms. Her hazel eyes searched my face, and she nodded.

I dropped my arms from around her, but needing the contact entwined her fingers with mine as she led me inside. The air was blessedly cool when we walked into the kitchen. She drew her bottom lip between her teeth and fiddled with the hem of her shirt. Was she nervous?

"Uh, you want something to drink?"

"Yes."

She nodded as if in agreement and went to the refrigerator. Staying on the other side of the counter, she slid a bottle of water across to me. I could take a hint and let her have the space she needed. She tapped her finger on the counter as I opened the bottle of water and chugged half of it down.

"Start at the beginning."

I sat down and debated where to begin.

"I'm gonna keep some of it vague because it has to do with the club."

Her eyes narrowed, but she motioned me to go on.

"Have you wondered where I got the name, Trigger?"

"Sure, because I'd feel weird calling you that."

"Believe it or not, I didn't look like this in high school." I gestured to myself, and she snorted a laugh. "I was scrawny, got picked on a lot and it pissed me off. I wouldn't take their shit, but it ended up with me getting my ass kicked. It wouldn't take much to set me off. Mom said I had a hair trigger with my temper."

"I guess that makes sense."

"She got tired of getting called to the principal's office every time it happened, which was a weekly basis. My dad talked her into getting me into martial arts. One, he thought it would help my focus and not be so quick to fight back, and two so I could finally kick their asses."

"Did you?"

"Eventually, and then they left me the hell alone. But I got good at fighting once I started filling out and grew about six inches. The fighting and martial arts were an outlet, a way for me to burn off the aggression that I couldn't get rid of. One day when I was at the gym, one of the other members, Jerry, came up to me to tell me a way I could make a quick buck. You ever seen the movie Fight Club?"

"Um, I think so. It was Brad Pitt and Edward Norton? What happens at Fight Club stays at Fight Club?"

I chuckled. "I think that's Vegas. That's kind of what this guy took me to, except it was more organized. There were rules and officials."

"Legal fighting?"

"Yes. We stood there watching two guys beating the shit out of each other while people cheered them on."

"It sounds a little barbaric. I've never understood the appeal."

I wasn't sure how I felt about that.

"The roar of the crowd cheering for the fighters just did something for me. Jerry introduced me to a guy named Darrell who was looking to add a few fighters to his roster."

Her eyes narrowed in contemplation.

"Yes, I did," I answered her unspoken question.

"I'm not sure how I feel about that," she admitted.

"Understandable."

"Is there more?"

"That's only the beginning."

She swallowed hard. I laid it all out for her, let her make her mind up whether she wanted to keep me around. Fuck, I hoped she did.

"I started fighting on the weekends. The first few I got my ass kicked. The guys were older and more experienced, but it was a learning lesson. Mom was suspicious when I came home with injuries."

"I bet. Us moms are a suspicious lot. What lies did you tell her?"

"I played it off as being more physical during training. Dad didn't buy it, though. He followed me one night and found out what I'd been doing. I thought he was going to kill me."

"I bet."

"He didn't interfere, though. He let me climb into that ring. It was the first fight that I won. Made five hundred bucks, and I felt like I was king of the world. It was a fucking rush."

"What did your dad say?"

"Nothing. He led me out to my truck and drove us home."

She winced. "That's worse than him kicking your butt."

"Once the adrenaline wore off, it was."

"How old were you?"

"Nineteen. Still living at home with my parents."

"Yikes," she replied with a grimace.

"We pulled into the driveway, and we sat there. The only you could hear was the tick of the engine as it cooled off."

I remembered it like it was yesterday. The dread that flooded me, waiting for him to say something, anything.

"And?" Sheridan encouraged.

"He turned to me, looked me dead in the eye, and told me we needed to work on my takedown skills because it was pathetic."

"Holy shit," she breathed out.

"Yeah," I laughed. "It was not what I expected. He told me he knew a guy that could help, and he'd give him a call."

"Your dad wanted you to fight?" she asked in disbelief.

"He said that he had noticed a difference in me a few weeks prior to watching me. Said that I was calmer, lighter. Whatever that meant." I shrugged.

"It helped you get rid of your demons."

"Maybe," I conceded. "I knew that I felt at peace in that ring and out of it."

"I still can't believe your dad was okay with it."

"Dad did it when he was in the army. He had some beef with another guy in boot camp and they ended up getting into a few fights."

"I bet that didn't go over well," Sheridan remarked before taking a drink. "They have rules against that sort of thing, don't they?"

"Yes. Dad said their drill sergeant took it out of their asses."

She winced in sympathy.

"The other guys were tired of paying for their fuck ups and had an 'intervention'." I did the quote marks in the air just like Dad did.

Her eyes widened. "That doesn't sound good."

"I'm sure it wasn't pleasant. Dad let me sleep in the next day and then drug me to this old ass gym that was on the other side of town. There I am, black eye, busted lip, nursing sore ribs, and moving like an old man. I thought he was just going to introduce me to the guy, but I was wrong, so wrong."

Just the memory still made me shiver with dread.

"What did they do?" Sheridan asked, wide-eyed, biting her bottom lip.

"They kicked the shit out of me," I laughed. "Not literally. He had me doing drills. I'd never been so tired in my life. We were there for three hours before Dad took me home. I passed out for the rest of the afternoon and was too damn sore to think about going out, much less finding any trouble to get into."

"You loved it, didn't you?"

"Why do you say that?"

"Because your eyes lit up when you were talking about it." Sheridan rested her chin on her fist.

"I went there every day after school. Even if it was to just watch the other fighters and see what they were doing, so I could learn. I even started working there after school to afford lessons."

"Did it keep you out of trouble?"

"Mostly. I still had some trouble with a few guys at school, but they learned not to fuck with me."

"I bet that made your dad proud."

"Yeah, it did. I started making better grades and giving a shit about school. Not that it turned me into a straight-A student or anything, but my mom didn't have to worry about me flunking out anymore."

"Do you still train? Obviously, you do something to look the way you do," she smirked.

"You like the way I look?" I teased.

"I'm not complaining," she laughed.

"I train with Hammer. We do drills, lift weights, and do cardio. I don't lift near as heavy as him, but I manage."

"He's the size of a freaking mountain. He could bench press my car."

"Not many guys can hang with him weight-wise."

"Do you still fight?"

"Not anymore."

"Why not?"

Fuck. I never wanted to relive this memory, much less tell her I killed a man.

"I just don't. I train Hammer at the gym and that's enough."

"Bullshit. What aren't you telling me?" Her eyes narrowed on me.

"Why do you think that's bullshit? Maybe I don't want to fight. I work out and I train with Hammer. That's enough."

"Something happened that made you quit what you loved doing. What was it?"

"Drop it," I barked out.

Her eyes widened at my tone. "Sorry. Forget I said anything."

Grabbing a towel and a bottle of cleaner, she started wiping down the countertop.

"I'm sorry. It's not something I like to think about."

Her hand stopped mid-wipe, and she looked at me.

"It was bad, wasn't it?"

"The worst thing I've ever done."

"Levi, look, you don't have to tell me now or ever if you don't want to, but I'm here. If you want this relationship to work, we have to be open with each other. I'm not going to judge you. The past is in the past. We grow and move on."

Why the hell did she have to sound so reasonable?

I placed my elbows on my knees and buried my head in my hands. What if she was mistaken? What if I told her and she looked at me in disgust? Taking a deep breath, I looked at her. The kitchen light created a halo effect around her. Maybe that's what she was. An angel sent down for me to be judged by. She would either be my salvation or would condemn me to a life of hell without her.

Did I dare take that chance? I'd already put her in the crosshairs of the enemy. I owed it to her to let her know why she was in danger.

"You might want to sit down for this."

She nodded her head and threw the towel at the sink. She sat down beside me, not touching but leaving a hairbreadth in between us.

"I used to be the club's fighter like Hammer is now. We hold fights at a place we own outside of town. A lot of people come from all over. It's a big deal. Lots of money to be made on betting. Other clubs, regular people, all different types, anyone can enter to fight if they pay. There was a club out of California that had come through one of the last fights and decided to enter. They'd come into town the weekend before the fight was scheduled, taking all kinds of shit about how their dude was going to win it all and take out a few of the other fighters. They were starting fights and trashing any place they were at. It was to where the club was ready to run them out of town because they were drawing way too much attention from the authorities. Two of their members were arrested before the fight."

"What did you do?"

"Ignored it and tried to keep our distance from them. They liked a bar on the other side of town, and we avoided it. But the shit they were talking still made the rounds."

I took a deep breath, building the courage to tell it all.

"They brought a few women with them. Some of us decided to start some shit of our own."

"Wait, what? You did something to the women?"

"No, nothing bad. We did uh," I rubbed the back of my neck. "We, uh, hooked up with a few of them."

She burst into laughter. Not the reaction I was expecting.

"I bet that pissed them off," she said.

"It did. Especially since one of them was the chick he was hooking up with for the trip."

"Oh, no." Her hazel eyes widened, and she covered her mouth with her hand. "Then what happened?"

"It happened the night before the fight, so the guys were hot when they showed up. Of course, that just meant we had to do some trash-talking ourselves. The way the fights are set up in rounds. First round has eight fights. Second round, the winners fight in the next four, and so on until only two fighters are left. After each of their wins, they talked more and more shit. The last fight came down to me and a man named Mamba. He was the son of the President of their club."

I stopped as I recalled Mamba coming into the ring. The smug grin on his unmarked face. He was around my size. He strutted into the ring like he didn't have a care in the world. The old Trigger would have pounced as soon as the bastard hit the inside, but I'd learned better.

"We both got into the ring. now these fights are pretty much anything goes. Not like you'd see for professional fights. It's brutal and bloody."

My mouth dried and hard for me to get the words out. I pick up my bottle of beer and down the rest.

"We traded a few hits, nothing too damaging. Kind of feeling each other out. Then it was like a switch was flipped. We were going at each other full force. It was me and him. Everything else was a blur. I don't even know how to explain what I was feeling. It was like someone else had taken me over. I hit him again and again, never letting up. He ended up on the ground. I stood there feeling elated that it was taking him so long to get back up, and when he did, I hit him one more time. I still see him falling over like it's in slow motion and his head bouncing off the concrete. The sound it made. I'd never felt like that before. Like I was on top of the world."

"I can understand that," she whispered, reaching over and covering her hand with mine.

"He didn't get back up," I uttered, voice cracking.

"You knocked him out?"

I looked her in the eyes.

"I killed him."

CHAPTER 21
SHERIDAN

It took everything I had not to flinch when said those words. How the hell was I supposed to react to him admitting to killing a man? His head dropped, waiting for my chastisement.

"Levi, I don't believe for a minute that you killed that man."

"It was my fault," his voice was a harsh whisper. "If I hadn't hit him—"

I squeezed his hand tighter.

"No one made him get into that ring and fight. You can't blame yourself. It could have happened with anyone he fought. It was not your fault." His shoulders lifted with a deep breath, and he let it out slowly. You've been carrying this around for a long time, haven't you?"

"For years, I had nightmares about it. I'd wake up and smell the blood, the sweat. Hear the crowd. At first, they'd be cheering for me, calling my name. Then it would turn into blaming me, calling me a murderer. As the years went on, they became fewer, but every once in a while, one will blindside me."

"I don't know what to say—"

"That's all I need you to say. Everyone always wants to try to fix it. I don't need answers on how to fix it. This guilt is a part of me now.

Rationally, I know that I didn't kill him, that it was a freak accident, but it doesn't change the fact that I was the catalyst for his death."

He looked up and me and he looked lighter. If that's what you could call it. As if a weight had been lifted. By the simple words I had spoken? Or that I didn't try to fix him? God, I wanted to, though. Wanted to rip the guilt out of his soul so he could find peace.

"I've put you in a dangerous position," he confessed.

"What do you mean? How?"

"Does the name Devil's Reign mean anything to you?"

"No, I don't think so? Why?"

"The man I killed was the son of the President of the Devil's Reign MC. They're based out of California." He searched my face as if looking for something.

"Okayyy," I drew out. What the hell was he getting at? "What does that have to do with me?"

"He vowed to make me pay for killing his son."

"But he's in California. What are the chances you're going to run into him again?"

"Higher than you'd think. He's here in Texas," he confessed.

"Here? Like here?" I pointed down. Levi nodded. "Why?"

"The club still holds regular tournaments. It's one way we make money."

"He's here for that?"

"They entered the tournament."

"But you're not fighting. Hammer is."

"Right. I don't know what their end game is, but I don't think it's good for anyone."

"Any chance they're here to try to win the tournament?"

"It may have been before," he hedged.

"Before what?"

"You."

"Me?" I took a step back. "What about me?"

"I've never had anything I cared enough about besides my brothers until you and Ellie came along."

"How would he even know about me? About us?"

"Remember our first ride and we went up to that diner?"

"Sure." I paused. "Wait. A group of riders came while we were there."

"Yeah. I had no inclination that they would show up there. It's so far out of the normal territory."

"That was them?"

He nodded.

"And they saw us together?"

"Yes."

"Are we in danger?"

"I'd like to say no, but I can't promise you that you're not."

He ducked his head. My gut churned. Had I placed my daughter in danger? I stood from the couch and walked into the kitchen. Liquor wasn't my usual go-to, but I pulled a bottle of Jack Daniels out of the cabinet and took a hefty gulp. My throat burned as I swallowed, and it landed in my stomach like a fireball. I took another for good measure.

"What aren't you telling me?"

I knew there had to be something else. he looked guilty sitting there on my couch, elbows propped on his knees and his hands clenched together in front of his face.

"I don't know how to tell you or if I should."

"How about this? If you don't lay all of this out now, you can walk out of that door and my life and not come back."

His eyes widened at my outburst, but I was tired of the bullshit.

"Ellie's father is a member of the Devil's Reign."

"Excuse me? What the hell are you talking about? How the hell do you know who Ellie's father is?"

"He showed up when your car was in the shop and paid for some repairs on your car."

My head spun. Whether from the alcohol or shock, I didn't know. My world was all topsy-turvy. Roger had been here? How the hell did he even know where the hell we were?

"I met Roger in Colorado. He lived in the apartment next door."

"With his mom."

I nodded and sat down on the floor. I stared at him across the room.

"He said you had no idea who he really was."

"He was fucking right."

Levi looked startled that I had cursed.

"His club is bad news. They're into all kinds of illegal shit. Nasty shit. When he found out you were pregnant, the safest thing for you and Ellie was for him to disappear before his club found out about you. His President is known to use their family members as leverage to get them to do shit they don't want to."

It made sense in a strange sort of way. Roger was such a nice guy when we were together. It was like a switch flipped when I told him about Ellie. He became cold. Not to mention he packed up and left in the middle of the night. I'd never dreamed that would have been his reaction. Shocked, yes. Not that I was expecting a marriage proposal or anything. He did it to protect us.

"I still don't understand how he knows where we are?"

"He's kept tabs on you. This house? He owns it."

"Come again?"

"He wanted to make sure you and Ellie had a nice place to stay. He had his agent reach out to you and faked some financial aid paperwork, so you'd be able to afford it."

"That son of a bitch," I laughed.

What the hell was happening with my life?

"He's put all the rent money that you've paid into a college account for Ellie."

How could I be mad about that?

"Is there anything else I need to be worried about?"

"God, I hope not," he breathed out and fell back against the couch.

"What do we do now?"

"I keep you safe. And that starts with that mother fucker Lansky."

"Levi, let the police take care of him."

"Assholes like him walk with a slap on the wrist. He won't care about a restraining order. It's a piece of paper. He'll have an expensive ass lawyer who'll have him out in a matter of hours. He needs to know that he can never come near you again."

"You're going to do something stupid, aren't you?"

"Me? Never."

Why didn't I believe that?

CHAPTER 22
TRIGGER

Like I thought, Lansky made bail and was out in a couple of hours. Mother fucker and his top-dollar lawyer. Hawk, our resident computer guru, had hacked into the police's system and gathered all sorts of useful information. Like his full name, address, and picture. From there, Hawk could hack the Department of Motor Vehicles and tax assessor's office.

Savage had been tailing the doctor since his release, keeping the club informed of the details of where he went and where he stopped. Savage had called when Lansky stopped and I headed in that direction with my brothers.

Peaches, the strip club the club owned, was on the outskirts of the city. How fortuitous for me that Lansky stopped there. The rumble of our bikes didn't cause a stir when our group rolled into the parking lot. Savage had propped himself next to the double doors, knee bent with his boot resting on the wall, smoking a cigarette. As we killed our engines, he dropped the butt and squished it with the toe of his boot, then picked it up and put it in his pocket. He walked over to us.

Savage was an intimidating mountain of a man. Roughly the same size as Hammer, he had the look of a man who would kill you and not blink.

"He still inside?" I asked, even though I had spotted his Audi in the lot.

"Yeah. Gina's got the girls keeping him occupied."

"Who we got inside?"

"Bear and Jesse are working tonight. As soon as I let them know the situation, they shut down the security camera and Hawk erased any sign that the asshole was here."

"Thanks for taking care of it, Sav."

"No one fucks with one of ours."

Sheridan and Ellie had both won over Savage in the short time he'd known them. Most men avoided him, but Sheridan hadn't hesitated to welcome him into her home. With the innocence only a child possesses, Ellie climbed into his lap and made him watch her favorite movie with her.

"Damn right," Raze added.

I looked at him in surprise. Not that I thought he wouldn't care about what happened to Sheridan, but he's been standoffish with her.

"What?" he barked out.

"Nothing, man. Just didn't think you cared all that much."

"She's yours. That makes her one of our family. No one fucks with family."

I nodded my thanks.

"How many inside, Sav?"

"Two regulars, but they're going to be occupied. Gina's got him in the Sapphire room."

"Let's get the show on the road."

We entered the building to fast-paced music and dim lighting. Jesse nodded from where he was stationed at the end of the hallway that led to the VIP rooms.

Jesse was a prospect for the club and hadn't earned a road name yet. He was young and eager to prove himself. He had received an injury that forced him to be discharged from the Army a few months earlier and needed the comradery that he had found there.

"Everything okay?" I asked as we walked up to him.

"Yes, sir. Bear is outside the door listening to make sure he doesn't try any shit with Lola."

"Lola was a good choice."

"She can handle that asshole," Jesse agreed.

Bear saw us as we approached and knocked twice on the door. A raised voice came from the other side of the door as Lola cut her performance short. The door swung open, and she waltzed out, breasts bared with a little scrap of red cloth covering her pussy and five-inch heels on her feet. Bear handed her a dark-colored shirt, and she graced him with a smile. A real one, not the practiced one she gave the customers.

"Thanks, Bear," she said as she slipped it over her head.

"No problem, Lo. He give you any trouble?"

"No more than I usually get. They always seem to forget they can't touch the merchandise."

Bear scowled at her admission.

Was something going on between the two?

There wasn't time to worry about that now as Lansky started banging on the locked door separating him from us.

"Skedaddle, Lo. We got some business to take care of."

She laid her hand on Bear's arm.

"Be careful, okay?"

She turned to the rest of us.

"Make the bastard pay," she ordered before traipsing down the hallway toward the dressing rooms.

Bear rubbed a hand over his head. "I let her know why we needed to keep him occupied."

"Bear, it's club business," I reminded him.

"I know, but she had a right to know what she was going into. He hurt one woman. I wasn't going to let her go in blind."

His dark eyes bored into mine.

"I get it, but if she talks—"

"She won't," he said without a second of hesitation.

"Let's do this, Brother."

Bear unlocked the door and shoved it inward. A heavy thud resulted along with Lansky cursing. The door opened wide to reveal Lansky holding a hand to his face as blood dripped.

"Oops, sorry bout that," Bear apologized with a smile.

"I want to speak with your manager, you incompetent ass," Lansky whined.

"No problem. They're right here."

Lansky's eyes widened in shock as we appeared behind Bear.

"You guys need to leave me alone. I'll call the police," he warned.

"Go ahead," I challenged him as I slipped past Bear.

Raze and Savage brought up the rear. As Lansky got a look at Sav, the front of his pants darkened as he pissed himself in fear as he stumbled back.

"That's just nasty," Raze sneered. "You're a fucking pussy. Can beat up on women, but when faced with men, you piss your pants."

"Look. I don't want any trouble."

"You should have thought about that before you put your hands on my woman. Or any woman, for that matter."

Lansky paled even further at my words.

"Yeah, I know all about you. Where you live. What you drive. How much money you owe."

With each word, the strength seemed to seep from him until he plopped down on the couch.

"What do you want? Money? I can pay you."

"I don't want your fucking money," I spat out.

"What do you want?" he stuttered out.

"For you to hurt," I replied with a smile.

CHAPTER 23
SHERIDAN

Waiting on the couch, I flipped through a paperback I'd picked up at the store a few weeks ago. The house was spotless, and I was antsy. A feeling of dread had been building all day, and I wasn't sure why. Levi had gotten a call a couple of hours ago and had taken off like his ass was on fire. I'd take his advice before he left and drew a hot bath with lots of bubbles to relax. My mom was due to drop off Ellie any minute and my anxiety had spiked.

I hadn't told her about the attack, just asked that she keep Ellie overnight. My mom was a Mother Bear and Lord knows she would have grabbed my bat and taken off to find Dr. Lansky for messing with her cub.

My heart pounded in trepidation when I heard Levi's bike pull into the drive. Ripper's ears perked up from where he lay on the floor next to the couch. He looked up at me with his deep brown eyes, as if asking permission.

"Go get him," I whispered and like a shot, he was out the backdoor.

I tossed the book on the table and stood, feeling awkward. Did I run and greet him the way I wanted? Did I wait for him to come to me? Last night, it seemed as if he was scared to touch me. As if he was worried I would break at his touch.

Didn't he realize I felt safest in his arms?

A double knock preceded the door opening. When his eye lit on me, his lips quirked up at the corner. I couldn't resist.

I ran to him.

He caught me up in his arms and I buried my face in his neck. It felt like coming home.

Neither of us spoke. We held each other close until our breaths synched. His hand cupped the back of my neck and kneaded the tension away, and I melted even further into him.

"I like the way you greet me, Sher," he murmured.

"I missed you," I admitted.

He squeezed me tighter at those words.

"Little Bit home yet?"

"Mom's bringing her home any second now."

"No time for me to ravish you then," he teased.

"Sorry," I chuckled, leaning back and looking him in the eyes.

Even knowing my daughter would walk through that door at any second, I couldn't resist kissing him. My lips touched his, the barest of touches, as I closed my eyes. The heady scent of him filled my nostrils. Leather, sandalwood, and the faintest hint of motor oil. It smelled like home.

After a few seconds, he didn't hold back and ate at my mouth. His tongue swept in and danced with mine. I wrapped my arms around his neck and pulled him closer until there wasn't a centimeter separating us. He palmed my ass with his hands and squeezed.

"Sher," he murmured against my lips when he pulled back.

I didn't want to hear it and kissed him again.

"Sher," he moaned. "I think your mom is here."

A bucket of ice water would have had less effect than his words. I dropped my legs from his torso and took a step back. My chest heaved, my nipples tight and aching as I tried to contain my lust. Levi reached down and adjusted himself just as Ellie burst through the back door.

"Momma!" she shrieked as she ran to me and hit me like a ton of bricks. For a little thing, she sure packed a punch. Her tiny arms wrapped around my leg and squeezed.

"Hey, baby. Did you have fun at Gigi's house?"

"Yep. We had pizza and ice cream. And Jensen tried to kiss me on the playground today."

"Um, okay. Who's Jensen?"

"My friend."

"Let's keep the kissing for when you get older, okay?"

She pressed the side of her face to my leg and spotted Levi standing to the side.

"Levi!" she yelled, abandoning me in favor of him. She launched herself and he caught her up and settled her on his hip.

"How you doing, Bit?"

"Good. Can we watch Elsa?"

"We'll see. It's up to you, Mom."

Both looked at me in question.

"Maybe—" I stopped short when I heard another voice beside my mother outside the door. Ray had decided to make the trip with her.

My heart pounded. My mother had met Levi before, but not as my boyfriend? Lover?

Suddenly, I left like I was in high school instead of an adult with a child.

Ray and my mom were still talking when they opened the back door, and it took them a second to realize another person occupied the kitchen beside me and Ellie. It should have been obvious someone else was there because Levi's bike was parked in the driveway.

"Well, hello there," my mother cooed. "I believe we've met before. Levi, right?"

"Yes, ma'am. Levi Jameson."

"That's right. You're the one who fixed Sheridan's car."

"Yes, ma'am."

"I told you before, call me Sheila. This is my husband, Ray."

"We've met," Ray barked out.

"Behave," Mom warned, as she smacked him across the chest.

Ray's steely gaze locked on Levi with what I call his cop look. It didn't seem to faze Levi, though.

"It's nice to see you again."

"I didn't know that Sheridan was going to have company," Mom continued.

"Levi's here all the time," Ellie announced.

"Really?" Mom shot me a look. "That means we're going to have to have dinner together soon."

It wasn't a question and Levi realized it.

"I would love to. Something smells good."

Mom blushed as she raised the bag containing the food she had cooked for me. It smelled like Italian.

"I made baked ziti."

"What happened to your face?" Ray ground out, eyes moving from my jaw to Levi.

Oh shit. I'd forgotten about it in the short time since Levi had arrived. My hand raised to cover my jaw.

"Let's talk about that when little ears aren't present," I said.

"How about I take Little Bit out back and we'll play fetch with Ripper?" Levi offered.

Ray unclenched his jaw. "Good idea."

"Ellie, why don't you go get his ball?"

She wiggled until Levi let her down and she took off down the hall, Ripper hot on her heels.

"Sheridan, you didn't mention that Levi had been coming over," Mom chastised.

"Well, I, no I guess I didn't." Heat crept up my face.

"How long have you two been seeing each other?"

"A few weeks now," Levi answered.

Mom's eyebrows shot up in surprise.

"A few weeks? Sheridan Diane, you should be ashamed keeping this young man a secret."

Levi smiled. "Keeping me a secret, huh?"

"No, I'm not.

Ellie saved me from further embarrassment when she returned with Ripper's ball clutched in her little hand.

"Okay, Little Bit, let's go out back."

When the door closed behind them, both my parents turned accusing eyes toward me.

"I wasn't keeping him a secret. Or trying to hide him, Mom."

"Then how come you haven't mentioned him?"

"I want to know how you got those bruises. Now." Ray barked out.

"It wasn't Levi, Ray. One of the vets at work attacked me."

"What the hell do you mean, attacked you? Why the hell didn't you call me?"

"Ray, the police took care of it. They arrested him."

"I want a name, young lady."

"Gerald Lansky."

Mom put a hand on his arm.

"Don't do anything stupid, Ray. She said they arrested him."

"Trust me, honey," Ray replied before kissing her forehead.

"I've heard that before," Mom muttered, then turned to me. "Tuesday night, our house. Dinner."

"Yes, ma'am," I replied.

"We'll be there," Levi said from the doorway.

"Good," Mom replied with a smile. "We'll see you then. Ellie, give us a hug."

"Bye, Gigi. Bye, Pops."

Ray smiled at her as he picked her up to hug her.

"Love you, Bug."

"I love you, Pops."

"Love you, baby girl. Be good for your mom tonight," Mom said as she kissed her cheek.

"I will," Ellie promised.

"We're going to head home. Have a good night."

Mom turned toward the door while Ray continued to glare at Levi.

"Come on, Ray." Mom grabbed his arm to lead him outside.

"Drive safe guys," I called after them as Mom pulled the door shut.

"Elsa?" Ellie asked, looking up at Levi.

He looked at me, and I rolled my eyes with a smile.

"Sure thing, Little Bit."

Later that night, after Levi had wrung me dry of orgasms, we laid in the bed with my head pillowed on his chest. His hand trailed up and down my back, lulling me to sleep.

"Do you remember the first time we met?" he asked.

"How could I forget? It was only a few weeks ago."

He chuckled.

"What?"

"The first time we met wasn't at the shop."

"What do you mean?" I asked, looking up at him.

"We met the night that you and Kenna went out to a country bar."

"I don't remember that."

"You'd had quite a bit to drink. More than I had realized when I asked you to dance with me."

"Oh my God." I buried my face in his chest. "How do I not remember that? I'm sorry."

"I guess you don't remember mauling me in the hallway either," he laughed.

"What?"

"You couldn't keep your little hands off me."

"You're kidding? Please tell me you're kidding."

"Sorry, Sher, but I had that perfect body of yours all over me."

"Kill me now," I groaned and buried my face against his hard chest.

"I couldn't get you out of my mind after that. Kenna wouldn't tell me jack shit about you. When you walked into the shop, I thought I'd got my wish of seeing you again. It was a blow to the ol' ego that you didn't remember me at all."

"I'm sorry."

"Don't be. It made me want you even more if that was possible. Then to find out that the heart and mind are just as amazing as the body. I think I won the lottery."

"I think I'm pretty lucky myself," I teased.

"You think?" He cocked his eyebrow in question.

His hand cupped the back of my neck and before I realized what had happened, he had me lying on top of him.

"Maybe I need to show you again, so you know for sure."

His lips met mine in a fierce kiss and he showed me again and again throughout the night how lucky I was.

CHAPTER 24
TRIGGER

TRIGGER

"Thank you for dinner, Sheila. It was delicious," I told Sheridan's mom when I didn't think I could eat another bite without busting the button on my jeans wide open.

"You're welcome. I'm glad you enjoyed it," Sheila smiled, and I felt her husband's gaze settle on me like a laser beam.

I hated to admit it, but it unnerved me. Sheridan placed her hand on my arm and squeezed.

Sheila stood and started picking up the empty dishes.

"Here, let me help," I offered, placing my napkin on my plate.

"Oh, that's okay. I can get it."

"No, ma'am. I'll help."

Picking up my plate and Sheridan's, I took them to the kitchen before she protested again.

Sheridan walked in behind me and scraped out the bowl she carried into the trash.

"I think you've won my mom over."

"How's that?"

"A man that cleans up without being asked. Winner."

"Ray doesn't help?"

"He does now. Mom said she had to train him."

"My mom trained me. She told my dad she wouldn't send out a couple of feral boys into the world without knowing how to take care of themselves."

I opened the dishwasher, placed the dishes inside, and took the bowl from Sheridan.

Sheila bustled in, carrying more dishes.

"Levi, Sheridan and I can get this. Why don't you and Ray take Ellie out back and play before it gets to be her nap time."

"Yes, ma'am." Trepidation sat like a lead balloon in my stomach. Alone with Ray? Not sure how that was going to turn out.

Sheridan hip-checked me with a wink, and I tossed a dish towel at her.

"He won't bite," she teased.

"But will he shoot?"

"You'll be fine," Sheridan encouraged. "His granddaughter loves you, so that's a point in your favor."

Out back there was a large wooden deck with a built-in outdoor kitchen, table and chairs, and a large television. Ray had turned on a show about car repair and sat at the counter-height table with a beer. Ellie was on the jungle gym that dominated most of the backyard. She was at the top of the yellow plastic slide, encouraging Ripper to climb up to her.

"Want a beer?"

"Sure."

Ray opened the middle part of the table and pulled out a bottle. He plunked it down on the table next to him.

"Take a seat."

"Thanks."

I pulled back the tall wooden chair and sat down across from him. He popped the cap off the beer and handed it to me. Taking a long pull, I let the cold liquid soothe my throat.

We sat in awkward silence for a few moments, and I felt relief that maybe this would not be the inquisition I had worried about.

"I looked into you."

Never mind, I was mistaken.

"Yes, sir. I figured you would."

"Did you kill that boy on purpose?"

I took another pull off the bottle.

"No, sir. I never meant for that to happen."

"You still fight?"

"No. I haven't since that night."

"Causing someone's death, no matter how inadvertent, is something that you don't get over."

"Sounds like you're speaking from experience."

"I was in the Marines. I've taken the lives of men and innocent lives have been caught in the crossfire. I'd hoped when I was discharged that would be the end, but I decided to go into law enforcement."

"If you don't mind me asking, why did you pick that for your career?"

"I hate injustice. The victims needed someone on their side. Having this badge means that I can help them. Within the confines of the law," he added bitterly.

And I had no words to add to that statement.

"What do you know about this Lansky?"

No, that was a loaded question. How much did I dare reveal to this man? Was he being Sheridan's father or an officer?

"Enough that if I'd done something about him the day he was mean to Sheridan at work, he wouldn't have had a chance to put his hands on her later."

"Why didn't you?"

"Our relationship was just starting. Hell, you couldn't even call it a relationship at that point. She was desperate when she called me to pick up Little Bit from daycare when she was sick. I dropped by the clinic to get the car seat when Lansky was running his mouth."

"And?"

"What if she resented me butting in? I wanted to pop him in the mouth, but I knew that wouldn't do any good. It may have cost Sheridan her job."

"It would have put you in a tough spot. I wish she would've said something to me about it."

"Have you met Sheridan?"

Ray laughed.

"Good point. Girl's too independent for her own good sometimes. Her mother and I were relieved when she moved here."

"I know Sheridan is happy about it, too. They both have y'all to fall back on if they need to."

"Has she mentioned Ellie's father to you?"

Fuck me. Where to start with that one?

"A little."

"Roger 'Duke' Ellington. Thirty-four years old. Lives in California. Member of the Devil's Reign MC. Been to prison twice for possession and manslaughter. I could go on, but something tells me you might know him."

"I'd never met him until he showed up at the shop wanting to pay for the repairs on Sheridan's car."

Ray's eyes narrowed on me.

"He what?"

"He's been keeping an eye on them from the shadows. He knows that it's safer for them if he's not in the picture."

"Sonuvabitch."

"His club may be into some nasty shit, but I don't know if he's a bad guy. He's been looking out for them as best he can without bringing it to his club's attention."

"And your club? Are they a threat to my girls?"

The underlying threat was there in his tone.

"They're safe with any of my brothers. They've come to love Ellie and they like Sheridan."

"Are the Devil's Reign going to be a problem?"

"Honestly, sir, I don't know."

"At least you're honest about it. Does Sheridan know you got someone watching her house?"

My eyebrows shot up in surprise.

"How did—"

"Son, who do you think you're talking to? I have cameras up around that house. On the outside," he clarified at what must have been a terrified look on my face. "I've seen a couple of your boys out there sitting on the place."

"I haven't outright told her about them, but she knows my history with them. The first time I took her out on my bike and made a pit stop to eat, the Devil's Reign decided to eat there, too."

"What the hell are they doing in this neck of the woods?"

"I asked myself that same question."

"And they saw you two together?"

"Yes. I tried to get us out of there before they had a chance, but it didn't work."

"Before your boys were sitting on the house. I think someone else was watching her house."

"Hammer's dad saw him, too."

"Hammer?"

"Michael. His parents live next door to Sheridan."

"His mom must be the lady that gives Sheila a run for her money in the Italian food department."

"She is one hell of a cook."

"Sheridan let it slip that she liked her baked ziti better. I ate ziti for a week while Sheila tweaked her recipe. I couldn't eat Italian for months after that," he groaned.

Laughter bubbled up at his pained expression, and I couldn't hold it in.

"Yeah, laugh it up. You'll be in her crosshairs now, too. She likes guinea pigs to try out her new recipes. Most are great, but there are a few…" His face wrinkled in disgust.

"Noted."

"I'm not going to ask your intentions toward Sheridan. That is between the two of you. And Ellie. You know they're a package deal. Ellie loves you."

"Really?"

"Talks about you all the time. Enough to make an old man jealous."

"I'm not—"

"I know. It's just that I've been the only father figure that little girl has had in her life. To hear her talk about how much fun she has with you, makes my heart hurt a little."

A mixture of pride and elation swamped me to know that Ellie talked about me.

"These girls may not be my blood, but they're my family. If you hurt them, I will end you. Badge or not."

His gray eyes bored into me. He wasn't kidding. Not even a little bit.

CHAPTER 25
SHERIDAN

Levi pulled into the gravel parking lot and backed his bike next to a line of others. Bass thumped through the metal walls of the building. The light outside the metal double doors illuminated the sign reading The Den Home of the Blacktop Brethren MC. Members only was stenciled in black on the gray doors. Apprehension settled in my gut like a rock. What the hell did I get myself into?

Levi opened the door and ushered me outside. Heavy Metal music drowned out the group of men gathered around the pool table. Several heads turned when we entered, and my steps faltered, causing Levi to walk into my back. When he made contact, I lurched forward and almost fell on my face. Levi caught my arm before my humiliation was complete.

"You okay?" Levi's breath whispered in my ear. All I could do was nod.

Wrench made his way over to us, carrying a couple of beers.

"Welcome, Sheridan, to our humble abode." He handed me a cold bottle.

"Quit trying to charm my girl, you asshole," Levi said.

"Can't blame a man for trying." Wrench shrugged. "Come on in. Almost everyone is here already."

"Even Demon?" Levi asked.

"He showed up earlier. I guess he's still around here somewhere."

Levi grabbed my hand and pulled me further into the room. Leather couches were scattered around the room. Several men were standing around the talking. One group at the back seemed enthusiastic as they huddled around something. I averted my gaze when a shirt went flying over their heads.

A wooden bar ran half the length of the back wall, and a younger guy was busy putting a bottle of beer on the scarred bar top. A staircase to the right led up to a hallway lined with doors. From the rafters, a vintage motorcycle hung suspended, and the walls were dotted with metal signs for various oil and gas products. Tall wooden tables were placed around the perimeter of the room. It seemed as if the theme from the Clubhouse had gone into the design of Shooters.

A set of glass French doors flew open and a topless girl in a bright pink bikini underwear came running through, shrieking with laughter. A tan, burly man came in after her with a shit-eating grin. I would've worried if she hadn't looked over her shoulder with a smile to make sure he was still in pursuit. She dashed through the crowd and up the stairs with the man hot on her heels. He caught her at the landing, swept her up into his arms, and disappeared into one room.

"That's not something you see every day," I uttered as my face heated and Wrench laughed.

"Regular occurrence around here," Wrench informed me.

"Really?" I looked over my shoulder and shot Levi a look. He ducked his head with a smile.

"Nothing you need to worry about, babe. All I see is you." He kissed the side of my head after he pulled me back to his chest.

"Bullshit," I laughed.

Thank God Kenna had somewhat prepared me for what I was walking into coming to a club party. Drinking, cursing, and raunchy behavior were just the beginning. She warned me that later in the night clothes would be coming off and it might turn into a porno flick. I thought she was exaggerating, but I guess I was mistaken.

Cat calls sounded from the other end of the room as another girl jumped on a raised platform and did a striptease. I sipped my beer, feeling both uneasy and aroused. The surrounding men seemed to enjoy the show, but I couldn't bring myself to look. Levi's arm wrapped around my waist, and I leaned into him. His touch was grounding, making me feel slightly less out of place in this den of debauchery.

"Anyway, make sure to grab some food. We ordered from the Mexican place downtown. Sheridan, whatever you want to drink, Frank can make you."

With a wink, Wrench wandered over to a table with a poker game going.

"You, okay?"

"Sure. Why wouldn't I be?" I hope I sounded fine, but when his brow furrowed, I knew I failed.

"We don't have to stay long. Just long enough to grab a quick bite and say hi to some guys," he reassured me. He placed my hand in his and led me through the crowd.

The men parted to let us through, some greeting us and some staring at me as if I were a bug under a microscope. The table with the food was close to where the strip was taking place. My gaze riveted to her gyrations. Her top was gone, and her breasts swayed with her movements.

"Never took you for voyeur, Sher," Levi teased.

"What?" I caught him grinning at me and my face heated. "It's just that, I ugh—"

"It's okay. I'm not judging you."

"Let's get some food," I rushed out as I brushed past him, even though I didn't have a clue where I was going.

Levi followed me to the table, a smirk on his lips. "You know, you're even more beautiful when you blush," he said, his voice low and husky.

I felt a shiver run down my spine, heat pooling low in my belly.

"Stop it," I said, my voice breathless.

"I'm serious.

"This place is . . . intense."

"I know," Levi said, his expression serious. "But you don't have to worry. I've got you." He leaned in and pressed a soft kiss to my forehead, his hand warm and reassuring on my back.

We made it over to the table with the food and I was grateful for the distraction. My stomach grumbled as the smell of the spicy Mexican food hit my nose. I grabbed a plate and loaded it up with tacos, beans, and rice.

Levi stood next to me, piling his own plate high with food. "Want something to drink?" he asked, gesturing to the bar.

I nodded, grateful for the chance to have a moment alone to compose myself. Who would've thought watching a woman strip would have been a turn-on for me?

As I lifted a forkful of rice to my lips, a flash of blonde caught my attention. lifting my eyes, I caught Nessa glaring at me from across the room. Would it have been too much to ask for her to not have the night off? My appetite vanished, and I placed the fork back down on the plate.

"What's wrong? The food not good?" Levi asked as he placed a margarita glass in front of me with a bottle of water. He pulled out the chair and sat beside me.

"No, I'm sure it's fine."

"Then what's the matter? Did someone say something to upset you? Cause if they did—"

"No one's said anything to me," I blurted out.

His eyes narrowed.

"I promise."

Picking up the fork, I ate a bite of rice. It tasted like sawdust, but I forced myself to swallow it.

"I just saw Nessa over there." I nodded my head in her direction, hoping he'd understand.

Levi's eyes followed where I was pointing. "Ah, sorry, she gives you such a hard time.

"It is what it is. Nothing you can do about it. You can't stop her from being a bitch," I said, taking a sip of my margarita. It tasted like heaven.

"I can keep her the hell away from you," Levi said, reaching over to take my hand. "I'll do anything to protect you."

I smiled at him, feeling the warmth of his hand against mine. "Thank you. I appreciate that."

"You know, we don't have to stay if you're uncomfortable. We can leave right now if you want to."

I shook my head. "No, it's okay. I want to stay. I want to see what this is all about."

Levi's lips quirked up in a smile. "Alright then, let's finish eating, and then we'll go play some pool. Maybe we can even get a game going with Wrench and Hammer if we can find them."

We fell into a comfortable silence, eating and drinking together. Every once in a while, one of his brothers would stop by to introduce themselves. Each one included me in the conversation and it made me feel more at ease the longer we sat there.

A sharp whistle came from across the room, and we looked over to see Wrench motioning to us from beside the pool table.

"Ready?" Levi asked as he scooted back his chair.

"Let's go kick some butt," I joked.

As we made our way across the room, a door upstairs slammed open and a beautiful auburn-haired woman stormed out of the room.

"Fuck you," she screamed as she marched to the staircase. Behind her, a man came out naked with his dick swinging in the breeze.

"Mads, wait, God damn it!" he bellowed.

"Shit," Levi said from beside me. "Stay here."

Levi moved toward the staircase and Wrench brushed by me.

The woman flew down the stairs, her feet barely hitting the treads. Raze grabbed her by the arm. She turned on her heel and belted him across the face.

"Fuck you, Seth," she screamed and stormed out the front door.

Levi and Wrench stepped in front of the man and stopped him from following her outside.

"Demon, knock it off!" Wrench ordered.

"Mads, get your ass back in here!" The man pushed against Levi and Wrench, trying to get free. Hammer came up behind him and wrapped his brawny arms around him in a bear hug. The men spoke, trying to calm the man down.

Movement at the stairs drew my attention. Two women stood there.

One wrapped in a sheet with a devastated look on her face. The other had on a man's t-shirt and a smug smile.

"You think you'll ever keep him satisfied?" Nessa hissed from my side. "Demon and Mads have been together for years and he fucks around on her all the time. It'll only be a matter of time before Trigger's back in my bed."

With a smirk, she walked back into the crowd.

My stomach churned at her words. Levi had told me about Demon and Madeline. He'd proposed to her, and they had been planning their wedding. And he'd been upstairs with not one, but two women?

The guys had gotten Demon calmed down and had him sitting on the stairs. The man Madeline had slugged continued to rub his jaw as he stood beside them.

What the hell was I doing here? I didn't belong with these people. The room seemed to shrink in on me and it made it hard to breathe. Escape is all I could think of. I made my way outside into the sultry night air. Pressing myself against the building, I took a deep breath as I slid down the wall and sat on the sidewalk. A million thoughts raced through my head as I slid down the wall and sat on the sidewalk. I'd been a fucking idiot. Levi wasn't like that, was he? He had a good heart, but was I fooling myself to think that we could be together?

I'm not sure how long I sat there drowning in my thoughts before I heard a voice beside me.

"Hey, beautiful," Levi sat down beside me and took my hand. "Too much for you in there?"

All I could do was nod.

Levi pulled me into his arms. "It's okay. I get it."

I rested my head against his chest.

"Why does everything have to be so hard?" I asked.

"It's only as hard as you make it. You worried because what happened in there?"

I nodded against his chest.

"Demon has issues. I won't condone what he did, but that's not the guy I grew up with. The man I know would've cut off his left nut before ever hurting Mads."

I took a deep breath and tried to wrap my head around everything.

The club, seeing the women, Demon and his girl issues. It all left a bitter taste in my mouth.

"Ready to go home?" Levi asked, helping me to my feet.

I inhaled his scent, taking the comfort he offered. Once we were back on the bike and headed back to my place, he placed his hand on my thigh. It felt right like everything was the way it was supposed to be.

It didn't take us long to pull into the driveway of my house. He killed the engine as I stayed wrapped around him. Everything was perfect at that moment, and I didn't want to let it go.

CHAPTER 26
TRIGGER

A FAMILY PARTY was much different than a regular club party, as Sheridan soon found out. I pulled up in the truck and put it in park. Over the top of the building, you could see the top of the bounce house I had ordered. A princess castle, especially for Ellie. The squealing laughter of children could be heard from the back when I opened my door. Sheridan eyed the building and kept her face composed. She didn't have the best experience here last time, but I hoped that would change today. To see it wasn't all that crazy most of the time.

"Levi, help me," Ellie whined as she tried to undo the buckle of her car seat.

"Hang on a second," I said and worked the snap loose.

Sheridan opened her door and hopped out as I helped Ellie. She picked the bag up from the floorboard and slung it across her shoulder.

"Are you sure we didn't need to bring anything?"

"No, Sher. It's all covered. There's plenty of food and drinks. I even hired a lifeguard to watch the pool."

She bit her bottom lip.

"It's going to be fine, Sher."

"What if your parents don't like me?"

"They're going to love you. Mom always wanted a daughter and got stuck with two boys. You're the first girl I've brought home since, well, ever, I think."

"No pressure there," she uttered.

"Come on," I laughed.

I led her and Ellie inside the building to the back where most everyone was. Several kids ran around and climbed the bounce house while others were on floats in the pool. The smoker was billowing out smoke and scented the air with cooking meat. A long table with a red and white checked tablecloth was laden with pans full of food. Another table was set up with desserts. The weather had cooled off enough that you weren't sweating to death, but several of the older family members sat under a canopy with a misting fan blowing over them.

"Can I go play?" Elli asked, tugging on my cut.

"Sheridan?" I asked, not wanting to overstep.

"Sure, Ellie, but be nice."

Ellie took off like a rocket toward the fun.

"You sure she will be okay?"

"Yes. We always have someone designated to watch the kids to make sure nothing happens."

I took both her hands in mine. "Everything is going to be fine, Sheridan. Try to relax. Want something to drink?"

"A Dr. Pepper?"

"Coming right up." I kissed her forehead and went to one of the coolers. As I opened the second one, I caught Sheridan out of the corner of my eye, helping my mom carry an aluminum pan through the door. Mom said something that I couldn't make out, and Sheridan laughed.

"Looks like your mom already put your girl to work," Dad said as he came up beside me.

"I haven't even introduced them yet."

"I bet your mom knows who she is. We don't get a lot of fresh faces on days like today."

"She's nervous."

"Why? To meet us?"

"She was with me the other night when Demon decided to be an ass. She didn't get the best impression of club life."

"That boy. Not sure what we're going to do with him. It wasn't a great introduction to the club life."

"She's been a little off ever since."

"Have you talked to her about it?"

"She says she's fine."

Dad busted out laughing.

"What?"

"Son, if a woman says she's fine, she's anything but. You need to get her to talk about what's bothering her."

"Why are women so complicated?"

"That's what keeps life interesting. Now, take her a drink and rescue her from your mom."

By the time I made it back over to the tables, Mom and Sheridan were putting paper plates, napkins, and silverware out for people to grab.

"Here, Sheridan," I said and handed her the drink.

"Thanks," she smiled.

"I see you've met my mom."

Sheridan's eyes widened in surprise before looking over at Mom.

"I didn't, I mean—"

"It's okay, Sheridan. I didn't introduce myself. I'm Sharon, Levi's mom. That's my husband Bruce behind him. You'll hear him called Rooster around here."

"It's, ugh, nice to meet you."

"Likewise, dear. Where's your daughter? I've been dying to meet you both."

"She's up there, Mom." I pointed to the top of the castle.

"Oh, my, isn't she adorable? She favors you, Sheridan."

"Thank you."

"A word of advice," Mom cautioned. "Get a plate early. Once these guys get started, there won't be anything left."

"Woman—" Rooster started, but was cut off when Sharon cocked an eyebrow at him. "Okay, you're right. Why don't you make you and Ellie a plate?"

"Sheridan, you fix yours and I'll get Little Bits."

The hardest part of the afternoon was getting the kids to quit playing long enough to eat. After fifteen minutes of cajoling, all the kids abandoned their toys with the promise of ice cream for dessert.

Once Ellie had sat down, she ate almost everything I had put on her plate. Sheridan had seemed impressed with my selections. I added some things that I knew were Ellie's favorites, including mac and cheese, and some ones I wasn't sure she'd like. She'd eaten the brisket as if it was her last meal.

The afternoon passed in the blink of an eye as Sheridan met several of the old ladies and other members of the club who weren't at the club party the other night. The club whores weren't invited to the family parties as it was in their best interest, as some of the member's wives were protective of their men. Most of the men were faithful to their old ladies, but there were a few who liked to have their cake and eat it, too.

Some old ladies turned a blind eye, but not always.

As dusk settled in, the kids went inside to watch and movie, and the prospects cleared off the large deck of the table and chairs. A few of the older members got out their guitars and played old country music. Before too long, a few couples were dancing along.

"Want to dance?" I asked Sheridan, as I placed my hands on her shoulders.

"I don't know how."

"You said the same thing to me last time I asked. You did fine then, and you will now."

I took her hand in mine and led her out onto the makeshift dance floor. Within a few steps, she had picked up the simple steps as we moved around the floor.

"This is nice," she said later as she leaned up against me and sipped a bottle of beer. Most of the kids had passed out inside watching a movie under the watchful eye of my mother and another old lady.

"A lot different from the other night, huh?"

Fuck, I should have kept my mouth shut, I thought when I felt her stiffen.

"Yeah, it is. We should be getting home. Ellie will be a bear if she doesn't get plenty of sleep."

She turned on her heel and walked away without another word.

"Damn it," I muttered.

"Apologize and mean it," Dad remarked as he came up beside me.

"How did you—"

"I'm a man. It's what we do. We fuck up and we apologize. The thing is, you must mean it. Saying to say it doesn't make anything better."

"I'm going to take them home and come back to help clean up."

"Drive safe. I love you, son."

"Love you too, Dad."

Inside, Sheridan was speaking with my mom. I made my way over to where Ellie was sleeping on the couch and picked her up.

During the drive back to Sheridan's house, no words were said. Country music played as Ellie slept in between us. Once we arrived, I carried Ellie into the house.

"Where do you want me to put her?"

"In her bed is fine."

I laid Ellie down on top of her comforter and covered her with a blanket. She looked so much like her mother, it made my heart ache. Kissing her forehead, I turned on her lamp and closed the door as I left the room.

In the kitchen, Sheridan wiped down the already clean counter.

"I'm sorry," I said, coming up behind her and wrapping an arm around her waist. She took a deep breath before she sagged against me.

"There isn't anything for you to be sorry for."

"If I hadn't said anything about the other night—"

"It's my hang-up. Not yours. You didn't do anything wrong."

"I have to head back and help clean up. It'll be late before I'm done. I'll see you tomorrow, okay?"

"Be careful."

"I will." I stooped and kissed the side of her neck. She smelled like smoke and sex. It made me regret offering to clean up tonight.

"Make sure you lock the door and set the alarm," I told her as I walked out the back door.

I didn't leave the backyard until I heard the lock slide into place and the beep of the alarm being armed.

CHAPTER 27
SHERIDAN

I WATCHED as Levi backed out of the driveway; mind heavy with my thoughts. After the club party, I was close to saying that I didn't think we would work out. Nessa's words had wormed their way in and wouldn't leave.

How could I be enough for him? A single mom struggling to make ends meet. A baby daddy watching in the shadows. It was a lot to deal with.

Levi had a choice of these beautiful women at his club who would strip naked and lay prostrate at his feet if he gave them the slightest bit of attention.

Then again, he was with me. He stayed almost every night in my bed and came over after work. If he didn't, he'd call or text to let me know he was thinking about me.

I hated feeling like this insecure little girl!

"Momma?" Ellie called from her room.

I threw the towel on the counter and went to her.

"Yes, baby."

She looked around her room with a frown.

"We came home. You slept the entire ride home."

"Where's Levi?"

"He had to help clean up. You'll see him tomorrow."

I ran my hand over her head. Most of her hair had escaped her braid.

"Why don't we get you in your jammies, go potty, brush your teeth, and go back to sleep?"

She didn't answer but climbed off the bed. She shuffled across the hall into the bathroom. The night light I kept in there was bright enough to not need the overhead light. We finished up and got her into her pajamas. Her eyes were already closing as her head hit the pillow. Ripper padded into the room and jumped up to his spot on the end of her bed.

"Good boy, Rip. Keep the bad dreams away."

He looked up at me with his soulful brown eyes as I scratched his head.

Finishing up a quick shower to get the smell of smoke off me, I changed into one of Levi's shirts and crawled into bed. I gathered the pillow that Levi used at night and fell asleep.

The following week was very different for Levi and me. Instead of seeing him every day, he was with his brothers. The fight was scheduled for the following weekend and there were a lot of moving parts that Levi oversaw. Five-minute phone calls had become our norm, and I didn't like it, but he had promised once it was over, we'd go out for a long weekend. Just the two of us. He already had it planned and all I needed to do was pack.

The number of bikers I saw around town had to have tripled in the last week, too. My awareness was heightened since I knew the Devil's Reign MC was supposed to have someone in the fight. I'd hoped Levi was mistaken and there wasn't anything to worry about. Kenna said the bar was packed every night with out-of-towners and she was racking in the cash. Ray had commented on the increased number of calls for fighting, public intoxication, and driving under the influence.

The next morning was Saturday. I wasn't in any hurry to do a damn thing. I'd tossed and turned last night, missing Levi's presence beside me. Dreams I couldn't remember teased my consciousness with bits and pieces that made no sense.

Maybe it was all the anxiety centering on the fights. I couldn't wait for them to be over and life to return to normal.

"Pancakes. I'm in the mood for pancakes," I muttered to myself.

I spotted my phone lying on the kitchen counter, battery dead since I hadn't put it on the charger the night before. Placing it on the charger, I pulled the pancake mix out of the pantry. As soon as I had mixed up the batter, I heard a bike pull into the driveway.

"If you cook it, he will come," I joked.

Hurrying to the door, I turned off the alarm and unlocked the door.

"Good morning," I said as I opened the door.

"Morning," he replied.

"You look tired."

"I am. I've missed you."

He pulled me into his arms and kissed me.

"When is the last time you showered?" I asked, as our lips parted.

"Trying to tell me something, Sher?" His lip quirked up.

"I'm making pancakes. Why don't you shower, and they'll be ready when you're done?"

"Sounds good."

He walked down the hall with his shoulders slumped and head down. Exhaustion was written in every line of his body.

Pulling out a skillet, I added bacon to the menu. When he reappeared, I plated him the bacon and pancakes. He walked into the kitchen with his shorts riding low on his hips and no shirt. Sex on a stick. Damn. He was in no shape for what I wanted to do to him.

"What time do you have to be back?" I asked, breaking the stare that I had on his body.

"Around ten, ten thirty."

"Maybe you can catch a quick nap after you eat."

"I'd rather spend time with you." He wagged his brows.

"Levi, you look like you're about to drop."

"You're right. A nap might be better."

"Eat," I laughed.

He polished off the plate of food and headed into my bedroom. He must have fallen asleep as soon as he touched the pillow because when I went into the room, he was already snoring. I covered him with the throw blanket I kept at the end of the bed. I pulled the door closed before Ellie woke up and became Tornado Ellie and woke him up.

From the kitchen, my phone dinged several times in a row as things I'd missed came through once it had enough power. I picked it up and saw several missed texts from Levi and five missed calls from Kenna. Speak of the devil. Her face lit up on the screen.

"Good morning. Why are you up so early?" I asked.

"Why didn't you answer my calls last night?" She shrieked enough for me to move the phone from my ear.

"Battery died, and I forgot to charge it."

"Listen to me." Her tone stopped me cold. My stomach dropped.

"Why? What's wrong? Did something happen to Mom or Ray?"

"No, this has nothing to do with them. If your phone was dead, I'm guessing you didn't get them," she gushed out.

"Get what?"

"Texts from Levi."

"No, they all showed up at the same time. I was about to check them, but you called."

"Don't look at them."

"What? Why? What's going on with you?"

"Please, Sheridan. Don't look at them."

"You're scaring me."

"Have you seen Trigger?"

"He showed up this morning. He's asleep right now. What the hell is going on, Kenna?"

"One of the club girls texted me last night. Nessa was bragging that she had ended your relationship with Trigger. That she had sent you some texts."

"From his phone? How would she have—"

"I don't know. Just don't jump to conclusions. She's a conniving bitch who's jealous of you."

Nausea bubbled up in my throat.

"I'm putting you on speaker."

"Sheridan, please. Don't," Kenna begged. "I'm on my way. Don't do anything until I get there."

"Okay," I lied.

"Five minutes."

The line went dead. I laid the phone on the counter and stared at it. What was on there? Could it be what would end Levi and me? I looked back at the hallway leading to the room he was sleeping in.

I had to know.

Opening up the texts, the first thing I saw was a picture of Levi lying in bed. His shirt was off, and I recognized the tattoo on his arm. The next was a feminine hand drawing down the zipper of his jeans with the button already opened. The jeans I recognized as the ones Levi was wearing when he came in this morning. I laid down the phone, not wanting to see anymore. Biting the nail on my thumb, I debated what to do. Keep looking? Wait for Kenna? Or wake up Levi demanding he explain?

The pancakes I'd eaten earlier threatened to reappear.

"Momma?"

So caught up in the thought, I didn't hear Ellie come into the kitchen.

"Morning, Ellie Belly. I made pancakes. Are you hungry?

"Uh-huh." She reached her arms up, and I picked her up. She snuggled her face into my neck.

"You needed a hug this morning."

"Uh-huh."

"We need to be quiet this morning. Levi's still sleeping."

"Okay."

I put her down on the stool and turned on the stove to make her pancakes. She reached over and grabbed a piece of bacon. Ripper's nails clacked as he padded across the hard floor and sat at her feet. He licked his muzzle and gave a soft whine.

"No way, Rip. Ain't happening. Ripper outside," I ordered.

He gave a little whine but did as he was told.

"Why can't Ripper have bacon?"

"Stinky toots. Remember?"

Her nose crinkled up.

"When Levi get up?"

Forcing a smile, I told her.

"In an hour or so. He's been working hard, and he's tired."

"Can we watch the cars when he gets up?"

I did a double-take.

"*Cars*? Not *Frozen*?"

"I like *Cars*. Mater's funny. Levi likes *Cars*, too." It was hard to keep my face passive and not show my irritation. Levi had ingrained himself in our lives and it would be my fault for letting him break her heart, let alone mine.

"What about *Beauty and the Beast*? That's my favorite."

"Nah. I wanna watch *Cars*."

Flipping a pancake, I kept thinking about what I saw on his phone. As I placed one on Ellie's plate, I heard tires screech.

"Please tell me that isn't Kenna driving like that," I muttered to myself, knowing that it was her.

The back gate slammed into the side of the fence, and she was stopping hard enough I could hear her flip-flops thwapping on the concrete. Ripper let out a couple of deep barks before Kenna shushed him. The back door swung, and Kenna appeared, hair sticking out in different directions, mascara smudged under her eyes, and wearing a threadbare t-shirt and booty shorts.

"Did you?" She asked around panting breaths. One look at my face and she groaned. "You did. I told you not to look."

"I didn't look at all of them," I defended myself. "But it was enough," I added.

"Damn it, Sheridan."

"Aunt Ken, you said a bad word."

"Sorry, sweet pea, but your mom did something stup-, silly," she corrected when I glared at her.

"Whad you do, Momma?"

"Nothing you need to worry about, Ellie. It's adult stuff. Eat your pancake."

"But—"

"Eat Ellie," I breathed out.

"It would help if you gave the kid a pancake," Kenna said, looking at Ellie's plate.

"Sorry, Ellie. Let me get you one."

I went back to the stove and turned down the burner.

"You want one?" I asked Kenna.

"No, I'm good. Thanks. I'm too tired to think about food."

"You can crash on the couch."

"No, my bed is calling me. Just don't do anything you're going to regret, Sheridan. Let him explain. You know what a horrendous b-i-t-c-h Nessa is."

"I will. Now be careful driving home. I don't need to worry about you falling asleep behind the wheel, do I?"

"I'm not that tired."

"Okay. I love you."

"Love you, too."

"What about me?"

"Love you too, Ellie Belly. Be good for your mom."

CHAPTER 28
TRIGGER

"HEY, SHER, WHAT'S BOTHERING YOU?" I asked as I watched her reread the same page of the book she picked up ten minutes ago. She'd been quiet since I'd woken up half an hour ago. Something was eating at her, and I needed to know if it was something I could fix.

"Where'd you stay last night?"

Not what I was expecting, but it was a start.

"At the clubhouse. We were getting the last stuff ready, and it was late."

"All the guys?"

"Most of them. Hammer, Wrench, Sully and Raze, and the prospects."

"Any of the club girls?"

Was she jealous? She had to know by now that they weren't a threat.

"Yeah, Vix, Candy, and Nessa were there."

"Nessa didn't have to work?"

"She came over after. What's with all the questions?"

She cut her eyes to me and tossed her book on the table.

"My phone was dead last night, and I forgot to put it on the charger. I got several interesting texts from last night."

"Who from?" I asked, not liking where this was going.

"You."

"Me? I didn't text you last night. I knew you'd be asleep when we finished."

"You might want to check your phone."

"Say what you want to say, Sheridan."

"If I do, I'm going to say something I'll regret."

"Fine," I said, standing up. I walked to the bedroom and picked up my pants, but my phone wasn't in the pocket. I checked the floor to make sure it hadn't fallen out, but there was no sign of it. Fuck, where was it? Had I left it at the Clubhouse? What the hell had I sent last night?

"I must have left it at the clubhouse by accident," I told her when I came back into the living room.

"Here," she barked out and tossed me her phone. "I stopped looking after the second text."

I pulled up her texts and selected the ones from me. The picture popped up and my stomach clenched.

What the fuck?

No doubt the man in the picture was me, but the hand undoing my pants was not attached to the woman in the room with me. Each picture became more and more damning, even in my eyes.

"Motherfucker," I breathed out. My eyes shot to Ellie where she lay on the floor watching cartoons.

"Sheridan, I don't know what to say."

"I think those say enough."

"It looks bad, I know, but I had no idea this was going on."

"Really? You expect me to believe that you didn't know Nessa was in the room with you taking your pants off? Please," she scoffed.

"Why do you think it was Nessa?"

"Because she hates me. And I don't see you sending me pictures of you and another woman."

"I'm telling you nothing happened."

But I could tell she didn't believe me. Hell, if the shoe was on the other foot, I'd have a damn hard time believing she was innocent, too.

"I know it looks bad, but you have to trust me. I didn't do anything with Nessa or any other woman since we've been together."

"I want to but . . ."

Now I was pissed off. Even if her shit was justified. I didn't need this shit on top of the fucking week I'd had getting all the shit for the club done for the fights today.

"Sheridan, you need to decide. I can't make that decision for you. You either believe what I'm saying is the truth and you trust me or this ends."

Her face paled at those words, but I pressed on.

"I'm going to spend time at the clubhouse. There are going to be club whores there. We're not going to kick them out because you want that."

"I never—"

"I don't expect you to like them. No one is asking that of you. The club is part of my life. It's always going to be part of my life and I want you to be part of my life. But if you can't handle that, I need to know now before this goes any further."

I turned away from her as the first tear slipped down her face. I put on my dirty clothes and slid on my cut. When I came back, she had moved into the kitchen and was staring out the back window.

"I've got to go."

Her shoulders stiffened, but she didn't turn around. Ellie was still on the floor watching cartoons, oblivious to the tension between Sheridan and me. As I walked by the window, she followed me with her sad eyes. God damn, is this what it felt like to have your heart break? It felt like I was dying inside. As I passed through the gate, I heard the back door close.

I swung my leg over my bike and saw her standing there, staring at me with her arms wrapped around her waist, not saying a word. Her eyes pleaded with me. For what, I don't know. To change my mind? To not go? I hesitated, waiting, but not one word passed those soft lips I loved to kiss. The engine roared to life. Without a backward glance, I drove away from what I had hoped would be my future.

Something I always would regret.

CHAPTER 29
SHERIDAN

COLDNESS SEEPED into my bones as he pulled out of the driveway. This was it, really? The wind picked up, whipping my hair around me, obscuring my view of his taillight, disappearing down the street. Goosebumps peppered my arms and legs, but I didn't notice. The only thing I felt was my heart breaking.

Ripper barked, breaking me out of the trance I was in. Levi was long gone. I wanted to break down, throw myself to the concrete, and scream about the unfairness of it all. How had I screwed this up?

A sound drew my attention to the house. Ellie had her face plastered to the window, lips smudging the glass. She banged the glass again and laughed at the prints her mouth left.

She was the reason I couldn't break down.

As soon as I stepped toward the back gate, Ripper's growl drew me to a stop. I'd never heard that sound from him before. Chills raced down my spine. My only thought was that my daughter was in the house alone. I glanced at the window, but she was no longer there. Terror unlike anything I felt before made me move my feet. Ripping the back gate open, I ran through, not sparing a glance at the enclosed yard. The back door was ajar, and I slammed it open. It bounced back as I barged through; the knob catching me on the arm, causing me to wince.

"Ellie!" My voice cracked with the scream.

"What, Mommy?" Her voice came from the hallway.

When I saw her peek around the corner, I wilted to the floor in relief.

"Mommy, you okay?" she asked, coming up to me and crawling onto my lap.

"Yes, baby, I'm fine."

"Where's Levi?"

"He had to leave."

"Well, isn't that convenient for me?" a voice said from the open doorway.

Ellie looked over my shoulder and whimpered. I gathered her close and stood.

And peered into the face of evil.

Ellie's arms clamped around my neck. His mouth quirked up at my gasp.

"Who are you? What do you want?" I asked, voice shaking. I took a step back toward the living room.

"Name's Cobra." He sauntered into the room and pull out a stool, plopping his ugly ass down. His flint-colored eyes narrowed on us as I took another step.

His cut wasn't like Levi's, so I knew he wasn't one of the Brethren.

Oh, fuck, I thought. What the hell do I do?

Outside Ripper continued to bark.

Why the hell hadn't he come into the house when the intruder did? That was the point of having him for protection. The thought crossed my mind, and he yelped in pain. Ellie's head whipped around.

"Mommy, Ripper."

"Shhh, I know, baby." I pushed her head down to my shoulder as she cried. "What do you want?"

He eyed me up and down and I felt dirty. He lasered in on Ellie.

"Over my dead body," I seethed.

Another man filled the doorway. His dirty brown beard reached down to where the material of his shirt stretched over his potbelly. He wiped the wicked-looking knife he carried across his jeans, leaving a dark red stain. Ripper's blood.

I closed my eyes. We were fucked.

"Everything settled?"

"Yeah, the coast is clear. Took out the guy outside."

"Witnesses?"

"Don't think so."

"Keep an eye out. Tell Crow to sit tight until we call. He can bring the van and we'll get them loaded up."

Who? Ellie and me? I had to do something. You're not supposed to let them take you to another location.

Where the hell had Levi put my phone?

Slowly, I backed up a step, then another, when neither man said anything. My phone or the alarm panel? My eyes were fixated on the one by the back door. That was a no-go. By the garage door? Front door? Could I make it carrying Ellie?

"Bitch, you better stop moving," Cobra barked out.

Freezing in my tracks, I stared at him. He wasn't even looking my way. How the hell did he know?

"Put the brat on the couch and take a seat. Our ride will be here shortly."

"Where are you taking us?"

His smile stopped me cold.

"Don't worry about it."

Heading to the couch, I sat Ellie down and unwrapped her arms from around my neck. Her eyes were red from crying and full of fright.

"Sit here, okay."

"Momma, I'm scared," Ellie whispered.

"I know, baby. It's going to be okay."

God, I hoped I wasn't lying to her.

"Where's Ripper?"

"Outside."

"Why won't he come in? He stays by me when I'm scared."

"He can't right now."

"Because of the bad men?"

"Yes."

"Make them leave."

"I'm not sure I can."

"Call Levi. He'll make them leave."

"Hey! You two shut up," Cobra ordered as he stood there, looking down at us.

"She's scared, asshole."

"I don't give a fuck. Shut up and sit down."

"Momma, he said a bad word." Ellie tugged on my shirt.

"Shhh, Ellie. Can I turn some cartoons on for her?"

"If it'll keep the brat quiet, fine. Keep your asses planted on that couch." His eyes darted to the chair Levi was sitting in earlier. "And I'll take this." He picked up my phone from where Levi had dropped it.

Damn. There went that idea. Turning on the television, I found something that would keep her occupied while I figured out my next move.

"Tell Crow to get a move on. We have places to be before the fights start."

Shit, I was running out of time.

My mind raced. I had to at least get Ellie out of this. If she was safe, that was all that mattered.

"Can I take her to the restroom?"

"No."

"She won't be able to hold it forever. You want her to make a mess?"

"Fine. Make it quick."

"Momma?"

"Come on, baby. Let's go." I grabbed her by the hand.

"But—"

"No buts young lady."

Picking her up, I pushed her head down on my shoulder so I could whisper in her ear.

"Ellie, I'm going to open the garage door and I want you to run to Evelyn's house, okay? Don't stop and don't look back. Just run. Understand?"

"Yes."

"No matter what happens, I love you, Ellie."

"Love you, too, Momma."

Carrying her toward the bathroom, I placed Ellie on the floor. With a deep breath, I opened the garage door and ushered her through.

"Remember run. Don't stop, no matter what. As soon as you can get under the door, go."

She stuck her thumb in her mouth and nodded. I knew she was terrified. So was I, but I needed to make sure that she was no longer in danger.

"Ready?"

Another nod.

I hit the button to raise the roll-up door. As soon as the motor kicked in, I whispered, "Go," and shut the door.

"What the fuck!?" Cobra roared from behind me.

His meaty hand clamped on my shoulder and spun me around. "Where's the girl?"

"Bathroom."

"Don't lie to me, bitch!"

My cheekbone exploded with pain as the back of his hand made contact. The impact sent me to the floor.

"Where the fuck is she?"

No way would I answer. The longer he guessed, the more time she had to get next door. I prayed Evelyn was home.

Tires screeched in the driveway and came to a stop inside the garage.

"Spider, see if Crow saw the girl outside. Find her. "

"Got it."

"Get up. It's time to take a ride, bitch."

Cobra grabbed me by the arm and hauled me to my feet. My head swam with the change as he maneuvered me through the door. A white utility van with the logo of a plumbing company sat in the space beside my car. Neither Spider nor Crow were to be seen. Cobra slid the side door open and shoved me inside.

"Stay put," he ordered. "I only need you alive. Remember that."

"Can't find the kid, Pres," Spider said as he came back into the garage, panting.

"I didn't see a kid when I pulled up. If she's out here, she's hiding good."

"Fuck. Check the house and get back here. We don't have time to fuck around. If she made it to someone's house, they could be calling the cops as we stand here with our thumbs up our asses."

Cobra's back turned to me, and I slid to the edge of the van. Without another thought, I took off like a shot out of the van and headed for the opened garage door. As I emerged outside, a hand wrapped itself in my hair and jerked me back. Crying out in pain, I landed on the concrete floor.

"Fucking bitch. More trouble than you're worth," Cobra ground out.

His booted foot landed on my ribs and I screamed with the pain. He stomped one more time, catching my arm across my chest.

"Pick this bitch up and put her in the van. Any sign of the kid?"

"No, we can't find her in the house."

"God damn. We ain't got time for this. Let's go. Get one of the guys to come over and sit on the house and see if the kid comes back."

Crow picked me up and threw me over his shoulder. Pain radiated through me, as nausea bubbled up my throat. Crow threw me into the van like a sack of trash.

"Crow, don't drive like a maniac. I don't want any unwanted attention."

"Straight to the warehouse?"

"Yes, and then I'll make the call and let Trigger know we have his girl."

CHAPTER 30
TRIGGER

I COASTED my bike to a stop behind The Barn. Even though it was early, several vehicles were parked in the lot. Food trucks lined the edge of the parking lot, getting ready for the day. The first round of fights was scheduled to begin after lunch. All the stress and hard work had paid off. After this, I had planned on spending more time with Sheridan and Ellie. Now if the threat of Cobra and his crew would only disappear.

Dreaming? Perhaps. But how long would Cobra's club put up with staying out of their territory? It had been weeks already. I'd tried reaching out to Duke with no response. The last time we'd spoken he had been sent on an errand for his club. It left me unsettled.

I parked my bike next to Hammer's truck. At least he would quit grumbling about not riding his bike after this was over. We couldn't take a chance that he'd have a wreck and get injured or worse.

The metal door creaked open when I pulled, revealing several of our Prospects placing folding chairs in a row. The bleachers extended on each side of the room and ropes cordoned off the two fight rings. Black chain link fencing enclosed each ring, and a thin mat covered the concrete floor. A gate was at both the north and south corners to allow the fighter entry.

Wolf, one of my brothers and a former Army combat medic, stood off to the side digging through a duffle bag of supplies.

"Wolf, you got everything you need?"

"Yeah. I replenished after the last fights. Plenty of saline and super glue to take care of the small stuff. Major stuff will be taken care of in the back room."

The back room was where Wolf would treat any major injuries or stabilize anyone before the ambulance could get here. He also used the room for veterans who shied away from doctors. Occasionally, he had a doctor volunteer to help him out with medications and the like.

"Hope you don't have to use it, Brother. You seen Hammer?"

"Prez's office, I think. Quite a few people were already in the locker room when he got here."

"Seen anybody you think we need to worry about?"

His brow furrowed.

"Not yet. Same guys that usually show up."

"Expect a few more. We had double the fighters sign up that we have had in the past. We all need to keep an eye on the Devil's Reign boys. Who knows what kind of shit they're going to start?"

"You got the girls squared away?"

All of my brothers knew about the threat that they posed.

"Oh, I almost forgot." Wolf reached into his back pocket. "Here," Wolf said, tossing me my phone. "Found this on a table at the clubhouse."

I looked at the damn thing like it was a snake.

"Something wrong?"

"Everything," I replied. "Sheridan got some texts from me last night."

"And?"

"I didn't send them."

"What were they?"

"Pictures of me with Nessa."

"What the hell, man?"

"I don't know. After we finished up, I went upstairs and crashed."

"Nessa was with Savage last I saw. But there are pictures of you and her having sex?"

"No, just her taking my pants off and pawing my dick."

"Have you asked her about it?"

"Haven't seen her."

"Nessa is a bitch, but why would she do that?"

"Sheridan has always said that Nessa considers all of us, hers."

"Maybe you should have listened. I'm guessing Sheridan saw them?"

"Yeah."

"And doesn't believe that nothing happened?"

I shook my head. "She's been on edge ever since the party when Mads caught Demon with Vixen and Sherry. Nessa said something to her, but she wouldn't tell me."

"This isn't the first time Nessa has messed with a brother's love life."

"You talking about Dagger and his wife?" I asked.

"She tried breaking them up several times."

"It must have worked since Jen took off after a couple of months."

"Something will need to be done if she keeps fucking with the old ladies."

"Well, we'll have to worry about that later.

I ran a hand across the back of my neck.

"If I may?" Wolf asked.

I arched a brow but motioned for him to continue.

"You have to listen and validate what she's saying. I'm guessing that she said something you didn't like and instead of hearing her out, you took off."

"What the fuck, man?"

"I've learned a thing or two over the years. Wish I'd learned it sooner. Maybe I wouldn't have lost everything."

Wolf had lost his wife and daughter in a car accident after he'd taken off and she'd gone looking for him. If anyone knew the guilt I was feeling, it was him.

"It's hard. I'm not used to having to account for someone's feelings in everything I do. If she doesn't believe that nothing happened with you and Nessa, there's not a lot you can do about it. You know the truth. You'll have to get her trust back and not give her anything to doubt about you. Do you love her?"

"Fuck yes, I do."

"Have you told her?"

"No."

"Scared?"

"Fuck, yes."

"I remember that feeling. You need to tell her. Otherwise, you may lose the best thing that's ever happened to you."

"I will, Brother." I reached over and squeezed his shoulder. "I better go check on Hammer. Let me know if you start getting low on anything and will get you restocked."

Wolf nodded his head, and I walked toward my dad's office. Knocking twice, I twisted the knob and swung the door open. Hammer sat on the leather couch opposite the large oak desk, a water bottle dangling from his hand.

"How you feeling, Hammer?"

"Good. Mom made sure that she fed me a good meal last night."

"Nothing heavy this morning."

"No, just some scrambled eggs, toast, and a protein shake."

"You're fighting in the second round against a guy from San Antonio."

"Rodrigo? I've seen him fight before. He's solid," Hammer said before taking a drink.

"You should be able to get him on the ground and tap out. Don't let him wear you down. You have a longer reach and should be able to avoid his kicks."

For the next half an hour, we talked about strategy and who we thought would advance to the next bracket.

"Anyone set eyes on the Devil's Reign guy?"

"Not yet," I answered. "We'll head to the gym in a few to get you—"

My phone rang with a video call from an unknown number. Gut clenching, my thumb hit the accept button before my brain registered the movement. Cobra's ugly face stared back at me from the screen.

"What do you want?"

"The same thing I've wanted since you took my boy. You dead," he snarled.

"Dream on."

"Oh, my dream is about to come true," he chuckled. "Unless that little bitch you've been fucking doesn't mean a damn thing to you. We both know that's not true."

My heart stopped at his words before kicking up a furious pace. Keeping my face passive.

"Not sure who you're talking about. I've fucked a lot of bitches. You'll have to be more specific."

Bile churned in my gut and crept up my throat with those words.

Cobra looked off to the side and spoke.

"You hear that, Sheridan? He's fucking so many whores he's not sure which one you are." He turned his head back toward me. "Need a refresher?"

He flipped the camera away from him and I bit back a cry. Sheridan was tied to the chair, her hair obscuring her face. Dried blood stained her white bra.

"Bitch, time to say hi," Cobra said.

A hand wrapped in her hair and wrenched her head up. Her face was mottled with bruises. Deep purple and blue had taken over her lightly tanned skin. Her left eye was swollen shut, and the right opened a sliver. Blood that had run from her nose and mouth had dried to a burgundy crust. He let go of her hair and her head lulled to the side as if the strings of a marionette had been cut.

Fuck!

How did they get their hand on her? And where the fuck was Ellie?

I chanced a look over at Hammer, who was whispering into his phone. He looked at me and shook his head.

What the fuck did that mean?

"Did that refresh your memory, Trigger? Or do I need to make her scream? She screams so prettily," he chuckled.

She whimpered as a hand caressed her jaw. He flipped the camera until his evil face filled the screen once again.

"What do you want, Cobra? She's not a part of this."

"You made her a part of this. You!" He screamed, spittle flying from his mouth. "You're the reason my boy is dead."

"I'm sorry he died, Cobra, but it was the fucked vein in his head that killed him. Not me and certainly not her."

"I'm not going to kill you either, but I will kill her, or maybe that sweet little girl of hers. I'm sure I could get a nice stack of cash for her."

Hammer caught my eye as he held up a piece of paper with his heavy handwriting on it.

Bear not answering. Savage is going to check.

Bear was the member of our club who I assigned to watch Sheridan and Ellie's house last night. In the middle of all this, I forgot about him checking in this morning.

"If you want to see this pretty thing and her girl again, Trigger, I need you to die."

I sat on the couch in disbelief after Cobra laid out his deal. After the last time, I swore to never get into the ring again, but that was a promise I had to break if I wanted to save Sheridan and Ellie. Even then, could I trust him to keep his word?

Fuck no.

"Savage got to Sheridan's house. Found Bear and his bike in the backyard."

"Dead?"

"No, he's alive, barely. They beat the shit out of him. Ellie's safe. She said her mom made her run to my parent's house. They called 911 after they figured out something was wrong.

"This is my fault," I whispered. Standing up, I clenched my fists. Fury washed over me.

My fault. My FAULT. MY FAULT!

"No, it's not."

I hadn't realized I'd screamed out the words until Hammer's hand landed on my shoulder. Jerking away from him, I turned and launched my fist at the wall, leaving a hole in the drywall.

"What the fuck is going on in here?" my dad bellowed, throwing open his office door.

"He has her," I screamed.

"Calm the fuck down, son. Who has who?"

"Cobra. He had Sheridan.

Dad sucked in a breath. I could hear the gears turning in his head.

"Talk to me."

"Cobra called. He—" My voice broke. "They hurt her. Bad. Bear, too. Savage found him in her backyard."

"And Ellie?"

"He threatened her, too, but she's with Hammer's parents." Fear threatened to overwhelm me, and my breath caught in my chest.

"Get it together, son. She can't afford for you to lose it."

He motioned to Hammer.

"Get Hawk to start tracing the call Trigger got. Find out what hospital they're taking Bear to and get some boys over there to sit on him."

"On it," Hammer said and started dialing.

"Trigger, it's time to call Ray."

Fuck my life.

CHAPTER 31
RAY

THERE ARE few things that will scare you more as a parent than finding out your child is hurt. As a law enforcement officer, it worried you that some criminal you had a hand in putting away would use them as a pawn in their revenge.

I always wondered what I would do if something happened to Sheila, Sheridan, or Ellie. After getting that call from Levi, I knew. In my twenty-five years as an officer, I was going to do something that could destroy my career and reputation.

My family was worth it. I pulled up the contacts on my phone and pressed a button.

"Dell, I need your help."

I rolled up to Sheridan's house in my truck. Several motorcycles were parked in the driveway and across the yard. One city squad car was parked at the curb. I recognized him as one of these younger guys on the force. As soon as I closed the door after I stepped out, two other trucks pulled up and parked at the curb. A pair of steel-gray eyes stared back at me through the windshield. My younger brothers, Dell and James, had gone the same route I had when I was younger. When I got out of the Marine Corps, I went into law enforcement, and they went a less conventional route.

"What do we know?" Dell barked out as he and James came up beside me.

"Not a lot, but we're about to get more answers."

Two older gentlemen walked toward us down the driveway.

"You must be Ray."

The black vest he had on declared him the president of the club my daughter had gotten tangled up with.

"I am. These are my brothers, Dell and James."

"I'm Rooster, Trigger's, er, Levi's dad. This is Brass, my VP. I wish we were meeting under better circumstances."

"What the fuck have you gotten my daughter into?"

Brass started forward, but Rooster stayed him with his hand.

"I'm sorry this has happened, but it wasn't Levi's fault."

"What the fuck do you mean it wasn't his fault? If she hadn't gotten mixed up with your boy, she'd be here with her daughter!"

"Ray, this isn't helping anything. What do you know?" Dell asked, placing his hand on my shoulder.

"As far as we know, Sheridan was taken some time this morning. Levi said he left around ten and they were both in the house. Bear was sitting across the street, keeping an eye on the place. We didn't know that anything had happened until Levi got the call."

"Who has her?"

"His name is Cobra. He's the president of the Devil's Reign MC."

"Rivals?" James asked.

"It's more personal than that."

"He has something against—?" James left the question in the air.

"Levi."

"And he's using my daughter to get back at him?"

"Yes."

"Why?"

"First, I need to know if I'm talking to the cop or her father?"

"My badge doesn't mean shit right now."

Rooster nodded at Brass.

"Levi and Cobra's son were in a fight a few years ago."

This I knew, but I motioned for him to continue.

"The other kid died after he hit his head and had a brain bleed. Cobra swore that he'd make Levi pay."

"And now that bastard has my niece. Explain to me how that isn't Levi's fault."

"Because her baby daddy is a member of that same club," I added. Dell and James looked at me in confusion.

"Wait, Sheridan said it was some guy she met in Colorado who was taking care of his mother."

"He was, but he never told her who he was. He took off when he found out she was pregnant to keep her safe."

"Fuck me," Dell uttered.

"What does Cobra want?"

"My boy to die."

"Then it's time for us to get to work and save them all."

CHAPTER 32
TRIGGER

THE METAL BENCH was cold under my ass as I sat there with my head in my hands. My ribs ached with each breath. My jaw popped when I opened it, and I swore some of my back teeth loosened and I tasted blood each time I swallowed.

"Stand up and let me put some of this on your ribs," Hammer ordered.

I stood and tried not to grab my right side.

The pain called up the images of Sheridan and the pain she must be feeling. It was all my fucking fault. If they'd never met me, Sheridan would be home, curled up on the couch with her daughter. Watching some movies. Not trapped with some psychopath who'd do anything to hurt me. My stomach clenched with the urge to vomit at the terror they must be feeling. Sheridan's sacrifice to save her little girl. She's too fierce of a mama to not have done everything in her power to get Ellie away from Cobra and his piece of shit club.

The muffled chanting could be heard in the dressing room. All cheering for the sight of blood and pain. Memories flashed in my head, the last fight I was in, the one where I killed Cobra's son, and he swore vengeance. Things had come full circle.

"You ready?" Hammer asked as he came over to me, unscrewing the lid off the container of liniment.

After each fight, Cobra sent me a new video. Sheridan was on her knees, bruised and bloody. Face streaked with tears as he threatened to do horrendous things to her and her daughter. The sheer desperation in her voice when she begged for them to leave Ellie alone. Jumping up, I ran over to the trash can and puked.

"Easy, man. You can't fall apart. Not now," Hammer barked out. "All the guys are looking for her. They think they have it narrowed down. It should be soon."

I wiped my mouth with the back of my hand and straightened up.

"What if they're too late?"

"You can't think like that, man. Sheridan wouldn't want you to give up."

"Sheridan is going to hate me after this. If I survive this."

"Don't fucking talk like that. They're going to find them."

"I know they will but—"

"But nothing. You gotta have faith, Brother. Your Brothers have your back."

Hammer squatted down in front of me. "Sheridan loves you. Ellie loves you. You can't give up on them because they wouldn't give up on you. They're waiting for you, for us to get them the hell out of there."

Tears stung my eyes. My dad, Ray, and the others were getting close to finding them. I had to believe that.

"Get your head in the game, Brother."

Hammer was right. I couldn't fall apart now. Not when Sheridan's life was on the line. I needed to stay strong and focused. I looked at Hammer.

"Let's do this."

I took a deep breath, trying to shake the thoughts from my mind. Focusing on the fight ahead, I stood up and flexed my hand. My knuckles were swollen and tender from the earlier fights. I couldn't afford for them to get stiff. Hammer rubbed the liniment into my right side, and I hissed at the pain.

"Give it a couple of minutes and it should start to cut the pain."

He straightened and inspected the cut above my brow that he'd glued together.

"Looks like it's holding. How's the head?"

"A little headache, but not too bad."

"You're going to need an ice bath after all this."

I bit back the retort that I may not be alive for it.

Whatever magical concoction Wolf had come up with warmed my skin and the sharpest pain faded.

"Have you eaten anything?"

"No. I'm not sure that I can."

"You can't fight on an empty tank. Drink this Gatorade and I'll try to round up something. I'm sure there's a protein bar or something that won't be too heavy."

As Hammer left the room, my dad appeared.

"Anything?"

"Hawk and James have it narrowed down to a two-mile area. He turns off the phone after he calls. They're having to see where the closest towers are, or some shit."

What he didn't say is there wasn't enough time to narrow it down before the last fight.

I knew what I was getting into when I agreed to this fiasco, but it was still a shock. Could I give up my life for Sheridan?

Abso-fucking-lutely.

They were more important than my life. Cobra had taken everything from me, and this was my chance to get it all back. Even if I wouldn't be here to enjoy it. Sheridan and Ellie would have a wonderful life.

"We're working as fast as we can. Her uncles are badasses. I'm glad they're on our side."

"I bet it's killing Ray to have to work with our bunch of criminals," I chuckled.

"He hasn't been too bad." My dad looked down. "I'm sorry, son."

"For what?"

"Not listening to you. If I hadn't agreed—"

"Dad, you're not to blame. He's been carrying this grudge for years. It was bound to come to a head."

"If I would have taken care of this back then, we wouldn't be in this situation."

"What do you mean?"

"I should have killed him when I had the chance."

"Dad—"

"I'm sorry I failed you," his voice cracked.

"You didn't fail me, Dad. Don't ever think that. You aren't a killer."

"For my child, I would. For that girl and her daughter, I will because you love them."

My throat closed up, and I pulled him into a hug. Words failed me.

"One of the food trucks had some spaghetti and meatballs," Hammer said as he walked in. "Oh shit, sorry. Didn't mean to interrupt."

"It's okay, Hammer," Dad said as he pulled back. "Levi, you get fueled up. There's about thirty minutes until the last fight. You're going to need your strength."

Thirty minutes? Could they pull off a miracle in that small amount of time?

CHAPTER 33
SHERIDAN

I'D NEVER FELT such agony. Cobra's fist came down on my thigh. Much more and the bone would break from the repeated abuse. After each fight that Levi won, Cobra went on a tirade and my body paid the price. A twisted smile would cross his face with every cry I emitted.

The only thing that kept me holding on was Ellie. I prayed Evelyn had been home when she escaped the house. And Levi. Poor Levi. I could only imagine the guilt he was feeling. The blame he was placing on himself. When Cobra had made the initial call and said he wanted Levi to die in the ring, a little piece of me died inside.

Our argument from earlier seemed inconsequential in hindsight. I believed him and I should have told him. I was hurt, even if it wasn't justified, and I wanted to hurt him. Damn, I was stupid.

I love him and I was too afraid to tell him. Now it could be too late. He would sacrifice his life for mine. Too bad it would be for naught. There was no way these men were going to let me go.

My mom and Ray would take care of Ellie, I knew. I didn't want to miss her growing up. I wanted to go back to school. Marry Levi and have another baby or two.

All a distant and fading dream. Within the next few hours, we would both be dead, and those dreams would die, too.

A tear slipped down my cheek and Cobra licked it off my face. Cringing away, he laughed at my disgust.

"It's the last fight," he taunted. "Time for Trigger to die. And you, too, my dear, but we'll wait until the end. I'll make it quick, one shot to the head."

He stroked the pistol down my cheek, the cold barrel stark against my heated cheek. Movement by one of the windows snagged my attention. As far as I knew, Cobra and Spider were the only ones here. The other ones were at the fight.

Who the hell was outside?

CHAPTER 34
TRIGGER

"IT'S TIME. You ready for this?" Hammer asked after he answered the knock at the door.

I had heard nothing else from my dad and I knew they hadn't found the girls.

"Ready as I'll ever be. Hammer, I want to thank you."

"For what?"

"Being my Brother."

"Don't you make this a goodbye," he bit out.

"I'm not. I'm holding out hope until the end, but if they don't find them, my life will be worth the sacrifice. Just promise me that you'll tell Sheridan and Ellie how much I love them."

Hammer nodded and led me out of the dressing room. The noise in the arena grew louder as we stepped onto the floor. I could feel the eyes of everyone in the room on me. They were all waiting for the show to begin. Waiting for me to fight.

The announcer stepped into the middle of the ring and the noise died down.

"Ladies and gentlemen, this is the fight that you have all been waiting for."

Cheering drowned out any other sounds and reverberated through me. My heart pounded.

"This last fight will be between Reaper of the Devil's Reign MC," he bellowed.

Cheers and jeers accompanied the announcement as the man stepped into the ring. He raised his arms and smiled at the crowd as he made his way around.

"And our hometown local, Trigger of the Blacktop Brethren MC."

I climbed into the ring and looked across at my opponent. He was a big guy, built like a tank. His face and neck were covered with tattoos, but what stood out was the grim reaper covering his torso. His eyes were cold and sent a fissure of fear down my spine. Never had I encountered someone with a dead soul. Steeling my spine, I looked at him dead on. Fear was a luxury I couldn't afford right now. I had a job to do. Get my girls back home.

The smell of sweat and blood filled my nostrils, and the adrenaline pumped through my veins. Reaper grinned when the bell rang, and we circled each other in the center of the ring. I could feel the anger boiling inside of me, and I knew I had to keep my cool if I wanted to come out on top.

Reaper threw the first punch, but I dodged it and landed a solid hit on his ribs. He stumbled back, and I took advantage of it by landing several more hits. The crowd went wild with each punch and kick that landed.

He grabbed me by the back of the neck and threw me into the ropes. I rebounded back towards him, and as I came close, he swung for the fences. One punch connected with my chin, and the world went dark. I stumbled back against the ropes. I blinked through the sweat that was dripping into my eyes.

"You're going down, fucker," Reaper snarled.

Bloodlust shone in his eyes as he lunged at me. I dodged him and sent a right hook into his jaw. The sound of his teeth smashing together echoed through the night. He staggered back, shaking his head. Eyes lit with rage, he threw a flurry of punches at me. I blocked most of them, but one got through and slammed into my eye. I felt the sting and a trickle of blood running down my face.

Reaper lunged at me, wrapping his brawny arms around my torso and throwing me to the floor. The thin mat covering the concrete did nothing to ease the impact of hitting the hard surface below. My breath left in a rush as Reaper's heavy body landed on mine. My ribs felt like they cracked under the pressure, and I bit back a scream.

Hammer's voice rang in my ears as he shouted orders at me. with my arms pinned to my sides, Reaper increased the pressure until I couldn't take a deep breath. Black dots danced in front of my eyes.

"Tap out and I won't kill you," Reaper ground out.

"I can't. I won't let her die."

His gaze met mine in shock and his grip loosed until I could take a deep breath. blissful air inflated my lungs and my head cleared.

"What?"

"I can't tap out. He'll kill her if I do. You're supposed to kill me."

"Who?"

"Cobra. He has my woman."

Confusion showed in Reaper's eyes, and at that moment, I could twist and free my arm. I jammed my forearm into the side of his head. With a grunt, he rolled off me. Rolling to my feet, I grabbed him by the back of his head and threw him to the floor. He scrambled back up just in time for me to slam my fist into his jaw. Blood splattered the ground as his face hit the mat. Before he could recover, I pounced, landing squarely on top of him. He looked up at me wide-eyed.

"Fake it," Reaper ground out.

"What?" I asked, surprised at his tactic.

"I'm not going to kill you. That's not who I am. Fake it."

"I can't take that chance."

"Building over on Grant. Behind the old meat packing plant. That's where they've been held up. I didn't know about the woman."

"You'd give up your brothers?"

"I'm not about abusing women. Go save your woman."

"It has to be believable," I uttered as I hit him, lessening the impact. He made a big show of it being worse than it was.

"I'll flip you over. Both of us get to our feet and I'll lay you out. Pretend whatever. I don't give a fuck but make it convincing."

He lifted a leg under me and flipped me over. I climbed to my feet as he did. Did I trust him? He seemed to be honest when he said he knew nothing about Sheridan.

He rushed me and I closed my eyes. I had to believe that he spoke the truth. My arms up in defense, I threw a punch he dodged, and pain flared across my jaw as his fist made impact. I let gravity pull me to the ground and lay still. The crowd booed and cheered as I breathed shallowly. Footsteps ran toward me.

"Fuck! Trigger talk to me, man!" Hammer bellowed.

"Play along," Reaper said. I slit my eyes open to see him look at Reaper as realization dawned. Each man blocked the view of the crowd as they gathered around me.

Hammer paused, then yelled for the medic.

Wolf appeared at his side within moments. Hammer spoke with him quickly, and Wolf motioned outside the ring. A couple more of my brothers came inside with a backboard and neck brace. I let them manhandle me as they placed me on the hard plastic surface. Each man grabbed hold and lifted me up. They rushed me out of the ring and into the back of the barn. My resolve almost faltered when I heard my dad screaming for me.

CHAPTER 35
SHERIDAN

THE ROPE around my waist was the only thing keeping me upright. Agony had become second nature and Cobra had tired of not hearing me scream when he inflicted his torture. Breathing had become difficult, and I felt lightheaded. That is what I blamed on thinking I saw someone outside. Or maybe that had been my last shred of hope. No one had come in to save me. It was a pipe dream. I was going to die in this abandoned warehouse with these assholes.

"Are you sure?" Cobra paced around the room as he spoke on the phone. "No, I want to know if that son of a bitch is dead or not. Find out."

He looked at me and smiled. God, I hated that smile. A mixture of crazy and evil.

"My boy Reaper took care of your man. They hauled him out of the ring on a stretcher," he said gleefully. "At last, my boy is avenged."

Rage burned a hole in the pit of my stomach.

He pulled the gun from the back of his pants.

"Now, do I kill you now? Or wait for the final word that he's dead."

"I'd wait, Pres. Let her feel it before you send her to hell. Better yet, let me take a turn with her," the other guy said, grabbing his crotch.

"Knock it off. She's not one of the whores. Go take a turn with one of them. But don't bruise them too bad. Customers don't like damaged merchandise."

"Fine. I don't see why I can't fuck this bitch, though. Not like we're selling her. Maybe we can still snag her kid. We'd get a pretty penny for a young thing like that."

Bile rose in my throat. I'd never prayed as hard that Ellie was safe. What these bastards would do to her made me sick to my stomach.

A shadow moved across the window, but neither man noticed. Most of the windows in the building were up high and coated in years' worth of dust and grime. The only windows at eye level were inside an office that was directly in front of me. With the door open, I could see them clearly. A streetlight must have been close to cast the shadow since it was dark. As the sun had set, the room had become gloomier since only three of the overhead lights worked.

An eternity seemed to pass as Cobra paced, waiting for the phone call. The one telling him Levi was dead.

Outside, a noise drew Cobra and Spider's attention. Both drew their guns.

"Go check it out," Cobra ordered.

Spider nodded and went to the side door. It opened with a loud squeak of the rusty hinges. He peeked out before taking his considerable heft outside. The door crept shut in his wake.

A thud sounded from outside.

"Spider, what's going on out there?" Cobra asked, staring at the door.

Glass broke from one of the upper windows and we both looked up. A blast from the end of a gun flashed in the darkness. Cobra stumbled backward; his hand pressed to his right shoulder. Bright red blood seeped between his fingers. His gun fell from his limp hand, clattering on the floor.

"What the hell?" he muttered.

The side opened and men dressed in dark clothing infiltrated the room. One rushed over to me, his gray eyes familiar behind the black mask.

"Ray?" I whispered.

"It's me. You're safe now, Sheridan."

"Ellie?"

"She's fine. She's with your mom."

"Levi?"

"Right here."

Relief poured over me, and my body shook.

"Wolf, get your ass in here!" Levi bellowed.

His hand cupped my cheek.

"You're alive," I gasped.

Footsteps hurried towards us, and I cringed backward.

"Easy, Sheridan. It's just Wolf. He's going to check you over."

His hand left my cheek, and coldness seeped over me.

"No, don't leave me."

"Never. I love you, Sheridan."

"I love you, too," I got out as the darkness consumed me.

CHAPTER 36
TRIGGER

"FUCK, she's in rough shape. Get an ambulance now," Wolf ordered.

Looking at her, I wanted to scream. The pain she had endured because of me.

"Got it. They're on the way," Raze answered from behind me. "What can we do?"

"I'm afraid to move her. She's, God, how could someone do this to her?"

I looked over to where Brass and Hammer had Cobra pinned to the floor. Dad came up beside me.

"You stay with Sheridan. We'll take care of this piece of shit."

Ray stood off to the side with his brothers.

"How are we going to swing this?"

"I've got it covered. Don't worry," Ray assured me. "You guys get out of here."

"I can't leave her," I argued.

"For now, you have to. I'll tell you which hospital they're taking her to, but I need you to haul ass out of here for this story to work."

I knelt beside where Wolf had laid Sheridan down. She was unrecognizable from the swelling and bruising. Bluish purple areas and blood mottled every inch of her exposed skin. I didn't touch her for fear of causing her more pain.

"Go, Levi. I promise I'll take care of her."

Leaving my heart on the floor, I followed my dad and brothers outside.

The barn was still a hive of activity when we returned, the after-party going strong. No one noticed when we pulled up and climbed out of the vans. Rooster and Hammer drug Cobra out as we created a human wall to prevent prying eyes from seeing. Inside, Jesse signaled the locker room was cleared.

Hammer flung Cobra to the tiled floor of the shower.

"You should be dead," Cobra yelled when his gaze landed on me.

"Hate to disappoint you," I snarled.

I started forward, but Dad placed a hand on my arm. I looked at him in question.

"This was about avenging his son. Now it's time to avenge mine."

Dad shrugged off his cut and handed it to me. Cobra stood, his right arm dangling. Blood dripped from the tips of his fingers.

Brass held Cobra from behind and Dad approached. It had been years since I'd seen my dad this angry. His fist landed again and again on Cobra's torso. Each hit sent a bolt of satisfaction through me.

My phone rang in my pocket. I stepped out of the locker room and into Dad's office.

"Ray?"

"We're at Methodist. They're taking her for emergency surgery now. She has internal bleeding."

"Fuck. I'm on my way."

Rushing back into the locker room, I saw Brass let go of Cobra and he dropped to the floor.

"Dad, I have to go."

"Go take care of your woman, son. We'll take care of this."

Rooster

The panicked look on my son's face told me it wasn't good.

"Raze, you drive. He's in no shape."

"Yes, Pres."

He rushed out of the room after Trigger.

I stood over the man who had caused all this pain and devastation. Cobra laid on the white tile with his eyes closed.

"Jesse, bring me a chair. Hammer, we need some chain."

"Yes, Pres."

"What are you thinking, Rooster?" Brass asked, coming up beside me. We'd been through hell and back together. There was no one else I wanted to have my back.

"You saw what he did to that girl."

He nodded as Jesse returned with the metal chair. Hammer let the length of chain he carried pile on the floor.

"Everybody out," I ordered. The fewer witnesses, the better.

It left Brass and me alone with Cobra.

"Let's get him in the chair. Secure his hands and feet."

Cobra's head tipped toward his chest as we secured him. Filling a bucket with cold water, I dumped it over his head. He came to sputtering. His dead eyes met mine.

"I should have done something about you years ago."

His eyes narrowed.

"He killed my son," Cobra ground out.

"No. It was an accident. If that ticking time bomb hadn't been in his head, he'd still be alive."

"An eye for an eye. Your son needs to die."

"That's not going to happen today. You, on the other hand, are going to meet your maker. I hope you've settled up with God. He may forgive but I sure as hell don't."

I pulled the knife out of my boot. The fluorescent light gleamed off the silver blade. When Cobra screamed, I smiled.

CHAPTER 37
TRIGGER

THE RHYTHMIC BEEPING of the monitor had become a comfort after a while. Sheridan seemed so small, lying in the hospital bed. During the surgery, they had discovered a laceration on her liver and had repaired it. The nurse came in, hung another bag of clear fluid, and hooked it up.

"It's an antibiotic," she informed me.

"Do you know when she'll wake up?"

"Don't rush it. Her body needs to heal, and sleep helps. She's been through a very traumatic experience."

"Yeah."

"Have you been checked out?" She eyed me.

I didn't blame her. Cuts and bruises marred my face and hands.

"I've had worse," I told her.

Her eyes widened. "Ugh, okay then. Call if you need anything."

Picking up Sheridan's hand, I kissed the cool skin. Her fingernails broke off into the quick and blood caked underneath.

The door slid open, and a gasp dragged my attention away from Sheridan. Sheila stood in the doorway, hand over her mouth as she stared at her daughter.

"My poor baby," she cried out, tears coursing down her cheeks.

"Sheila," I said, my voice rough as I stood.

She dragged her gaze from her daughter to me. I braced myself for her condemnation, but she shocked the hell of out me when she rushed me, wrapping her arms around me.

"Oh, Levi," she sobbed.

"She's going to be okay," I told her, hugging her back. "How's Ellie?"

Sheila leaned back. "She's doing okay. She's worried about her mom, of course, and Ripper. Evelyn volunteered to stay with her while I came up with her. I didn't know how she'd react to seeing Sheridan like this. Ray said it was bad, but I wasn't prepared."

"She's alive, Sheila. That's all that matters."

"How are you?"

"I'm okay."

"You look like hell," she quipped.

"Thanks," I chuckled. "Sheridan is going to have a long recovery ahead of her."

"She's a fighter," Sheila said. "She'll be fine."

"I'll leave you alone with her. Want anything from the cafeteria?"

"A Dr. Pepper if you wouldn't mind."

"I'll be back in a little while."

Walking out as Sheila took my seat, I breathed a sigh of relief. She was right. Sheridan was strong and would overcome this. The only question was, would I be in her life to see it?

CHAPTER 38
SHERIDAN

"DAMN THIS ITCHES," I griped, trying to reach the cast to the itch with a pen.

"Sheridan Diane, stop that. You'll end up getting an infection or something."

"How much longer do I have to wear this thing?"

"At least a couple more weeks."

I'd been home from the hospital for over a week and Mom had practically moved in. Not that I minded at first, but now I was tired of her hovering.

I'd spent a week in the hospital after my surgery. Between the blood loss from my lacerated liver and spleen that was missed during the initial surgery, it had been a long road to escaping the place. I'd gotten this annoying cast on my left arm for the broken wrist and a leg immobilizer for my right leg. My femur wasn't broken, but it had taken quite a beating that they wanted me to keep my weight off it to let it heal.

The bruising on my face had faded to a sickening pea soup color, and the swelling had gone down.

Ellie said that I looked like her mom again. The first time she had seen me at the hospital, she cried and clung to my mother. I'd decided then she wasn't coming back up there. It was too traumatizing for her.

When they had wheeled me into the house, she'd stared at me for a minute before climbing onto the wheelchair with me and sitting in my lap. Then I cried. Mom was scared to death that Ellie had hurt me but, in reality, it was with relief. Joy that I was alive to hold her.

"You ready to take a shower? Your appointment is in a couple of hours.

I groaned in annoyance. "Fine."

I pulled the wheelchair into place and transferred into it. Placing my leg on the outstretched part, I grabbed the wheels and pushed myself towards the hall.

"Good grief, Sheridan. Could you at least wait for me to help you? The doctor said not to strain yourself."

Thank goodness she was behind me and couldn't see me mimicking her words with a scowl.

"It's fine Mom."

We'd found out that the house was easy for me to maneuver around in the chair. As long as I was careful, I didn't bang into the doorway with the wheels. Slowly, I made my way into the bathroom, Mom hot on my heels.

The water turned on with a hiss.

"Do you want me to help you?"

"Maybe getting the leg brace off?"

She made quick work of the Velcro tabs and pulled it out from under my leg. She wrinkled her nose.

"This thing is getting a little ripe."

She got a glare for a response.

"I'll let it air out for a bit."

She turned her back as I took off my shirt. After a few minutes, I stood on my strong leg and let my pants and underwear drop to the floor. I pivoted and sat on the shower chair that now had become part of my routine. Steam fogged up the glass of the shower enclosure.

"Shit," I uttered. "Mom, I forgot that cast shield thing."

"Here," a different voice answered. I looked up to see Levi standing there with an amused grin. "Slide your arm in."

The hard plastic slid up my arm.

"When did you get here?"

"A couple of minutes ago. Your mom said she's making lunch if I wanted to help you."

"And you couldn't say no, huh?"

"And miss the chance to see you naked? Not a change in hell."

He stripped off his clothes piece by piece as I stared. All the bruising he had received from the fights had faded and he only had a couple of scabbed areas remaining. He walked in behind me and grabbed the shower wand. Testing the water first, he let the water run over me.

"Want to do your hair?"

"Yes, please."

He washed every inch of me until I was squirming with the desire to jump his bones.

"Not until you get the all-clear," he whispered in my ear.

"Tease," I muttered.

Ever since I'd come home, Levi had hardly left my side. I knew the guilt was eating him alive, but I did my best to reassure him I didn't blame him for any of it. And I believed him about Nessa. He'd confronted her about what she had done, and she'd admitted to sneaking into his room and taking the pictures. She wanted me out of the picture so things would be like they were before. Rooster had banned her from the clubhouse for a month. He couldn't ban her from Shooter's since she worked there, but she wasn't in the club's section anymore.

It made me glad that I didn't have to deal with her anymore, unlike Kenna.

Dr. Collins had stopped by to check on me after hearing what had happened. I'd cried as he told me my job would be there when I was ready to return. He'd returned with Ripper a little worse for wear. Dr. Collins had taken care of the stab wounds and kept watch over him until we were settled at home. Gladys had sent over enough food to feed an army and said the office wasn't the same without me.

No one had heard from Dr. Lansky. Apparently, he had left town and his house was for sale. Good riddance. When I had mentioned it to Ray and Levi, neither would meet my eyes. It was better if I didn't ask questions.

Levi grabbed a towel and dried me off. He wrapped the towel around me and picked me up. Instead of putting me back in the wheelchair, he carried me to the counter and sat me down. His eyes swept over me from the faded bruises to the healing incision on my stomach. He stroked a finger down beside it, careful not to touch it.

"I'm okay," I reassured him.

"If I had lost you—"

I placed a finger on his lips to silence him.

"You didn't. We both came out on the other side of this, alive and well. It's something we'll never take for granted."

"I love you, Sheridan Diane Taylor."

"I love you, too."

"If you two don't get a move on, your food will be cold," Mom yelled from the hallway.

I couldn't stop the smile from forming as he rested her forehead against mine. Life was good.

EPILOGUE

WRENCH

I THREW myself down on the bed, not caring that I was getting grease on the sheets. These sixteen-hour days were kicking my ass. Demon's bitch ass had disappeared, leaving me to run the shop alone. As my eyes closed, my phone rang.

"Fuck," I groaned. "What?"

"Wrench, my man. How goes it?"

"Who the fuck is this?"

"I'm crushed," he laughed. "It's Colter."

"Shit, sorry."

"No worries. Heard you needed some help up there."

"Yeah, I do."

"I'm sending Van your way."

Van? Which brother was that? My brain had decided to switch off.

"She'll be able to help you with all the painting and detail work."

"Sounds good. Thanks, Colt."

"You sound tired. Get some sleep and I'll talk to you soon."

My eyes were already closing as he hung up. I must have been hearing things. I thought he said *she*.

ALSO BY SAMANTHA CONLEY

Silver Tongued Devils Series

Down in Flames

Break Me Down

Down on My Knees

Crashing Down

Whiskey Bend Series

Pieces of a Broken Heart

Beat of My Heart

Blacktop Brethren MC

Pull the Trigger

Wrench in the Plans 2024 release TBD

Straight Shooter 2024 release TBD

ABOUT THE AUTHOR

Samantha is a multifaceted individual, balancing the roles of a devoted wife, nurturing mother, and compassionate Registered Nurse. Beyond her professional and family commitments, she shares a deep passion for the world of romance novels. When not tending to patients or spending quality time with her loved ones, you'll likely find her engrossed in the pages of a captivating romance book. And, just between us, she's been known to sneak in some reading during work hours, though she hopes her boss never finds out!

Her household is a bustling haven filled with the warmth of family and the presence of adorable fur babies who bring joy and chaos in equal measure. In her moments of relaxation and inspiration, she dedicates her time to crafting enchanting love stories that transport readers to worlds of passion, emotion, and romance.

One of her little secrets? An addiction to Dr. Pepper Zero and a penchant for sweet and spicy pickles, providing a delightful combination of flavors that fuel her creativity and satisfy her cravings.

www.samanthaconleyauthor.com
www.facebook.com/authorsconley/
www.facebook.com/groups/SamanthaConleysReaders/
www.instagram.com/author_samantha_conley/
www.bookbub.com/authorsamanthaconley/

www.ingramcontent.com/pod-product-compliance
Lightning Source LLC
Chambersburg PA
CBHW052047240626
47153CB00006B/2246